the tyrant's novel

NAN A. TALESE | *DOUBLEDAY*

NEW YORK LONDON TORONTO SYDNEY AUCKLAND

the tyrant's novel

thomas keneally

PUBLISHED BY NAN A. TALESE
AN IMPRINT OF DOUBLEDAY
a division of Random House, Inc.

DOUBLEDAY is a trademark of Random House, Inc.

Book design by Dana Leigh Treglia

Library of Congress Cataloging-in-Publication Data

Keneally, Thomas.
The tyrant's novel / Thomas Keneally.—1st ed. in the U.S.A.
p. cm.
1. Fiction—Authorship—Fiction. 2. Detention of persons—Fiction.
3. Political prisoners—Fiction. 4. Novelists—Fiction.
5. Despotism—Fiction. I. Title.

PR9619.3.K46T97 2004
823'.914—dc22   2003059670

ISBN 0-385-51146-9

PRINTED IN THE UNITED STATES OF AMERICA

June 2004
First published in Australia by Random House Australia
First Edition in the United States of America

10 9 8 7 6 5 4 3 2 1

To my brother, John Patrick,

the good practitioner,

with fraternal love

contents

the tyrant's novel

the visitor's preface

It's a truism almost embarrassing to repeat that a particular government might find it suitable to have an enemy in-the-midst, more imagined than real, whom they can point out to the populace as the threat. And from that threat, only this party, this view of the polity they manage, can save the innocent sleep of the citizenry.

That's how it was with us when there appeared in our plain outer suburbs and our desert towns double-walled gulags. Those who, sincerely or opportunistically, came from afar to seek asylum in our community were detained and isolated there as a virus too toxic to be released. They were isolated not for six weeks, not merely until it was discovered whether they had dangerous powers or connections, or were carrying antibiotic-resistant TB; not for six months, to allow the watchers to observe their behavior. But for years. The apolitical infant fugitives were detained with their complex and supposedly dangerous parents.

The government was officially proud of these installations. Yet there were no signposts to them. In the deserts they were remote. In the cities they seemed to be surrounded by industrial parks with many cul-de-sacs and unexpected crescents leading back to the street you recently left. But at last persistent visitors came suddenly, amidst small engineering works and warehouses, upon the high walls of steel mesh and razor wire. I say walls with reason— first an outer wall topped with the static buzz saws of razor wire to a height which Afghanistan's, Iraq's, Iran's, Bangladesh's champion pole vaulters could not possibly clear. Then an intervening road down which trucks could patrol or go on maintenance errands. And finally an inner wall, similarly exceeding an Olympic-standard clearance. And one now knew why the proud government did not signpost these places. One minuscule sign from the Hume Highway, and another one from Woodville Road, white-on-black and designed to defeat all but the sharpest eye, gave the driver an indication of the location of these prison walls in our city. Rarely had such a vote-engaging venue, never such a glory of policy, been so well hidden from common gaze. There was something about the miles of wire, and its height, which might shock a citizen who, until this moment, had put the merely abstract power of his vote behind the project. And it was not advertised either that citizens could visit the inmates under certain conditions, with photo ID, bringing them perhaps a picnic (wine excluded) and a book or two.

To get inside these walls, apart from presenting photo ID and the name of a detainee, pockets need to be emptied of anything metallic and the visitor passes through a detector. The hand is stamped with an ink which shows up in the ultraviolet-lit intervening room between the front desk and the visitors' compound.

On some days the shape stamped on the hand is of a teddy bear, on others of a dolphin, on others of a dog. That stamps of the kind used in a classroom are used here is one of the absurdities which always seem to cling round the flanks of noxious institutions. And so one goes from the ultraviolet chamber to a gate, and thus into the compound.

At tables and chairs on dusty ground the visitors sit—in some cases relatives of the internees; various nuns. Immigration lawyers are pointed out by other visitors you get to know. The lawyers can tell the full, irrational story: who is locked up, and for how long, and who is let go. How the detainees are rendered crazy by the inconsistency of it all, and might become desperate.

The first time I went there, I went with a friend, another writer, a woman named Alice. She introduced me to a refugee, very competent in English, who insisted that he be addressed as Alan Sheriff. (The reason for the Western-style name will soon become apparent.) He had been in this place, and in similar enclosures out in the desert, for more than three years. The government would neither give him asylum nor send him back to his country, for fear of what that regime would do to him. So he was caught here, with his lively eyes and his smile into which irony easily crept. He was the sort of man, said my companion, the writer, whom women found disarming and, to use her word, "cheeky." She also told me that he had got into trouble with the regime he'd fled over some "writing business." Since the regime he had escaped from was led by a man whose name was a synonym for gratuitous tyranny, it was an easy idea to believe.

So at a table under a eucalyptus tree we sat with this Alan and skirted round his motives for skipping out on the tyrant. He was dark in complexion and that seemed to suit his intensity. He gestured in a way which made it possible for me to see five marks on his wrist, dots of scarring. I decided these were tribal marks.

Was the president where he came from as bad as they said? I asked. Oh, of course, he replied, but though I would have liked him to elaborate he didn't. So we moved on to his immediate life within the wire here, in sight of small engineering works and distant bungalows. It became clear that he was one of the leaders of this enforced community of refugees. He talked about his informal counseling of men who had trouble sleeping, who were racked by the uncertainty of the immigration process, which they saw as a lottery and thus a tyranny of chance to match the tyranny of intent or danger they had run, floated, or flown away from. Sleeping was difficult here in the four-to-a-room huts, he said. Men often lay awake from three o'clock, when the need to urinate woke them, until dawn, fretting about their visa applications and families left behind.

There's a library, I suggested, still wanting to think of our polity as civilized enough to provide that kind of refined facility. People could not concentrate to read, he told me. Even I, he declared, I find it hard to read. If I read, say, African history, or Irish history, or the history of Crazy Horse or some other figure, I begin to feel the injustice in my gut, and I can't read further. It's stupid, but it's true.

Religion—Assyrian, Christian, Islam, Baha'i—was any of that a comfort?

For some, Alan admitted. Sadly, not for me. He grinned in apology. I'm such a weak Mediationist.

I asked what that was.

Just one of the sects at home, he told me. Scratch a Mediationist, he explained, and you'll find an agnostic.

I didn't have the expertise to argue this point.

After a while, as the afternoon heat grew thicker and Alice and I leaned forward to catch his fairly reticent voice, we got him talking about other camps he'd been held in during his detention years. This is a holiday camp, he said, compared to the ones in the west and in the desert. I have seen the guards for no reason and in ill will separate families till a husband breaks a bottle and puts it to his neck and pleads to be reunited. Then the government can say, See, see what sort of people are these? Instead of reunion, he is charged with disorder. I have seen them put a father and his four-year-old in an observation cell for ten days. I have seen them start a fight with young men in a dining room, over nothing. For the guard and the prisoner, you see, for both of them, boredom is the great problem. For the guards, blows, and what you'd call the theater of blows, are a great opium. A morning's entertainment!

We ate some of the mandarins and nuts Alice had brought. The pungency of the rinds scented the heavy air. Your name? I asked. Alan . . .

It's a good name, isn't it? he asked.

Of course, I admitted.

Look at it this way. It's the name of a man you'd meet on the street. I would very much like to be the man you meet in the street. A man with a name like Alan. If we all had good Anglo-Saxon names . . . or if we were not, God help us, Said and Osama and Saleh. If we had Mac instead of Ibn.

I did not mention then that I understood Sheriff to be originally an Arabic name. I think he knew that it, like him, had made a transition and he liked the idea. I did not refer to his other and real name we had used, Alice and I, when we signed ourselves in.

I asked what he used to do before he fled his country. I wrote some short stories, he said, dismissing the idea of short stories. But I liked subtitling foreign movies for the broadcasting network.

I said, Oh?

That's the great neglected art form, and generally left to the literalists. The sort of people who could translate menus but don't understand the text below what is said. I liked that work. A lot.

But on what made him decide to become a refugee he was as discreet as about a love affair.

My colleague Alice had an unblemished olive complexion and huge, limpid, oriental-like eyes. How could a man in detention not half fall for her? And she confided to me by telephone when next I asked her how Alan Sheriff was that he had taken her wrist gently and said, Alice, this recent marriage of yours . . .

She had been married a year to a book editor. Is it serious? Alan had asked. Will it last? I think we two are fated.

I imagined the scene, his half smile, but the jollity probably desperate and a bit demented. Meanwhile her laughter would be lighter than air, the wafer-thin, half-wary, half-flattered laughter of a woman who possessed the automatic confidence of the beautiful, taking account of the desires of men almost as dispassionately as a nurse might take temperatures. I have to say that she told me his story not so much from vanity or condescension but to make the point that Alan, this normal man, had the same predictable desires as men walking free in the streets, and so could fit easily into open society.

The next time I saw the man who insisted on being Alan Sheriff, I went on my own. I brought him science fiction books, since he'd told me they were least likely to distress him and make his stomach churn. He said, as we sat at one of the tables in the yard, Did Alice mention I touched her wrist and spoke of destiny?

My hesitation in answering was itself an answer.

He scratched his reddened hands, which seemed to suffer from some kind of eczema, probably brought on by internment. He said, If only she knew, she has so little to fear from me.

I think she realizes that, I said.

From my side, he said, it was like the hand of an amputee. The palm feels itchy but it means nothing, because it's gone. One day I might tell you a story. Man-to-man. No confidences to Alice or anyone else.

Do you know me well enough?

Well, you like to talk, but . . . Do you know, my story is the saddest and silliest you would ever hear.

I remembered a book by Ford Madox Ford, one of the great and now unread classics of the early twentieth century, *The Good Sol-*

dier. It had made the boast in its first line that it was the saddest story the reader would ever hear. From what I remembered, Ford Madox Ford hadn't quite delivered on the promise.

I found out that Alan Sheriff had become well known in the pro-asylum-seeker community for his work in trying to keep his fellow internees sane and healthy. He had written essays against detention, some published in the daily press, and now was to receive a UNESCO Human Rights Award.

Twenty people, including Alice and myself and one opposition politician, went out to the detention center for the award ceremony. But the minister had decreed that only three persons could enter the center, and they, of necessity, were members of the UNESCO committee. Nor could a camera or tape recorder or anything else designed to leave an image of the event be brought in. Alice and I and fifteen others waited in October sunlight by the very outer wire near the car park, shifting from foot to foot, engaged in desultory gossip and badmouthing the minister. Someone said, If I wanted to be a citizen of a pre-Fascist country, I'd rather be a citizen of a big, dramatic, baroque pre-Fascist country like the United States than of a little, pissant, head-stuck-up-the-arse pre-Fascist country like this.

Yet the guard who operated the gate seemed typical of our jovial culture and got into quite friendly and ironic conversation with us. He said, I know you jokers would like to close this place down, but then where would I go for a job?

At last the UNESCO officials emerged from having given the man with the saddest and silliest story in the world his award.

Alan is in good spirits, said one of them. Though there was another name on the certificate, his myth of Anglo-Saxonism was becoming slowly pervasive.

Alice now wrote a long magazine article about her visits to the detention center. Most of its readers considered it a generous article and praised it for presenting the intimate human features of the detainees whom the government wanted people to see as an inhuman, peevish mass. Alan Sheriff played a considerable part in the article. She identified him to the readers by true first and second names, his patronym and name of the hearth, and explained why he had adopted the name Alan. She admitted that some thought this grotesque, but she defended it as a brave stratagem designed to demand the sort of regard the minister would no doubt pay to all the suburban Alans who voted for him.

In another attempt to give Alan human identity, she mentioned that he sometimes took her wrist and absorbed her with his sad, ironic eyes and wistfully considered her breasts. She was chastened to find on her next visit, with a copy of the magazine in her hand, that Alan Sheriff was appalled specifically at that, that she had mentioned the dialogue of eyes and touch between him and her. Laid down on paper, he said, these things made him seem *silly* to the minister. This man who had sustained other detainees through their depressions, and was credited with having prevented many suicides in the center, now announced to her, I am so depressed. I don't want to see you for now.

He was not angry, she told me. She wished he had been. She could then have expected him to recover soon.

She had somehow earlier smuggled a mobile phone in to him. She hinted it had been done with the help of a generous female guard who also admired Alan. Though she kept on calling this number, she did not get a response for days. Alan is sick, a young Palestinian refugee to whom Alan had entrusted the phone told Alice. She began to visit other detainees in the hope that Alan would wander into the visitors' compound. She heard from the young Palestinian that Alan was feeling a little better but not ready to come out into the visitors' area yet. I think he does not know how to face you, said the young Palestinian.

I don't know how to face him, Alice said. Tell him that. He must think I'm a very stupid woman.

At last she called me and told me Alan had said that he would welcome a visit from me. I made the drive and went through the rigmarole and waited in the visitors' compound for him. When he appeared he still retained what I always thought of as an air of gentle proprietorship, his moral right to this dusty space, its scattered plastic tables and chairs. He was wearing shorts this autumn day and seemed to have put on weight during his depression. Jailhouse stodge had no doubt helped. In his accustomed way, murmuring, offering his hand, he greeted immigration lawyers and other visitors. He still had the respect of his fellows, one could see. They obviously forgave his calling himself Alan. They obviously overlooked his reported interest in Alice's breasts.

Then he came to my table. He spoke my name gently, sat, and pulled out his cigarettes. I smoke too many of these in here, he told me. You know, before the escape I never smoked. It's the truth. I suppose you read the article by Alice.

Yes, I had to say. I'm sorry it hurt you.

Miss Kiss-and-Tell, he said, grinning forgivingly. But no. It's so silly. It set something off in me. I don't know.

I said, She didn't mean any harm. And neither do I. You have to understand, Alice needs you, Alan, as I need you. I imagine grandchildren I may never have asking, What did you say when the government locked up the asylum seekers? And my grown daughter, their mother, can at least say, Well, he visited Alan. He made an attempt. He went to the detainees.

I don't like that word, said Alan. *Detainees.*

Neither do I, Alan.

He said, Alice said those things about me because she thought it meant something. A human touch, I suppose. I wish it meant what she thinks it means. She is an innocent girl.

In our terms, I told him, she's worldly.

He made a balancing gesture with his hand, indicating either that innocence and worldliness were mixed in her, or else that my idea of both qualities didn't match his. He said, I decided while I was ill that I wanted to tell my story. I thought I would tell you. In confidence. You are not kiss-and-tell. I do not wish to kiss you anyway.

He laughed.

I'm relieved, I said.

And I don't want to kiss Alice either. Though she likes to think so. If I touch her wrist, I do it to be courtly. What's another word for silly?

Useless? Futile?

Futile. My English has gone off a bit. It was better, or seemed better, in the old days. I translated my own prose.

Oh? I said.

But he covered his eyes. He didn't want to talk about that.

He savored the word. He said, *Futile.*

A crow flew above the nearby bush, mourning dryly.

You like to talk man-to-man, said Alan. I like fellows who enjoy gossip but have obviously managed to keep secrets. You're that sort of man.

I conceded, I've kept a lot of secrets. Though it's hard to do so when they have a good punch line at the end of them.

Punch line? This hasn't a punch line, he assured me. And you won't keep this secret forever, but long enough. You'll want to tell it in the end. Because it is the saddest and the silliest.

So he began.

alan sheriff's story

A tyrant builds up around him more titles than the most slavish subject could possibly utter or remember. Tyrants abound in superlatives. Chosen One, Commander-in-Chief, Regulator of Laws, Supreme Judge, Overchief. If the tyrant goes on naming himself with names implying broad power and intimate connection with the people, he will come up in the end with a title which can be used ironically. In my land, *Great Uncle* was it. Everyone remembered that one. Great Uncle of the People. I suggest you call him Ian Stark, since Stark is a name associated with tribalism and toughness, and he came from a tribal, tough background—the clan symbol of five dots was incised on Great Uncle's wrist.

Great Uncle was, as the name implies, both kindly and justly severe. Imagine you're far back, two hundred years ago, when in the West the bodies of criminals were displayed. Not a long time ago, two hundred years. Remember that then when I say it happened in my home city, when Mrs. Douglas's nephew was so displayed for wronging Great Uncle. The nephew was in charge of the fountains and swimming pools at the Bellevue Palace, and Great Uncle had not spent any time there for the past two months. The chlorine and pH levels had built up under Mrs. Douglas's nephew, whose mind was on a particular soldier's wife living two streets from the Bellevue's broad, lion-engraved gate. Great Uncle made a surprise visit to Bellevue one afternoon and began to swim in his pool—his favorite exercise now that his hip and back were said to be playing up. He came out of the water with a rash between the legs. Various members of the Overguard stood above Mrs. Douglas's miscreant nephew while the pH levels were tested, and then he was taken in a van to Wolfmount, the prison, and shot dead, and his naked corpse displayed from the ramparts of the place. Wolfmount was often called the Palace of Disappearance, but the nephew's body was all too visible. He would have better been employed in California, where clients, though litigious, do not usually resort to capital punishment for a high pH. Not that Great Uncle or any of the Overguard gave an explanation of why the well-molded young body hung from the outer walls of Wolfmount. Great Uncle did not choose to have the people know about rashes, pimples, hip twinges, or any other sign of mortal squalor. Mrs. Douglas had got the information only from her sonless sister, for her dead nephew, as displayed on prison walls, was not readily identifiable. She had then, returning from the shops with a few modest bags of groceries, with tears in her eyes, whispered it to my wife and me on the interior stairwell of our block of flats.

Wolfmount was seven miles west of us in a working-class area and we did not like to think of the exposure of corpses there. We did not often drive there and could forget the place. Mrs. Douglas was determined not to let us do so.

His mother is crazy, Mrs. Douglas told us. She would like to see the body released, but they won't release it yet. Not till the birds have had their way with the eyes and the tongue. Poor boy! Poor boy!

She rolled her eyes as if she feared someone might be listening, and lowered her voice. Too much chlorine in the water, she said. I thought he liked chlorine.

It was a subtle reference to Great Uncle's bent for chemicals, most particularly in making war, and I coughed at the recollection of gas from my service to the state as a soldier.

And then Mrs. Douglas suddenly abstracted herself from the tragedy, as our people had learned to do. She resigned herself to events and removed herself from them. Her hunched shoulders descended, whereas ten seconds before they had been raised high with the sense that some serious explanation was needed. For anger was a one-way street for us. It descended from heaven. It did not have the right of ascent. She turned to my wife.

We all miss you on the telly, she said.

I could see that Sarah was still fixed on the story of the chemically negligent nephew. She had not left it yet. My wife was a dangerous woman, a woman of conviction.

Oh, said Sarah abstractedly. My wife was a well-known beauty, who would have been more so in a saner place, where she did not need to frown about retribution being so summary. It's very hard work, you know. Television. I'd been in that series for years and years, since I was a child.

I understand that, Mrs. Douglas conceded. But we still miss you, Mrs. Sheriff.

The truth was that Great Uncle had summoned the producer of the series, *Daily Lives,* and asked that my wife's character acquire a betrothed who had fallen in the final days of the war against the Others. (Great Uncle had insisted the enemy be not dignified by any other name than that.) The producer was so instructed in the hope that this plot shift might console the widows and girlfriends of the men, aged between fifteen and sixty, who had given their lives in the final, deadlocked campaigns in the straits, not far from where I had fought some five years earlier.

A woman of Sarah's craft, a woman who had read for the stage and settled for television and film, could spot the lie behind the direction the daily television show took. She could not blame our friend the producer for wanting to go along with Great Uncle's production notes. He had three children. And besides, there *were* thousands of casualties, deaths and life-shortening injuries to be absorbed into the social fabric, to be sucked in, swallowed, and somehow reconciled by the populace. My wife had lasted four episodes as the bereaved fiancée, and then had pleaded overpowering migraine—untruth does produce overpowering migraine— and refused to appear further. It took some considerable skill on the part of the writers to explain her absence on the fifth night, but they achieved it through the mouths of the other characters, opining that not only had the Others unjustly deprived her soldier sweetheart of life, they had suddenly, through a brain clot which, without the grief, might not have formed, removed the fiancée from life as well.

A doctor of our acquaintance testified to Sarah's migrainous condition, but she was not forgiven, and had no trade in television now.

I am working on the stage at the moment, my wife told Mrs. Douglas.

Indeed, she and a small group of her friends were rehearsing Tennessee Williams's *The Glass Menagerie*. It would be played in a warehouse for two nights, before an invited audience. My wife would earn nothing from playing Laura.

But I had no complaints. My wife was my wife. I had come through the war with nothing worse than eczema of the hands and a vague loathing. As for the matter of Great Uncle, caution drew its veil. I saw the two women, the pool keeper's aunt and my wife, look at each other out of their haunted eyes. Such eyes were Great Uncle's gift to our nation's splendid women.

Actors are mysterious people, and, as I said, my wife, Sarah Manners, had indeed taken on the symptoms of severe headaches. The attacks were regular, although they improved when her small theater group was at work, particularly during rehearsal. But the complaint, and the diminishment of appetite which accompanied it, made her seem gaunter than she had been when she was a famous and ample television goddess. Great Uncle, by his intrusion in the script, reduced her to the haunted girl he meant her to play, but we had been to the best doctors, and they said it was no more than a phase, that people often passed through a peak of migraine in their lives and emerged from it with a clearer head. One even suggested that the chemicals released by pregnancy would prove to be the cure. Although my wife was willing, we had not been fortunate in that regard.

So here I give you, through this one encounter with Mrs. Douglas, what it was to live with Great Uncle on one's shoulder. He had the power to make water soft, and if for an hour it turned hard, that was soon amended. He had the power to separate dead sons from their mothers. Having served in the Summer Island campaign, I know that to be the truth. And he had the power to bend actors according to his imagination, whether they consented or not.

Every second Thursday, we still dined at Sarah's old producer's, Andrew Kennedy's, house. Andrew had been promoted to head of the National Broadcasting Network, and so was a man to reckon with. Yet I knew also, because he told me once, that though middle-aged and with a wife and three grown children, he had considered at the time of his promotion becoming an escapee, fleeing north into Istria and seeking asylum. But on a late summer's evening, as one sat around his swimming pool in the midst of his five acres of ornate and devoutly tended garden, one could understand why he might have inhaled, taken his new post, and decided to stay another winter. In the spring he could review whether he really wished to travel as a nobody, by truck, hidden amongst cargoes, over the final border where he would declare himself a refugee, a man adrift, a man with no resources but those he carried by suitcase or in his pockets.

These days, Andrew met with Great Uncle at least once a week, and chatted with people in the outer office both before going in and after leaving. People were, of course, very careful not to say too much, but even the most wary bureaucrats and Overguard gave away something more than they intended. That, combined with what he observed himself, made Andrew Kennedy increasingly hopeful that Great Uncle might die. He put what I can see now was too much hope in the possibility. But he knew that, as well as other aspects of age, such as short sight and the need to have frequent recourse to black hair dye, Great Uncle had persistent hip and back problems—by all reports a slipped disk—which made it painful for him to walk even in the office. He was getting paunchier too, a fact he disguised with tailoring and a corset when he appeared in his military uniform.

It was at one of his meetings with Great Uncle that Andrew Kennedy had been given the helpful suggestion that Sarah should be turned into the grieving victim of the Others. Great Uncle had frequent production and programming issues to raise with Andrew. And all the time Andrew made notes his eyes flicked over the face and body of Great Uncle, looking for subtle indications of death. Great Uncle, said Andrew, could not be sleeping too well, since he increasingly asked for certain favorite films of his to be programmed for late-night television. The *Godfather* gangster films, *The Old Man and the Sea* (Great Uncle the fisherman, and the ruthless, murderous fish representing the body politic), *The Day of the Jackal, The Conversation, Enemy of the State*. Knowing that Great Uncle had an expert grasp of and interest in the Stalinist era, Andrew had at one stage run the wonderful Russian film of the Stalinist purges, *Burnt by the Sun*, and Great Uncle asked him not to do it again, because it sentimentalized the whole issue of treachery in subordinates.

Great Uncle, said Andrew, was exceedingly mild in these demands—they could sound very nearly like requests. Only in prison, or against the wall, did you discover that what had been suggested had actually been an edict.

Anyhow, at his home, and around his pool during the summer in the piny hills of Forest Tops, Andrew Kennedy still ran his regular salon, which gave all his friends a sense of stability. I had been asked to join the circle after the publication of my first book, a series of connected short stories about our campaigns at Summer Island. At Summer Island I had seen bravery and savagery and crimes I did not dare mention even in the book, even in fiction covered by disclaimers. Thus I felt an impostor to an extent. But it was there at the Kennedys' that I first sighted but barely spoke to Sarah Manners, who became my famed wife.

What I liked about Andrew's gatherings was that they were like the literary or artistic salons one read about, and while we were there we felt we had freedom of choice and speech, and we felt creative. In the old days, prior to our rebellions against our British-controlled monarchy and during the post–Great War British Mandate period, our Anglophile parents and grandparents had engaged in such gatherings, and city people with resources tried to sustain the urbane habit. In various ways, even though English was not their first language, the British Mandate period made the bureaucrats, the lawyers, the professors, other well-off city people like my father—the chief surveyor of the city—nearly as British as, say, a Canadian, a New Zealander, an Australian, or a member of India's ruling class.

At the time my book was published, by the way, the United States was our ally, since the Others had interned U.S. citizens and sunk American tankers on their way through the Hordern Straits to collect our oil at the Summer Island terminals. Our army was momentarily glamorous, for unlike the Others, we had no suicide troops and could be imagined as normal frontline soldiers, if such creatures ever existed. Hence my short stories were published in the United States, and sympathetically reviewed on page five of the *New York Times Book Review*. Since then, however, because of his experimentation with chemical weapons, Great Uncle, and our nation, had lost our standing in the American press, and policy had taken a total reverse.

I had in the past three years been working on a novel, now virtually completed, for which I had received an advance against royalties of forty thousand U.S. dollars in the days of our alliance, and that money, stored in a U.S. dollar account in a bank in the city, was a godsend to Sarah and me and gave us our latitude. (I would be receiving a further thirty thousand dollars on delivery of the manuscript and thirty thousand on publication.) My advance had liberated me from our Cultural Commission, and its head, Old Billy Salter, lawyer and disappointed author. Giving support to writers and poets, the Cultural Commission acquired the right to read and censor books, and Billy, who had begun as quite a nice old fellow, a good host, liberal-hearted and widely read, seemed, over the past five years, to have come to enjoy his power over the word, his management of the national literary farm.

Matt McBrien, a very talented young man nearly ten years younger than me, told me that as he presented the draft sections of his novel to Billy, Billy's calm, sage, avuncular comments were all about Matt's need to ensure his future as a writer in receipt of the commission's largesse. Billy would present Matthew with editorial notes which, in terms of subtlest propaganda, out–Great Uncled Great Uncle. Though the oratory of state might itself be an interesting art form, Old Billy was suggesting prose of a kind that he would have once mocked. But his eyes gleamed these days. He had found his vocation as a functionary.

Sonia McBrien, though young, had sometimes displayed the haunted look of a woman whose husband suffered from unpredictable moods. Sometimes, at the Kennedys', Matt would defend his past submission to Old Billy, and any future ones he might have to make. How much different is it, he asked, than having a Western publisher who wants to smarten up a manuscript according to what's fashionable? Besides, there's always something wrong in a novel. A few sentences from Old Billy, a required shift of emphasis for the sake of the McBriens' safety and Matt's work security—these were not major intrusions in a book of over three hundred pages, the young writer would argue. He never talked about fleeing, but I had a strong instinct he daydreamed about it. He had a first cousin in Los Angeles, and Sonia had a brother in Melbourne. Facing the giant task of displacing themselves, people often wore the sort of aged weariness one had seen recently in Sonia's young eyes. As she could work out for herself, beyond the possible, dangerous exodus and the harshness of processing in some other country lay the destiny of a career as a hotel maid in some New or Old World city; and for the barely exportable literary talent of Matt, a future as parking attendant or cabdriver.

Sarah and I parked our Fiat and were on the way to the door together when, choosing her moment, in view of how much I enjoyed these get-togethers and forgot all other problems while I was at them, Sarah told me Mrs. Carter had called again. You think we could go and see her, together?

She watched me sideways, knowing that the name Carter created in me an unreasoning flurry of irritation. In my eyes, this crow of a mourning woman, mother of Private Carter, harassed me, wanting to see in me her lost son. And every few months she wanted us to go and visit her. It had been more than six months since we last did, because I hated these meetings. When we visited her, Mrs. Carter would look at Sarah, who was innocent of any battlefield secrets, and clutch at her wrist and say, My son would have married a woman as good and handsome as you, had he not been captured by the Others. But there may still be time.

Indeed, tens of thousands of our troops were still prisoners in the POW camps of the Others, and as much as the Red Cross and our government tried, they remained for years on end over there, beyond the straits.

What I hated was the crazy glitter of hope in the old lady's eyes, the subtle chastisement of her berserk smile. I'd often thought of bribing someone in the Ministry of War to send a telegram saying Hugo Carter had died in captivity, and thus put paid to the reproach of that daft, lips-parted smile. But I knew she would want to retrieve the body, and feared that this resolution of the matter would bind her to me more solidly still.

With a tentative grin, not daring to look at me for long, Sarah said, Mrs. Carter suggested Saturday afternoon.

Fuck her, I said. I could feel the blood in my cheeks. That old witch! That succubus!

Don't be angry, she urged me. It's only for an hour. I'll say we have an appointment afterwards. Maybe you could have a glass of vodka before we go.

Mrs. Clarke, the Kennedys' housekeeper, met us at the door, created a restraint on my anger, and led us through the house and out to the pool, its apron, its cabana, its cocktail bar—all painted by the last rich pink of the low, dusty sun. Grace Kennedy, Andrew's full-bodied, mothering wife, greeted us and accepted our order for drinks. Sarah, her hand firm on my wrist, asked for apple juice. I asked for a bludgeoning Scotch to suppress the memory of the crowlike, carnivorous, parted lips of Mrs. Carter. But I was already charmed to see a pair of Andrew's familiars, Toby Garner, the architect, and Hope, his wife, with glasses in their hands, sitting on lounges, looking content. Andrew Kennedy himself bowled up with his casual brand of fraternal courtesy. In what I was sure was an entirely paternal way, he was besotted with Sarah. When I asked him how he was, he said, Thank God for the European soccer semifinals. They have Great Uncle transfixed.

He coughed then, and Sarah obliged him by walking away to greet Hope Garner.

Collins is gone, Andrew told me. Three days ago. Got into Istria in a chartered Cessna.

He shook his head at this further attrition amongst his friends. The dead and fled were too numerous for a moment. Peter Collins was a cultural favorite of the people, a poet who cooperated with rock bands and folk musicians to give his verse the extra dimension of music. He had written some good novels as well, translated into English, French, and German, and when I was younger I had very much envied and been impressed by him. His going was devastating but in a way hard to define. It certainly made me forget Mrs. Carter and left a rent in the air. If Robert Frost had left Maine to live in Lapland, or Philip Larkin had left Hull for Tajikistan, the shock could not have been greater.

Kennedy continued. I think his German editor helped him with the necessary, he explained. Maybe we should all have such friends. The whole thing is, he took his wife with him.

Wilf Apple, a slim figure though fifty years old, emerged from the cabana, a wet towel in his hand, beside his young boyfriend, Paul. He came with purpose to where Kennedy and I were standing. He asked, Did you tell Alan? I nodded to let him know I had the news, and did not need a further recital. I shook my head with wonderment, tilted it back, and opened my throat to the acidic comfort of liquor.

He took his wife, Wilf insisted on telling me. He was separated from her, and he ended up taking her instead of his girlfriend.

Andrew had an opinion on that. He said, The editor in Frankfurt must have told the wife. Not knowing about their split and that young singer of his. And once the editor let her know . . . well, dear God, did she have a weapon?

Andrew said, He loved that little singer though. He idolized her. And so why did he take the opportunity to go just now? I mean, the fellow's so popular with the kids even Great Uncle has to pretend to be a fan. The Overguard adopted one of his songs as their own. And I didn't know he was under any sort of threat.

Even if the German editor said, Here's a packet of U.S. dollars, so go and charter a plane . . . why would he need to go? And take that bitter wife of his?

Wilf Apple had his ideas. He said the Germans probably had a chair lined up for him at Tübingen or Konstanz or somewhere else. All those literary theorists loved Collins's work. He could speak German too. He could perform for them. He could write his own ticket.

No dishwashing for Peter, said Wilf. Straight into the heart of the intelligentsia, and an instant rock star as well. Elvis Collins meets Derrida Collins. And he can bring his little chanteuse to him later maybe.

Andrew Kennedy shook his head. If the Overguard don't decide to interrogate her, he said.

Andrew's bafflement and Wilf's knowingness added wings to my depression. I wanted at least another half glass of Scotch. A man does not take the trouble to come amongst his friends for the sake of getting as blue as I now felt. There was anger as well. I, who rarely had a fight with Sarah, felt as if I wanted now to take her home and start one over Mrs. Carter and Peter Collins.

The young McBriens appeared on a pathway—they had been walking amongst the pines. This evening, they both looked cheerful and animated. They started speaking to the Garners, the architect and his wife, and slowly we all coalesced over in that direction, some standing, some sitting on the sun lounges.

As we moved, I saw Sarah semaphore to me with a small wave her regret at having piled Mrs. Carter on top of the story of Collins's absconding. Beloved, I thought—though a minute earlier I'd wanted to take issue with her.

To the group, Andrew said, Whatever you thought of him, you have to agree the cultural landscape's changed for good.

Toby Garner agreed. You're going to have a few gaps in your programming, all right, Andrew.

Grace Kennedy said, He could be a pompous shit.

Yes, said Andrew, but he had gifts which nearly justified it.

In the midst of this anxious hubbub, Matt McBrien seemed possessed of a rare serenity. There's always someone to step into the breach, he told us. Even genius isn't indispensable. I wonder did he think of his audience, anyhow, before he left them in the lurch?

A certain uneasiness overtook the company, and many began to abandon their reverence for the escaped icon.

To hell with him, said Wilf Apple, with a stuttering laugh. Some of his lyrics were absolute crap. *Love of the twilight, love of the night, love of the East in predawn light...* Only the music saved them from banality.

Some of us nodded. He was too prolific. But we were, in the end, not consoled. To help us out, Hope Garner said, Toby's had an interesting few days. Cheer them up with your story, Toby!

Garner was the supervising architect on the Northbourne Palace restoration. He always had interesting tales about Overguard officers turning up with new and, to a normal person, gratuitous demands from Great Uncle. A poor sleeper, Great Uncle, who had determinedly developed a gift to read English, would skim through *Architectural Digest* or books of architectural pictures late at night, and by morning would issue orders that an entire terrazzo floor be pulled up, or that the molding of the state banquet hall—there was one such in each of Great Uncle's twenty palaces—be done in the style of the Frick museum.

But before Toby Garner could tell us his latest experience of the way absolute power encourages absolute gratuitousness in architectural taste, the housekeeper and caterers appeared with our dinner of rice and salad, fish and lamb. Set out on tables by the pool, it consumed our time, as we advanced one by one along the line asking the normal questions of the buffet—what mayonnaise is this? Is this a marinade? I carried my refilled glass of Scotch, pecking away at it, feeling its false but vivid consolation behind my sternum and thinking as ever, Why do you need consolation? You have Sarah.

When we were all seated attacking the food, and Mrs. Clarke, the housekeeper, moved around filling wineglasses, Toby Garner sat up with the anticipatory glow of the storyteller who has the chair. But Sonia McBrien, sitting on the same side of the table and thus not able to see Toby's move to begin, said in a shrill, young voice, We have news. Matt has news.

Matt waved the statement away, but it was apparent the news was effervescing in him too, and must froth forth soon. Almost aggressively, Grace Kennedy asked that Matt McBrien cough it up. Matt still pursed his lips in amusement and shook his head as if he didn't want to. Sonia said, Tell them.

You tell them, said McBrien.

The two of them were annoying us more than was customary.

Sonia announced, Old Billy Salter has asked Matt to take the appointment of Acting Commissioner of Culture.

If they had worked themselves into a state where they expected us to be prolix with congratulations, they were a bit confused by the silence this announcement produced. Why shouldn't we be enthusiastic though? After all, Andrew had achieved a big state job, and the house to go with it. We said, Well, that's remarkable. Congratulations, Matt. You must be proud, Sonia!

But Wilf quickly got to the point. Don't do it, he advised.

Matt's smile frosted. Do you say that, he asked, because you're not in favor at the moment?

Wilf declared, I say it because I have not sought favor. I haven't consented to become an apparatchik.

And when was your last feature film? asked Sonia, offended for her husband's sake.

I make my films with handheld cameras. So do my assistants. We are documenting this age, and it will be interesting to those who come after us.

Sonia said, So you look for your rewards after you're dead?

Wilf Apple said, No, I get my rewards now. By being free of people like Old Billy Salter.

As the dialogue grew poisonous, Toby Garner sat forward, a genial soul. As much as I admire that, Wilf, he said, we have to live. After all, like Matt, I took Great Uncle's shilling, I'm afraid. But whose shilling am I to take if not his?

Wilf Apple said, Your work is not as censorable as ours.

Toby Garner cast his hands up, passing judgment on no one. Of everyone at this table, he said, you'd be the hero of the future, Wilf. Your name will be justly honored. You create the record of intolerable times.

Wilf Apple murmured, It's not only Great Uncle. The Western sanctions are shit too.

Garner said, I should perhaps welcome young Matt to the circle of government employees, but my story, the story I want to tell—listen to it well, Matt, because you're not just joining a payroll. You'll find yourself squeezed, sooner or later. I thought I was squeezed by having to alter a colonnade here and there. But what happened to me two days ago, it was the true damn squeeze!

He laughed confidingly in his wife's direction. He said, It made me light-headed with exhilaration, because I could be dead now, the bullet angled up into my brain. So I'm ecstatic.

This compelled our attention.

He told his two-days-old tale. At the Northbourne Palace he had supervised the installation of Courtney Witt's brilliantly designed bronze gates: dazzling with the reflected sun, opened and closed by means of electronic devices embedded in their stone columns. So that something so brilliant would not be tarnished, he had left a road, a gap in the stone wall, either side of the gates for the trucks bringing their cement and steel, their milled cedar, their mosaic tiles, to enter and exit, all without the risk of collision with Witt's lovely work.

Two afternoons before this party of the Kennedys, as the day shift of construction workers was going off duty, three vanloads of Overguard men in their red berets so feared by the populace, their camouflage kit which implied that some peril to the state was imminent, and their automatics carried in the particularly ominous way, the butt poking up over their shoulder blades, arrived outside Toby Garner's prefabricated on-site office. Eight of them crowded in, others milled in the dust outside.

They told him that an hour earlier, Great Uncle had passed the site on his way somewhere. Great Uncle's location was of course always secret, to the extent that the chefs of each of his twenty palaces, soon to become twenty-one with the completion of Northbourne, prepared three meals a day, just in case someone malicious were watching for a clue to Great Uncle's whereabouts.

Anyhow, an hour before, Great Uncle had passed the Northbourne site and remarked to those who were riding with him that there was a gap either side of the great bronze gates, and that this detracted somewhat from them, and made him angry on the lovely gates' behalf. He told the Overguard escorts that when he passed by again, sometime after nine P.M., certainly before ten, he wanted to see the gaps between the stonework walls and the dazzling gates closed.

When they declared that they, all of them, were there to help Toby get the job done, he began to see that they were under the same pressure as himself—not that that was much consolation. He told them straight out it couldn't be done. He appreciated their offer, but the day staff was gone and he needed a further delivery of the honeyed sandstone of which the fourteen-feet-high walls were built. Work on the swimming pools and fountains would continue through the night, and wiring in the main residence. But the stonemasons themselves had all gone home. They were in coffee bars, driving their cars, shopping in supermarkets (or selling cigarettes on the black market).

Give us the lists, said an Overguard officer. We'll find them.

The stonemasons? asked Toby.

Every bastard you've got on the payroll. We'll get those lazy damned Overalls working too.

(The Overalls were the lowly city police, who wore blue overalls.)

He opened his computer personnel files and printed them off page by page, as the officer distributed them to his three dozen men. Toby could well imagine the quantity of fear that would arrive at each hod carrier's or bricklayer's door in the person of an Overguard officer. Are you Ted Williams? Then please accompany me, sir. The red beret, the great splotches of martial camouflage, the hefty holster, and the submachine gun carried upside down on a belt between the shoulder blades. Timidly, Is there a problem, sir? And if the Overguard were a little genial: You're wanted at work. Tell your missus to keep the dinner hot.

By five o'clock the workers were largely back at the site. Overguard officers with experience of pneumatic drills were helping out the stonemasons. Everyone in this together. Waves of fear and light-headedness overtaking Toby. It can't be done, I tell you it can't be done. And the Overguard demonstrating that in a sense they *were* warriors, saying it could be done, the redoubt could be taken, the walls closed up to those gates whose dignity demanded it. To hell with Courtney Witt and his fancy gates! thought Toby.

You might remember it was a hot evening, he reminded us.

Fine dust of sandstone fragments democratically clogged the lips and nostrils of workers and Overguard. The stacked and abandoned weaponry was humanized with orange grit, which seemed to hold out a promise that when the impossible job was not done by nine o'clock, or five past, and all or some were put against the wall, the weaponry might benignly clog. Further cement trucks arrived, and winches pulled large friable blocks onto foundations of wet cement. It was impossible. Ten yards either side to be closed, and closed with the same quality as the rest of the palace walls, no sloppy cement, no leakage, no hasty trim on the sandstone itself, no faulty symmetry.

About six-thirty, Toby said, the job was quarter done, one side closed up but only to human height. Unqualified men were trying to erect scaffolding to take the wall higher. Then the officer of the Overguard suggested they bring in workers from other government sites. There was a Ministry of Oil building going up on Viaduct Bay. An army of riggers and scaffolders were working there. We'll get them! promised the Overguard. Toby did not bother saying, There's not time to get them here. The Overguard officer was sanguine. He said that half the delay had been logistics, the job would move faster now. Even if they could bring in workers who would be effective for an hour and a half, that would be a contribution. More riggers were in any case needed to assemble scaffolding in line on the far side of the gates, where the other stretch of space was to be walled.

Throughout their labors, the workers on-site were largely silent—no whistling, no pop songs. There were occasional sudden surges of rage. You stupid prick, pick it up! But ultimately each of them came to realize he needed every stupid prick who could be mustered. Some upper wall stones were miscut, were raised, broke the uniformity of the capstones, too narrow or too broad to dignify the gates they were reaching for. Fear took the craft out of some of the craftsmanship. They had to be all hauled down, recut or discarded. It was the Overguard who shouted at mistakes and grabbed their holstered side arms. And Toby amongst them, the only man who had the entire plan in his head, found he became suddenly excited, this challenge meaningful, transcending the mere building materials. Be calm, everyone! Get the measurements right! Nothing to fear! And he heard a stonemason say under his breath, Balls!

And so the cement was poured on the far stretch of wall, and suddenly the stone began to ascend to the correct height there. Hope was traveling to meet hope, along dug foundations. After the sun went down, lights were brought in from other parts of the site to illuminate the area. The electrically competent amongst the Overguard worked at this and got them shining. A new kind of constructive energy emerged amongst the workers. When a man's hand was crushed in its leather glove, others felt they had time to express commiseration. Whereas two hours before they might have punished him, the Overguard sent for an ambulance. A further work gang, including stonemasons, arrived from the Ministry of Oil site. It was astonishing how much work they got done in an hour, given that everything was already set up for them, the total scaffolding in place within the site, on the blind side of the wall from the street, where it would not offend the gates. The last stone was set at eight-fifty-five. A mason and a bricklayer watched it settle for five minutes to ensure it would not play false. On the street side of the wall, Toby and the Overguard officer watched for mortar seepage or crookedness of the capstones and found none.

I could, said Toby in telling us the story, have kissed the fellow. As it was, we embraced like brothers.

The officer told Toby to get out of the way before Great Uncle came by again. Out of obscure duty he remained within the walls, as the tired Overguard cleaned their weapons of fragments of stone and dusted their camouflage kit and stood before the closed walls and the splendid gates to give the salute as the President passed. From a point on the inner scaffolding, Toby watched. He was exhilarated, he said. At that word, *exhilarated,* his wife reached out and touched his arm, as if she both feared his exuberance and had benefited from it, yet hoped it would not last too much longer. Toby said, I thought at the time, Frank Lloyd Wright never went through this. This is real architecture.

And what's the moral of this for Mr. McBrien? asked Wilf Apple, his eyes narrowed.

That if you work for Great Uncle, declared Toby joyously, one day you'll get a *real* deadline.

What's your smile for then? asked Wilf. You've been tyrannized over, and just because you get some obscure kick out of it, you tell this kid to join the club.

Sonia McBrien said, My husband is not a kid.

Apple was unkind enough to assert, He sounds like one.

Andrew Kennedy, the doyen, intervened. Oh come! All Toby's saying is that anyone who works here should be ready for some exceptional deadlines. We know that to be the case.

He raised his glass to Toby. I congratulate you that you have survived yours, Toby. My life would be hard to sustain without you.

This gesture made us all kinder to other, although Wilf Apple said, Our friend Alan Sheriff doesn't have to worry about a deadline, not with his Yankee advance.

For a second I wanted to answer, but I saw Sarah's eyes dissuading me.

Don't worry, Wilf, I told him. The dollars will no doubt run out soon.

Yet it was true that I had a certain security. I had reached the end of the penultimate draft of ninety thousand words, and thus was close to the conclusion of my novel.

My Sarah. She had already been a classically trained actress and a television and film notable for some years before I talked to her in person and in passing at a Kennedy salon, the first I was invited to. I had recently returned from military service and considered myself lucky to be patronized by old hands like Wilf Apple on the edge of that circle of fraternity and hope the Kennedys provided. Sarah moved in her own sturdy orbit amongst us. Her astonishing eyes lay on me during a twenty-second introduction. She ascertained that my few stories published to that time had dealt chiefly with the war but, said Andrew, placed it in a full human context.

He manages to get a lot of women into them, said Andrew.

She said with what I thought of as an inevitably cold, fake earnestness, I'll have to read them.

Then I found we were members of Professor Duncan's same drama seminar at the university. She would say at the start of each session, Hello, Alan. At the second or third meeting of the group, she told me she had read one of my stories, had tracked it down in *Writers' Magazine*, which the National Broadcasting Network had published for a while under Andrew Kennedy's aegis, until lack of funds and some official disapproval closed it down.

I said, That's very kind of you.

She gave a rare laugh. I'm reading Chekhov's short stories too, she said. Should Chekhov feel it's very kind of me?

But he's dead, I said stupidly.

When called on to read the few times the group had met, she read from *Uncle Vanya*, so flatly and tentatively the rest of us were stunned. Professor Duncan asked her to stop after a while, and told us that she was doing honor to Chekhov's text, letting it dominate as a monotone which suggested meanings, contours, and points of departure to it. That's the way she rehearsed for television and film. Isn't it? Professor Duncan asked her. Yes, of course, she said, not making a fuss of it.

Only amateurs like the rest of us, said Duncan, had the luxury of imposing emphasis instinctively on the texts they read. We were right to do so, but we ran the risk of making too many misreadings. But she was right in her method.

Sarah kept her eyes lowered like a schoolgirl. She did not like being defined as distinct from the eleven other members of the seminar. She had begun to sit near me in the seminar because, some instinct told her, I was too poleaxed to be as annoying and importunate as I would have liked to have been.

I had a problem of honor. I had met at the university's primitive radio station, still then operating under sufferance (though its days were numbered), an enthusiastic girl named Louise James, who managed to combine her studies with broadcasting a two-hour interview show six days of the week. Her father was a famous broadcaster who had done the same sort of show on the National Network, and had then become a television interviewer. Louise was tall, full-faced, with wide, hopeful eyes. After the interview she took me to a coffee-and-cake soiree at a wealthy student's house. There had been other such events, a walk, and a visit to the cinema. I have to say that these outings were sedate. We students laughed at country people who seemed to consider that if a man courted a woman for an evening or two, he was bound to marry her, a proposition often enforced with *chardri*s and shotguns. But unlike the Western countries, there was, for all of our university bravado, a code of concern that one must not, for one's own safety, lead women on. Once you were introduced to the parents, you incurred the debt of marriage. I could see on the rational plane why I should ultimately marry Louise James, who had shown signs of thinking along the same lines. She was a brave young woman, temperamentally much maturer than I, and of a good, positive cast of mind. She was also a leader by nature. Her features were pleasant, particularly when lit up by intellectual curiosity. When she folded her arms polemically across her full breast, I was entranced and hoped to become more so. But that was it. I could not argue myself into being sufficiently entranced, and that fact made me feel both guilty and hapless.

At the university library one day I watched my fellow classmate Sarah Manners move across the vivid tiles of the reading room. There was a tension and a sort of unconscious cooperation of movement and static color between her and the expanse of eighteenth-century tiles. They added to her mystery, but then everything that had happened at our few meetings had done that. She really did have, as they say in America, the sort of bone structure the camera loves. Even I, as a fan of European and American film, could see that. And she had that look that I've noticed in other beautiful thespians—offstage, offscreen, they moved negligently but warily, and were less made up than many others, less beringed, with a fine paleness created partly by residual television or stage makeup, and by long hours in the studio. She created an impact in men, or at least in me, transcending sex. Really! The appetites she evoked were subtler by far. I wanted to be consumed and to consume, yet I did not think at first of this communion in sensual terms.

Besides, I was a speck of mustard and she, so obviously, a sea of nectar. So there was no use dreaming.

As well as by her beauty, she terrified me by her offhandedness. Just let me say that had I been as beautiful as that, I would have simply stood still and absorbed like benign oil the regard washing my way from the reading tables, from librarians emerging from the stacks, from browsers on the galleries of books above. Beauty is something I have never been able to work out. I know the clichés about how those beautiful folk who live for their own splendor are destroyed by its passing. Et cetera. Et cetera. But I still could never understand why Sarah didn't pause in midstride, self-stunned.

There were about eight of us from the drama studies course in the library that day, all attending to our Chekhov assignment. Sarah passed me without a look and went to sign on for an hour's use of one of the library's two computers—this in an era when the Internet was something mysterious to many of us, and the bite of oil and other sanctions meant that public facilities like universities and high schools and hospitals were losing ground. In any case we had limited access to the Internet—the articles and catalogues considered necessary to our work were downloaded and catalogued by trusted librarians, according to the guidelines of the Ministries for Education and State Security.

Sarah and I happened to be the stars of the course. I spoke plentifully to Professor Duncan and gave the subject the greater share of my energy merely to impress her through impressing Duncan. The strategy had had no impact, but I could not abandon it. Yet she later astonished me by saying that it was from a sort of respect that she spoke to me that day in the library.

Hello, she said. Mind if I sit down? I'm waiting for the computer. Don't let me disturb you.

I immediately hid my hands, red and less than handsome from a skin condition I'd caught during the war, under the table.

She held a photocopied and stapled mess of pages entitled *Chekhov: The Short Stories.* I hoped for the sake of her grandeur that whoever had translated them had done a good job.

You're very welcome, I assured her.

She riffled the pages but did not settle on one in particular. I closed my copy of *Chekhov* by Ernest. J. Simmons. The point of Chekhov was to attract a word from Sarah. That having been achieved, I was willing to abort any further studies.

So we got talking properly. The most astonishing thing about her was her joy in sharing information. She had researched Chekhov as part of a Russian tradition—something that I hadn't thought to do; I and the others just took him as he came, as if he were Shakespeare or Eugene O'Neill, and that was that. She sat down to tell me, plainly and without vanity, of Chekhov's debt to A. S. Suvorin, a newspaper publisher, a debt both as an individual and a short-story writer and dramatist. The relationship would split up because of Chekhov's revulsion at the trial of Dreyfus and Suvorin's enthusiasm for it. You can make a note of that name, if you like, said Sarah. It might impress Duncan.

Holding my breath, I began to take notes. Perhaps she could become habituated to passing on enlightenment to a plain fellow like me.

I'll never forget the details of her educating me. For as the battered, improvised edition of the great writer's tales she held in her hands indicated, she had also taken the trouble to read all Chekhov's short stories and was involved in making a comparison between a range of Chekhov's prose, including "A Boring Story," which she said was brilliant, and *Uncle Vanya.* In "A Boring Story," the old professor of medicine, Nikolai Stepanovich, bemoans the split between science and the humanities, which undermines the ability of graduating physicians to give proper care to their patients. She pointed out to me Stepanovich's statement "Feelings I never felt before have built a nest in my heart. I hate, I despise, I am filled with indignation." She looked at me significantly after reading that passage—as if there were someone closer to home in whom such sentiments could be rooted. She was frank, but fortunately not rowdy, in her dislike of our President for Life. Pointed to it by her, I read with unutterable longing Chekhov's short story "The Beauties," which I would never have read to this day without Sarah. "An Attack of Nerves" was next. A law student, visiting whorehouses with friends, becomes obsessed with the problem of prostitution. His moral agony is such that his friends take him to a psychiatrist, who numbs his outrage with bromide and morphine. By doing that, the psychiatrist proves that certain immoralities abhorred by many members of society are actually necessary to the functioning of a community.

Everything in Chekhov seemed to Sarah and me suddenly to relate to *our* community, *our* fraught nation. Tales of false love— "The Two Volodyas," for example—seemed in their way to be a critique of the *Hour of Devotion* on our televisions. Sarah had also found and given me a copy of Chekhov's second full-length play, *The Wood Demon,* which was unsuccessful and later proved the basis for *Uncle Vanya.*

Meanwhile, most of the rest of us were willing to accept whatever we could find in the university stacks. I began to think, She's really no flippant girl, this one. And she wasn't, either.

Were you wounded? she asked suddenly. In the battles for the straits?

Oh, no. I was very lucky. We were well dug in.

She smiled. You won't become like one of those old soldiers in Russian stories, talking about nothing but their cavalry wounds.

No, I agreed. I don't want to sound dramatic. But most of the wounds down there were not of that clean . . . that gallant variety.

What's your best story? Maybe not the one I read, "The Water Truck Driver." It was good, but it didn't sound like the last word you had to say.

Please, I said, making a gesture of literary modesty, hands to forehead. There's one coming out in the university newspaper next week.

———————

After my session in the library with Sarah, I knew I could not string Louise James along any further. I was in agony over that. I knew that if anyone dumped anyone else, it should so obviously be glamorous Louise dumping me.

I found her at the end of her show. As she emerged from the gimcrack studio her eyes were alight with the joy of what was so obviously her craft—broadcasting. Another show transmitted without mishap.

I took her to the student café. Inevitably, to outsiders, my speech would have sounded a little Jane Austenish. Louise, I said, after we'd ordered Turkish coffee, I can't go about with you anymore. It would imply I had intentions which I don't have.

She leaned forward, arms still folded in that way I had always admired, and frowned. But I wouldn't need you to have intentions, she said frankly, a modern woman, not dropping her eyes.

I can't meet them, I said. I was almost ready in my panic, as her wide eyes grew wider still, to claim some problem arising from the war, some obscure wound of flesh or spirit.

I'm very sorry, then, she told me through near-closed lips. Do you imagine to yourself you've got the power to break my heart? No one has that power.

You're worthy of—

Don't dare finish that sentence, she warned me.

She imitated a male voice. *You're worthy of someone better than me.* All that means is, I've found someone I like more.

There were tears in her eyes now, but she refused to dissolve. She would not be a weak woman.

Go to hell, then! she told me, and she got up and gathered her things together without any of the urgency of a wronged woman, though with her considerable jaw set and her eyes blazing. Then she walked away. No scene. No thrown crockery. A warrior woman. I had given up someone admirable in the empty hope of someone transcendent.

I would later see her around the campus, always busy, always genially vocal, though not in my direction. She did not lack for company, and she was said to be engaged to a young doctor. But then, for whatever reason, her family fled, and her esteemed father took a university job in America.

But back now to Sarah. The short story I had told her about in the library, the one about to emerge, was one which Peter Collins would later call a classic—"The Women of Summer Island," that is, the women who staffed the oil refineries, within range of enemy artillery. The story was in fact utter truth. Not as true as the story of Private Carter, which I dared not tell and thus covered with this other true tale.

One evening during my military services, a medical orderly and myself—purely because I happened to be talking to him at the time—were ordered away from our company, supporting a battery of seventy-two-millimeter cannon, to help one of the women in one of the oil workers' dormitories give birth to a baby girl. I was to be the driver, and he was to show due regard for the midwife but intervene in the case of emergency. After all, the midwife would not have such resources as painkillers, muscle relaxants, and blood-clotting agents. The story dealt with the way the ultimate birth, and the drinking of tea with the other women later, brought out a frankness that was not the frankness of those who cower, but the honesty of those who generate life. Thus the orderly and myself talked with the women about the question of staying on the island or fleeing. The voices of children not born urged us all to get out, and the new baby had brought that impulse close to the surface of our skin. And then, as a truck came to take the mother away to suckle her baby in a rear area, various women laughingly proposed that the orderly and I provide them with a similar means of exit—even though we knew that an offensive from the other side would occur long before they could complete their pregnancies.

This was extraordinary behavior in terms of the suburbs and rural towns they came from, but their closeness to the guns and their loss of men in war had altered them. And according to this comforting but un-acted-upon idea of fortuitous pregnancy, they sat on our laps. Even Intercessionist girls far from their clergy bounced around to simulate copulation. It was as if the tea had been gin. The medic was slightly shocked. Like me, he wished they would either behave themselves or that singular women from the crowd would take each of us by the hand to a more hidden place, if there was any such thing in the refinery complex of Summer Island. And then a woman of nearly sixty said, Well, girls, our shift starts in six hours. And we've all got to stay here for the oil.

The orderly and I drank the lees of the tea, said good-bye, and drove back to our company, drained, and knowing we, like the women, had to stand to at first light.

Why the oil? the medic asked me in real life and in the tale. Why do we live for it?

This tale appeared in the student newspaper soon after Sarah's and my delightful session in the library. The next day she told me that the University Drama Society had voted to turn it into a play. In return she would teach me how to download and print computer files. After a week, she had already created a play script from my short story. And so it was rehearsed over three or four weeks.

Produced by Sarah Manners, the foremost youngster of the National Theater, who played one of the young women. Old Billy Salter, Cultural Commissioner, let it run ten nights, attracting people from throughout the city, before he closed it down in response to complaints that the students took the play's ritualized sexuality beyond the limits of propriety.

That production sealed the closeness between us. I was by now enchanted not by her casual splendor but by the energy and nobility of her soul. To my delight and bemusement we became a couple. I thought myself mere protective covering for her, and I restrained myself through breathless fear I would be dismissed from that high office. It was only by her unambiguous signs that I realized my job was more dazzling still, that of intended lover. There was more wonder in that idea than I could use in a lifetime.

We walked, delightedly enyoked, as one creature. Sarah and Alan. What a phenomenon! He with a grin of idiot delight, she with the slight frown of her art producing one small crease across the bridge of her nose, a harbinger of doubts and pains years from revealing themselves.

We had not made it to the Kennedys' for the Thursday night gathering following the one at which Toby had told his astonishing tale of walls and gates. And on Friday, Sarah went to bed early, half blinded by migraine and the normal sickening yellow blotches of light in her vision. I had until now unjustly associated migraine with neurotic thyroidy women and was surprised by how profoundly Sarah had recently been struck by the complaint. I would sit beside her on a chair, since any sudden weight shift on the bed caused her pain, and place cold cloths of the lightest cotton on her brow. Once I said, Maybe you should have gone on with that part in the soapie, and she laughed painfully. I regretted the joke, of course, since nearly every human gesture was agonizing when these bouts came upon her.

She had been to our doctor, who gave her some potent capsules and a form of suppository, but none of that worked very quickly when she was at the apogee of her pain. Instead they made recovery quicker and then gave her some eight hours' seamless sleep. I have to say, part of me dared be gratified that Friday night—the attack was severe enough to justify canceling the next day's visit to Mrs. Carter. In case it did not, I had recourse to the black-market vodka bottle.

The next morning, however, Sarah dragged herself up and took extra painkillers, specifically because she did not want to give me an excuse to put off Mrs. Carter. She did not want to cancel one stressful appointment and then have another in a few weeks' time hanging over us. Best for all our sakes, for the ease of my questionable soul and her clearing brain, that we get it over today! To brace myself I drank some more, and Sarah declared herself more than well enough to drive. The yellow blotches had disappeared and her head felt clear.

Mrs. Carter lived in a seedy but interesting old building where the young intellectuals of the Fusion Party had gathered in the 1940s and 1950s for rumored free love, irreligious drunkenness, and political discussion and subversion. Mrs. Carter had once been, during the time of puppet governments, clients of the West, a famously beautiful woman, favored by the monarchy but also a lovely presence in the early party from which Great Uncle came, which he had ultimately perverted and subsumed.

Parenthood had changed Mrs. Carter, and loss of her son, Private Hugo Carter, had transformed her too. Her eyes were full of an unreliable glitter as she greeted us at her door, and sullen as a teenager visiting an aunt I stepped across the threshold. You both look so well, said Mrs. Carter, but to me that sounded like a reproach.

Leading us into her living room, she chattered about the honey cake she had bought at the market, and the fig pie. There was enthusiasm in her voice, as if she had hopes of sweetening the entire earth. Then, stepping back from the table set for afternoon coffee, she examined me head to toe. When I see you, she told me, I feel as if Hugo is closer to home than ever.

I could only nod and accept that role.

I feel it can't go on forever, she said. They're holding our men out of pure spite. But please, you must be so thirsty and hungry.

That was one of the poor thing's tricks—to build up the weight of this reunion by pretending that it was such a trek from our place to hers. In a psychological sense, she was right. It was too much of a journey there and back for me. Maybe it had been my earlier tension which had given Sarah her spasm of headache. It had certainly made me a sot for the day.

Mrs. Carter indicated we should sit at the table, with its tablecloth, cakes, oranges. My gorge rose when I faced this little feast. Mrs. Carter lived on the pension of her late husband and, a victim of inflation, no longer had unlimited means. Yet all this was painfully and expensively assembled. Faced with the imminent duty of tasting it all, my throat was stung by the returning acid of vodka.

She sat us down and mercilessly plied us with good things, and poured hot coffee from a silver pot, and stared, feeding on us, devouring our presence. I was sure that she daydreamed it was her thin son, returned from imprisonment and ready now for life's full flow, whom she was feeding in feeding us—that was her fantasy, an understandable one which nonetheless filled me with panic.

Let me show you, she said.

We were already chewing sweet things, and she had not had a mouthful of anything, or even a sip of coffee. This seemed to me unjust. I would have crossed to the other side of the table and urged a plate of pastries on her, except she was away too quickly. She went to a drawer in a cabinet, opened it, and took out a familiar file, one I knew well. I had been shown it many times. It was years old, brown and worn, and full of her letters of hope—to the Secretary General of the United Nations, to the Ministry of War of the Others, to the Secretary of State of Sweden, and ministers from every honest-broker government on earth. The Scandinavians and Canadians in particular seemed to be the world's honest brokers—at least, Mrs. Carter had spent a long time writing to them.

She opened the file and brought a fresh, obviously cherished page to me. I wiped my hands on a table napkin in preparation to receive her latest attempt to liberate Private Hugo Carter. It was a copy of a letter addressed to the Director of Prisoner of War Repatriation, International Committee of the Red Cross, Geneva.

> *Dear Sir,*
> *I ask as a mother for the considerate attention of the*
> *Director to the case of Private Hugo Carter, 53rd Infantry*
> *Battalion, captured in the Summer Island battles in the*
> *Hordern Straits. Private Carter has now been held prisoner*
> *for six years, since the spring of 1992.*

It had come to her knowledge, she continued, that the repatriation of prisoners of war was supervised by the International Committee of the Red Cross, and she had heard that it was sometimes possible for them to bring the attention of the holding nation to the case of a particular captive, and to seek his repatriation on compassionate grounds. She had been told by her own ministry that her son was held in a prison somewhere in Dona Province. As a sufferer of osteoporosis and hip-joint impairment, doctor's certificates regarding which she attached, she referred her earnest request to him that he would do everything he could . . .

She signed the letter, *Yours sincerely, Emma Carter.*

I looked up to see that haunted glow on her face. Good, I conceded, a very fine letter.

He would have no reason not to listen to me, would he? she asked. I mean, there's no international agenda that would make it hard for the Red Cross to do their work fairly and earnestly. There wouldn't be, would there, Alan?

I couldn't see why there would be, I told her, but then tried gently to build up an idea of the difficulties involved. The Others do make it hard for the repatriators. They move prisoners around. Sometimes they assign them in groups to farmers to work on the harvest. There were even rumors they've changed prisoners' names to make them harder to find.

I know, Mrs. Carter insisted, her faith remaining unshaken and expressing itself in a wan, determined smile. But after six years, she continued, the Red Cross must have sorted out all their little tricks.

The crease running between her eyes like a threat of coming pain, Sarah said, I hope they listen to you this time, Mrs. Carter. I can't see why it's taken so long.

No knowledge of the reality, however, haunted Sarah. She, like everyone else, thought I had put the whole truth of Summer Island in my short stories. I had a second cup of coffee and ate two pastries as quickly as I could—the sooner I made the gesture, the sooner we could get home. At last, to Sarah's relief as well, I suggested we had to go—we had an appointment at six o'clock at a fish restaurant on the river.

Soon Hugo will be back, murmured Mrs. Carter, saying such things as that. He'll be saying, I just called in for a moment, because I have an appointment . . .

Without having intended to, I found myself babbling the old story, the story which was a mere gesture to the truth but which I uttered with a genuine guilt. Hugo had been forward at the outpost that morning, the second day of the battle. I had been up there the morning before, when it all started. But I was resting that second dawn in a bunker farther back. Stupid luck meant that Hugo was overrun, and I had time to take part in a reasonably organized consolidation. How unfortunate for Hugo to be captured during a temporary tactical emergency of a won battle. Hugo *would* be going to a fish restaurant, instead of me, had the Others started the Summer Island offensive one day earlier. It's so stupid, I said. It's so stupid.

That was at least a proposition I could believe in thoroughly.

I saw Sarah staring at me. Mrs. Carter's face had become somber, not before time. I know, Alan, she said. I know. I don't ask you here to explain these cruel things. Just to bring me the scent of my son. It's selfish of me.

Never, I asserted, and I hugged her like a mother.

Then, thank God, we were on the stairs. The line of pain between Sarah's eyes was now very evident, but I was still tipsy. And so she had to drive.

———

We were lucky not to be dependent for health care upon the chaotic public clinics. On top of that, Sarah's uncle, a renowned cardiac surgeon, had a neurosurgeon friend to whom Sarah went with her head pain the following week. She told me afterwards that she was to have a CT scan at Mount Mediation Hospital, the hospital of the privileged and the home of a set of all the earth's advanced medical machines.

Do they think it's cancer? I asked in unheeding panic. A brain tumor? Surely not.

She laughed at my fears. They want to have a look at the vessels at the back of the brain, she said, the ones that have been seizing up on me.

On the eve of her scan, we went to the very fish restaurant we had used as an excuse with Mrs. Carter. I was buoyant. My novel was as good as finished, and as I'd gone I had proudly done a translation into English, though American editors sometimes said they found my usages odd. I wanted to hang on to the thing for another month and look at it calmly, a little at a time, before sending it to Haddow and Sons, the national publishers, and to my American publisher, Random House, who might then give me a further eighty thousand dollars or more for a new book, ensuring our future.

My late mother had been in her way a less star-crossed version of Mrs. Carter. It was not so much due to her, though, but because of Sarah, who was so courageous in her choices, and who now survived on small payments from the films she had made in her late adolescence rather than act to the tyrant's script, that I had a taste for heroic women. I had spent a lot of time researching the families who lived on the far slope of Beaumont, above the oil pipes running down to the great crude oil terminal of Ibis Bay, a sentimentally named but utterly dingy and polluted stretch where no birds flew or dared land, ibis or otherwise.

My novel began with a Mother Courage figure, Rose Clancy, wife of a former naval officer and activist.

Carrying her pitcher, Rose advanced in sandaled feet to the pump at the end of the street. She stepped across the clods of rubble which proved that the adobe houses were falling inwards upon themselves, and met Mrs. McPherson, a young mother of two, already standing by the pump with an empty pitcher. No water, said Mrs. McPherson.

No water, really? asked Rose.

Mrs. McPherson, who was of strong Intercessionist stock from the southern farmlands, grasped the handle of the pump in a no-nonsense way and began to work it. Again, from the pipe's mouth, nothing emerged.

In the meantime, her husband, now on a pension and the head of his street committee, is reduced to selling black-market cigarettes in the Eastside markets to raise money for pharmaceuticals, a gesture against the grotesque sanctions which the West somehow thought would make the people aggrieved enough to over-throw Great Uncle. The truth being, of course, that they cemented Great Uncle in place, gave him an outside force to blame for the country's condition, and compelled the brave endeavors of Mr. Clancy.

I knew my manuscript was not *Ulysses*, that it belonged to the school of social realism which would be more tolerated in me than in a Western writer. But when I daydreamed, I daydreamed that my book would remind the *New York Times* of Hemingway's *To Have and Have Not*, or of Steinbeck.

Sarah and I had our meal at the fish restaurant. She seemed to eat better than normally, and to be free of discomfort. The CT scan, she said, would probably prove unnecessary. We left the restaurant by eight-thirty, since at nine our friend Andrew Kennedy was programming on national television the final of the European Cup between Italy and France, which meant too that he would have an indulgence from Great Uncle for cutting the *Hour of Devotion*, the reading of tributes to Great Uncle, to half an hour.

As we ascended the stairs to our apartment, we heard howling from within Mrs. Douglas's place, and knew that our neighbor was nursing her demented sister. In that wail, Great Uncle's potency was recalled to our memory. Surely the remains had been removed by now from the stone walls of Wolfmount. Surely the birds had taken the nephew's eyes, and he had gone blinded into the netherworld.

Come on, I told Sarah, taking her by the arm.

Home, she was in the kitchen making tea as I tuned the set to the football match. I heard a cup fall, and a squeal from her, as if she had been cut.

Thus began the worst enduring moment of my life. I found Sarah on the kitchen floor in a swoon, and carried her in to the bed, believing absolutely in her surviving this faint. Even Mrs. Douglas, who was fast becoming a professional comforter, came upstairs, leaving her demented sister, and made me tea, stoking it with sugar for what she already knew to be my loss. Our general practitioner, Dr. Colless, turned up with the police medical examiner. They asked would I leave the room a moment. I stood up as they emerged from visiting her. What is it? I asked them. Did she have access to any poison? asked the medical examiner. Are there any pills in the house? Could I please see the bathroom?

I denied poisons, and any particular pills except her painkillers. But yes, he should feel free to go to the bathroom. I realize now I was grateful to him for introducing the possibility of human culpability into what had happened. Not that I believed she was gone. Oh no. She would be up again at any second, squeezing the line of pain between her eyes with forefinger and thumb, before directing her eyes in my direction. Dr. Colless lowered his voice, comforting me. It was probably an aneurysm, I'd say, Alan. There'll have to be an autopsy to find out one way or the other.

She was having a CT scan tomorrow, I suggested hopefully.

Well, the autopsy will show any problem in that regard.

Does that mean they'll take her brain out of her skull? I asked, my voice rising, I knew, to the level of primal hysteria Sarah and I had both heard on the stairs only an hour or so ago.

Alan, said Dr. Colless. You'd want to know, wouldn't you?

I shook my head. I did not choose to know cause of death, since I had not yet accepted death. If they were just to let her lie, she would recover. I do not need to detail, from this distance of time, the craziness of my bereaved ideas.

With Sarah, there had been that strange business by which she occupied the place in my emotional landscape previously taken up by the entire variegated tribe of women. I forgot my few army experiences with prostitutes, and Louise James and other failures of flirtation at university. This was surely what marriage was meant to be, a profound and exclusive reliance underpinning the occasional physical frenzy. In a confused way, I had always understood my good luck. Now she had made a noise no more than as if the pad of her thumb was pierced by a little shard of china, or a small knife for cutting oranges. Foreseeable and acceptable minor harm had been overtaken, outswamped a billion times, by something more gross and world-devouring, some accident under her skull. I could not have been more awfully dismayed if the dropping of a cup had destroyed her by causing nuclear fission. I possessed the normal craziness of someone whose love is taken in a banal second, with the television warming up to the postkickoff argy-bargy of a European championship final. By some terrible means, I suspected, the blowing of a referee's whistle in Lyons of itself produced this prodigious result in *our* hemisphere, in *our* kitchen.

One of Sarah's aunts, the tender one, Maisie, turned up with Sarah's brother, Jimmy. The aunt laid Sarah out for the rest of the family to visit, while Jimmy plied me with whiskey—on top of some vodka I had already drunk that day, but so what? Everyone was welcome to come and say good-bye to her, her brown hair combed back from her forehead, so that the brow could be kissed. The medical examiner would go away and come back with his men in a few hours' time, said Dr. Colless.

Before I could stop him I was aware that Jimmy was on to a school friend of his. Yes, Jimmy apologized to the friend, tears in his eyes, I know France and Italy are playing. But it's my sister.

His face was drenched with his sorrow. But his way of dealing with it was to begin arranging the funeral tents and refreshments. He must have therefore really believed that she was dead. Of course, our type of people, what you might call the remnants of the city's middle class, unlike the farmers, preferred coffins, but that was something, he conceded to his friend, I would need to have a say in.

Put the phone down, for God's sake, Jimmy, I pleaded. But he could not renounce its comfort.

Put the fucking phone down, Jimmy, please. I can't stand it.

He made hurried excuses to his friend, who, one of death's accustomed helpmeets, was no doubt pleased to get back to the football.

My poor fellow, Alan, he told me. I would never have started this had I known it would get you upset.

I prevented myself from saying that had he murdered her, he couldn't have wanted her in the ground quicker. The relatives came, Sarah's mother and my late mother's brother, my uncle Ted, and his new wife. Ted had aged and was not doing well living off his savings. Jimmy surreptitiously gave me a mint to take away the smell of liquor—some of the older people were strict about temperance.

The visitors said the same things I had about the impossibility of believing it, and asked me had I had any hints. Stupefied by now, I told them about the headaches. The headaches must have had something to do with it. I found myself saying, They'll see what it was at the autopsy. And at the blasphemous, dreaded word, her mother began to wail and beat her head and try to rip the stitching of her dress as if she were a farmer's wife. Her behavior reminded Mrs. Douglas to rejoin her bereaved sister downstairs.

And then, more of the same. How could it have happened? She was such a beautiful girl. And not finished with the stage, by any means. I wept with them, but also considered either telling them to be quiet or rending my own clothing. But I did not have the luxury of being an unrestrained peasant. We had been partly Westernized—all our class must have been—by watching the calmer, mere sniffling of mourning which characterized American and British films. And unlike the Godfather, beloved film character of Great Uncle, I knew I had no one to shoot. Curiously I kept coming and going to look at her and kiss her forehead, and believed crazily that if I just stayed away long enough, she might be encouraged by my absence into waking.

Jimmy seemed relieved to be given the job of taking all the visitors' identity cards to the nearest metropolitan police station to get permission for them to be on the streets after curfew. Of course, Jimmy knew a lieutenant in the Overguard whom the Overalls would be able to call for verification that our grieving and our journeys were licit, and not a conspiracy against the state. As for the Kennedys, who had permanent laissez-passer for all days and all hours, they turned up just after Jimmy went away. Their intimate solicitude formed the necessary screen between me and the relatives. I had been propping up the Manners family, and they had been propping me up. Now we had two people present who were sad but not demented, and I resolved to take advantage of that. To the Kennedys I could somehow reveal my true misery, and exorcise my doubt that she was not dead in the bedroom.

She's dead, I told Andrew and Grace, the first people to whom it could be admitted.

I heard Mrs. Manners declare, from amongst the arthritic remnants of her loveliness, She goes to join her father now.

I'd never really met Sarah's father; he had been struck rather young by some sort of disabling aneurysm, and the once or twice he had addressed me before his death, he did so painfully, with partially paralyzed lips. Sarah's mother had borne all this and had been loyal to her daughter's decision to retire as a television actress, although in the circles in which she moved, she must have been plagued by questions about it—about why one so beautiful and successful should want to get off the merry-go-round. I got up, crossed the room, and embraced her. And we wept together. The Kennedys came up and told both of us, her and me, that they would take me home to stay with them.

The medical examiner's men arrived and reticently put us on notice that they would soon be removing Sarah. The relatives all milled into the bedroom and queued to kiss Sarah's face, and at last departed the room so that I could remain with her. I noticed increasingly her look of faint astonishment, not an astonishment of sudden pain or unpredicted treachery, but the surprise of a person who has received a sudden gesture of friendship and grace.

She had decided, for some reason, in the last moment, that death had been kind to her. This idea struck me as so pitiable and innocent that I covered her face with kisses and tears, and Dr. Colless came in and held my shoulder, and swore it would not be the last time I saw her. He swore that when her body was released, she would look as she did now. So we watched the men enter and carry her away, and I could hear her aunts and her mother in the doorway of the flat, telling each other that at this hour of the night they should try and control their tears for the sake of other residents. Since I was incapable of it, Grace Kennedy gathered some things of mine, and again I embraced Jimmy Manners and his mother, and my elderly uncle, and we all stumbled down the cold steps together, fleeing the site of the tragedy.

In the car I said to the Kennedys, I'm liquored up. Please don't dope me up any more. I need to be clear in the head.

But they assured me, No, we won't. Promise, Alan. Unless you ask us.

And Andrew shook his head over the steering wheel.

In our country it was customary, even though refrigeration made the rushing of the dead into the earth unnecessary, to bury the deceased quickly. It seemed a denial of God's will to spin out the process, and even the medical examiner's people, urged along by Dr. Colless and Jimmy Manners, worked fast. By Tuesday I was visited at the Kennedys' by Dr. Colless, who brought the news at last that the medical examiner had released Sarah's body. It had been a cerebral aneurysm that had hemorrhaged. She had died of a massive and nearly instantaneous stroke. Hence the headaches, he said—the aneurysm would have caused those before it burst. A tragedy, he said. She should have come to him earlier, and organized the CT scan. Her blood pressure must have been abnormally high for her age group—genetics would have influenced that. Hadn't her father died of a stroke? It was rotten luck. He took my arm in both of his hands. There was nothing that could be done when a subarachnoid hemorrhage came on like that. Had she somehow lived through it, she would have been . . . well, a breathing shell. She wouldn't have been there at all.

Colless must have known a trick or two about the irrationality of mourning, because I did find in this reflection a sort of marginal comfort.

Since I had Colless's word that the system which underpinned Sarah's existence had massively failed, I opted for the bourgeois practice of embalming, which was frowned upon by all but the most liberal clergymen. Inanely, I did not want the most corruptible regions of the body to hasten decay. The Mannerses' local clergyman, within the limits of what the older Mediationist clergy told him, was a decent fellow and it would not worry him. Religion was not frantically practiced in the cities in any case, and most people were intermittently devout. The centuries-old split between Intercessionists, who believed their priests spoke for God not merely on matters moral and social but even on politics, and the Mediationists, who merely saw their clergy as somewhat better informed than the average person on matters theological, was something I had not bothered studying in detail, and so I was unsure what would be required of me ritually now.

I insisted on a pure white coffin, though Jimmy said they were generally for girls. She's my girl, I told him. He had meant, of course, virgins, but then Sarah and I had barely begun on our agenda of marriage. I did not know her as a widower of eighty might know his lost wife. I felt she had taken most of her supply of secrecy with her into premature death.

Jimmy Manners, whom I was beginning to appreciate more and more, and dear Grace Kennedy prepared the flat for Sarah's body to spend its last morning at home. She was brought into the living room in her coffin, and it was placed on trestles. She lay fully enshrouded and bound except for a fringe of her hair and her face and temples.

Occasionally members of the family would adjourn to the kitchen to drink tea or, in Jimmy's and Andrew's case, brandy. All the old friends came to say how beautiful she looked: Wilf and his companion, Paul; Toby Garner, the architect who'd avoided being shot for gaps in walls; the McBriens, Matt having already acquired a good suit and a new bureaucratic dignity. He regarded me across the room as if weighing how much like me he might become should his Sonia drop down dead.

Mrs. Manners, reasonably enough, still spoke of the congenital flaw which had deprived her of a husband and her daughter, two of the finest people she had ever known. Then, towards eleven, there was at last a knock on the door—the undertaker's men were here. Her mother kissed her a last time, Jimmy, the aunts and uncles, Grace Kennedy. Then they left me alone with her for a final time. The undertaker called softly, Just tell us when, Mr. Sheriff, and closed the door behind everybody, leaving me within.

I gazed at Sarah, but whatever they had done to her, it had removed the girlish look of surprise from her face. In a funerary sense she was now a statue, an artifact, and yet the only artifact I owed anything to. I went to my desk in the living area and packed up what had been until then my life as defined in the public sense, the printout of my novel in the original and in English and the two disks on which it was stored. Then I called up the ten files of the novel on the hard drive and obliterated them one by one as a funerary tribute. Later that night, I thought, I would drop the laptop in the river so that nothing could tempt me to retrieve the cyber ghost of my work. I had barely begun to think that I might owe the publisher the advance. If the publisher wanted it, I would pay it back perhaps. And I would not receive the further payments for delivery and publication. That did not matter against the fact that I already intended to end my life too. If not, I would be a life-long laborer to repay Random House. But the manuscript did not belong to them anymore. Only Sarah had heard and read this tale of the tyranny of sanctions, and the cruel jokes of the black market under the broader tyranny of Great Uncle. I put the whole thing and the disks in a huge envelope and took it to Sarah's capacious white coffin, which I had doubted, at the point of purchase, would fit her, but within which she was a waif. I owed her my work, plain as it might be, to fill out the space, and, of course, I owed her myself.

Now I went to the door and invited the undertaker and his men in, and they clamped down the coffin lid over Sarah, removing her and my banal offerings to her from the world's light. The mourners on the stairs made way and then followed the white sepulchre, jolting on the bulky shoulders of balding but experienced men, down the stairs. Mrs. Douglas joined us meekly on her level, muttering condolences to me. She was so beautiful, she looked so young. And such an actress!

We passed through the lobby, sobbing, and piled into cars, myself and the family into the undertaker's limousines. But before we reached the gates of the cemetery, according to the gracious custom, we all got out, appropriately for a species so flawed that its most dazzling member could be obliterated by a little venous defect, and so we walked the last quarter mile, the sun burning the bared scalps of the men of the party, behind the pallbearers and into the cemetery gates, where the Reverend Cooper and, a little more distantly, the white tent set up for the funeral feast waited.

When I was a student I predictably thought that clergymen invoked our helplessness chiefly as a means of keeping us in our place. But this was the right morning for me to hear that all our splendors were accidental ones, and could be so easily erased, leaving only God remaining in a universe in which all other voices had been quenched. I could almost imagine myself a believer. Later, at the funeral repast in the tents on the edge of the cemetery, I saw Dr. Colless give Grace a prescription, and she came up to me and said, Now it's final, Alan, you must take something. You must sleep.

For I had been wide-eyed and mute for days, held in insomniac suspension between disbelief in and the certainty of this hour we had now reached. I would certainly take soporifics. I would take the lot.

I drank grape juice into which Jimmy had humanely inserted a considerable quantity of vodka. I had resolved my destiny. I was, in my head, halfway in the presence of my love. Colless had kindly written up a means of exit. Comforting myself with the certainty of my own obliteration, at ease with the idea that nothing could cause me fear or delight, I was surprised by the sudden jolt of blood brought on by the sight of someone from the past, the antique times of a week or so before. Mrs. Carter wore a shawl, and was coming to comfort me. In my crazed condition, I was convinced that she carried on her face a look of awful appeasement, and was delighted to welcome me, her substitute son, into the cold ring of victimhood. She appeared to me pleased that though I had had the impudence to avoid becoming one of the lost of Summer Island like her son, Sarah's faulty human vascular system had evened the score for me. The idea of her coming touch, of her taking my hand, filled me with terror. I dropped the glass of fortified fruit juice I had held, and rushed from the tent without apology. I weaved amongst graves to make pursuit difficult, then out the cemetery gates, and into the small garden farms beyond. Andrew Kennedy caught up with me as I stood gasping by an irrigation culvert.

Don't worry, he said. Get your breath. Everyone understands, Jimmy and Sarah's mother understand. You're lucky in your in-laws.

I didn't have any in-laws anymore. Andrew assured me we could go back to the car from here without risking any contacts. No one expected more of me.

Since nothing much had been demanded of me for some days, I forgot about my laptop and about drowning it, and spent the rest of the day and early evening in the Kennedys' screening room—it wasn't large, but it was curtained and had one of those huge television screens generally seen only in the international hotels in town. I watched famous soccer games, war and murder movies. I sneered at love stories, laughed bitterly at everything—every depicted human concern and demise. Andrew sat next to me for a good part of the time, drinking whiskey, and Grace brought tea and food.

As, towards midnight on the day of the burial, we watched a re-run of the last World Cup final between Brazil and Italy, Andrew filled me in on the details of the last time we failed to make the World Cup. The Others from across the straits had beaten us 3–2 with a penalty kick and, almost instantly afterwards, a goal, after we had been ahead 2–1 with five minutes to go. When our team arrived back at the airport in town, they and their officials were collected instantly by the Overguard, even before they had claimed their baggage, and driven in a bus from the tarmac to the Winter Hill Palace. Bemused wives, girlfriends, and children, gathered to console the heroes, still waited at the airport, expecting them to emerge from Customs, even as they were ushered into Great Uncle's presence. According to Andrew's story, Great Uncle sat behind a polished table with the Minister for Sport, one of his dumber stepbrothers, Albert Jenkins. He reproached the team and its management, particularly eyeing off Red Campbell, his remote kinsman, and Tony Barker, the unpopular team manager, known for a certain close-lipped arrogance. They all felt humiliated, one of the team's young defenders told Andrew later. It was a terrible thing for any man, simply in terms of his self-regard, to be despised and chastised by his head of state. They also felt a professional weight, knowing they would need to play with unchallengeable brilliance for the next four years if they wished to contest another World Cup. One would have thought they were adequately punished by now, said Andrew.

But then Great Uncle called in Sonny, sometimes known in our polity as Football Sonny because of his passion for the sport—though he could also have been called Cocaine Sonny or Bimbo Sonny. If Great Uncle had been unhinged by power, having once been a halfway normal though rather thuggish social democrat, according to all available evidence Sonny had been quite crazy from childhood. His father's fierce tribal nature had been restrained by powerlessness, his childhood governed by want and lust for literacy. Sonny had experienced none of these constraints. Though Great Uncle was rarely photographed unless he wore a holstered pistol, and in some pictures held in his hands his legendary old AK-47 from the days of the revolutions (two of them), Sonny seemed to carry an arsenal, and was seldom photographed without a joyously caressed M16. When he came into the team's presence that night, Sonny looked grim, but they knew him from many a locker room visit he'd made, and expected nothing more than angry words.

Instead, the young man came from behind his father's desk and shot Red Campbell through the head. Then Tony Barker, who had stood firm, either defiant or stunned, was similarly shot. Some of the players had blood and gobbets of cerebral matter on their clothing. Members of the Overguard came and removed the bodies, Sonny had a quiet word with his father and then went off to a party, and the rest of the team was ushered to their bus again and driven back to the airport. They had instructions to tell Mrs. Barker and Mrs. Campbell that their husbands had been delayed at Ankara, and a story was published in the *Gazette* that the manager and the captain had been arrested by the Others in Straits City for crimes against underage girls. Other team members soon enough told the bereaved families the truth, but by mutual consent the story quickly died. The widows received a sumptuous pension, and lest recruitment of young players stop, the Minister for Sport was authorized to tell the national side, on an informal basis, that they had nothing to fear, that the Campbell-Barker case had been a special one.

The national side had never looked back, making the quarter-finals six years ago, and being beaten in the semis at the last World Cup. Semis were good enough for national credit. After all, Great Uncle didn't want absolute victories. He wanted only a showing of honor. One way or another, said Andrew with an acid laugh, it couldn't be denied that the cement of the national team was fortified with the blood of Campbell and Barker.

Later still in the night, Grace brought in the sleeping tablets she had had made up. She laid them on the table beside a glass of liquor I had nearly finished. Then she took both my hands in hers. Alan, she said, I'm not going to treat you like a child. But you have to promise you'll use these tablets purely to help you to sleep. God knows you need it. Do you promise me that? Andrew and I can't afford to lose you.

Of course I gave my promise. I had spaces of time ahead of me in which to act. I had the leisure of choosing the moment.

Don't forget, she told me, you have a book to publish. You can dedicate it to Sarah, and through it she will live.

I nodded. It would be a miserable enough gesture, my book momentarily in the world. That was why I had decided to give it to her pitiful, violated shell. But for Grace's sake, I drunkenly decided that yes, it would be a bad thing, or more accurately uncivil, to make an end of things here, in the Kennedy household. Like most potential suicides, I thought upon my exit purely in terms of causing minimum inconvenience. I did not believe that anyone would be too aggrieved. I had typically ceased to believe in the mystery of human affection.

I could not impose on the Kennedys too long. Nor did I want to become their child, though I had a sense that they were willing, from the kindest motives, to transform me into a damaged son.

After I had watched a few more of Andrew's videos, and received and absorbed some more of his diverting Great Uncle tales, I intended to go up north to Scarpdale, where an old friend, a doctor, had a state medical post. I could stay with him in what I thought of as that city of crystalline air, beneath mountains of blue snow, on avenues as straight as my intentions. I was coming, Sarah, to where you were, to the nothing you enhanced. Was delay fatal to the would-be suicide? I did not believe so.

When I went home to pack, I waited till eight at night and took my laptop out across Republic Bridge, and without hindrance from the Overalls or anyone else, dropped it into those deep, ancestrally owned waters which had carried three thousand years of culture down to the sea and would have no trouble destroying the cyber ghost of my novel.

I caught a plane up to Scarpdale, and the city did not seem as pristine or well planned as it had been in my imagination. (Why not abandon an earth whose cities let a man down?) My friend and I drank too much together in the thin air. But he had a very pleasant government villa to do it in, and was occasionally visited by a brown-eyed woman friend, the young widow of an officer killed in an ambush by one of the tribal liberation fronts in the mountains far beyond the city. She possessed a wistful expectation that she and my friend would marry, but he told me when we were drinking together that he did not choose to acquire a ready-bred family. It was not the widow who frightened him—it was her boy and girl, with the memory of the brave father in their eyes.

Oh how we drank! I came to the conclusion my friend was a sot—as was I, but that didn't count, since I had abandoned all expectations of health. He was good at disguising his daily intake of alcohol. He told me that in Scarpdale a great deal of alcoholism prevailed amongst bureaucrats and officers. The ski run reserved purely for military officers and officials went underused. Scarpdale was one of those places bad for morale, a town in which people felt exiled unless they were natives of the region, as indeed

Great Uncle had been when young. One took a mere three days to examine comprehensively Scarpdale's fourteenth-century temples. Then the chill of being remotely posted on a flank of mountains began to enter the bones.

When we were deep in drink one night, he suggested we visit a brothel. If he thought the idea would appall me, it didn't, and there was enough nihilism and drift in me to go along, as disgraceful as such an idea was. I was so far gone with vodka that I spotted little connection between any intimacy I had ever shared with Sarah and what I might be expected to do with a stranger on a whorehouse's linen. My friend joyously called ahead and ordered two women—for sharing, it seemed, in the same room. He wanted to welcome me back to the commerce of flesh, and treat my grief with orgiastic therapy. A more serious, less childlike man than he would have laughed at the idea. This, in fact, helped make it a matter of indifference to me whether I went with prostitutes or not. Later, with a clear head, I could see he had probably planned the night, rather than falling into it by impulse, but had then eased me along to the right point of stupefaction.

But it was I who went.

Somehow, in spite of his drunkenness, he drove us to a house near the old university. We were politely received by a stylish woman who called my friend *Doctor* and summoned our girls to come and meet us in the drawing room. I can't even recall their faces except for the fact that they were particularly handsome northern, semitribal women, and I assumed they had been deliberately recruited from their villages by some whoremonger. They led us, one each, by our hands to a spacious room towards the back of the house.

I somehow found myself sitting naked on a bed, caressed from behind by a wild-eyed peasant girl, her legs slotted around mine, her pelvis grinding against my spine in simulated urgency. I watched my friend the doctor—mind you, an expert in communicable diseases—drop to his knees before the fairer, less raw, more formal of the two young women and begin mouthing her in a manner which seemed to bring her unfeigned pleasure. Her groans so dominated the room that the second mountain girl and I gave up our own unenergetic rites and simply gazed at the event on the other side of the room. No question but that I had displayed the normal, half-interested animal reactions when caressed, but the extra dimension of eroticism orgiasts were supposed to lend each other by their parallel acts had been replaced by bemusement. For my friend's feral appetite was somehow horrifying. Not that such usage exceeded my atlas of erotic possibilities. Nor was it the matter of hygiene alone, either, the fact that this same woman my friend was devouring had probably accommodated many officers, technicians, and departmental employees. The reaction in me combined all elements: remotely felt lust, nausea, revulsion, a sense of futility. The girl herself broke the obscene spell by withdrawing herself a little from my friend and twisting his ear, saying, Gentle, gentle, Doctor. There's time!

But that was it. He had behaved like a man in a panic, a man who believed there was no time left. My friend, I decided, would in the end destroy himself, consumed by his own hunger. A peculiar insight, you'd agree, for a man who, as I did, intended imminent suicide in a day or week or two. I saw dreadful weariness now enter the face of the doctor's prostitute and a line appear just below her jaw, the beginning of a jowl. She was disappointed at herself for believing, however briefly, in my friend's goodwill, his apparent democracy of lust, which had now turned totalitarian, his teeth biting tissue.

When I saw this, I got up, ran into the bathroom, and vomited across the floor. This brought to an end the tolerance the women had so far extended to us. As I raised my face, I could read in my friend's irritable and flushed countenance that it was the end of his tolerance for me too. I must now either end my life at altitude, in Scarpdale, or return to the city to do it.

On my last night before flying back to the city, my doctor friend, as if embarrassed by our recent mutual adventure and by what I had seen of him the previous evening, muttered some excuses about a dinner invitation he had and how bitterly he regretted we could not spend my last night in the town over a shared meal. I found it easy to tell him to keep his appointment, and if I had hurried to the curtains to see him make his way to his garden gate I am sure I would have seen a man with lightened step. No doubt he was off to visit the widow, who did not understand the sort of fellow she was interested in marrying.

I was drunk by a little after seven o'clock. The hollow air of the city seemed somehow to leave room for much liquor. I watched a video of *To Kill a Mockingbird*, which was like enjoyable science fiction to me. The film was not dubbed, and the skill of the screenplay was continuously betrayed by the banality and literalism of the subtitles. I had become so crazily and alcoholically affronted at the damage done not only to the original English but to the translation into my own language that by the time the trial scene began I stopped the tape and called Andrew Kennedy. I told him, with all the miscued fury of too much grief and too much liquor, my brain seeming to creak with malign heat, that I was watching a taped version of *To Kill a Mockingbird*, as broadcast by his National Network, no less. Under your ultimate responsibility, I said. And the subtitling's utter shit. Who does these things for you?

He was of course taken aback by the lack of greeting and, in my view, wasted time asking how I was. But I wouldn't be swayed from the point. Who does your subtitles? I insisted.

Half the English department at the university, he confessed. And then, Ellen Cassidy at Haddow and Sons.

I scoffed at this. These aren't creative people, I told him. You have to employ creative people. Movies aren't comic strips, you know. For the viewer, the shit of the subtitles leaks into the very texture of the film.

I'm sure you're right, Alan, he conceded. But we have to take what we can get.

Because, no doubt, you pay them shit.

You wouldn't believe how low the budgets are. Except for the *Hour of Devotion*, of course.

Give me the job, I said. I'll work for nothing or close to it. For the time being, anyhow. Say I subtitle four classics for you. At least you'd have four films to show that aren't shit.

What about French films? Andrew asked.

I can handle French films, I assured him. I can read Camus in the original. But I somehow like the American stuff.

Andrew laughed. Like Great Uncle. What about finishing your novel?

I thought of it, keeping company as it was with unimaginable Sarah, underground. I began to weep.

I can't tell you what an armpit of a place Scarpdale is. Everyone's a drunk. And it's so damn cold. Don't worry about my novel. Let me do some films.

We'd be very honored, Alan. I'll see if I can get an extra pittance out of the board. Perhaps we could present them as the Alan Sheriff Quartet.

None of that shit, Andrew. I don't have a quartet. I don't want a quartet. I just want to watch films without needing to go to the university to strangle the stupid subtitler.

I heard Kennedy laugh. Grace will be pleased you're in such robust form, he said. By the way, did you know Peter Collins has made a hit appearance on the leading German talk and variety show? He's done a bit better than Stenhouse.

Even though I numbered myself, short of subtitling four films, amongst the dead, I had room to be depressed by this proof Collins was elsewhere. Stenhouse, by contrast to Collins, was a renowned biophysicist who fled to Paris. His body was found quartered and sectioned and enclosed in two suitcases, but no one knew if it was an exemplary project of the Overguard. It was said for a time to have prevented flight by other scientific specialists.

Kennedy said, Grace and I have missed you.

You haven't, I told him. And if you have, you shouldn't have.

But I could sense his humane warmth over the telephone.

I flew back to the city, with its vistas and larger sky and more sensible climate, and returned with some dread to my apartment. Before Sarah had died, I could not imagine being a person who went back to the house of the beloved dead. My instinct would have been to burn it down, either literally, as the poor Intercessionist farmers in the south do, to expunge and liberate the ghost, or else to go to a new place. I knew now, however, why people did return to the houses of the accidentally deceased, as if to find the terrible events revised and amended as they opened the door. And, in any case, there are no houses that do not belong to the dead.

So I returned home, and parted the air beyond the front door of my flat, and walked into the kitchen as if nothing had happened there, lighting a flame under the same kettle Sarah had died tending.

True to his promise, Andrew organized me a pass to the National Broadcasting Network, so that within a day of my arrival home I was met at reception at the television studio by one of Andrew's assistants and instructed before a video machine and a specially programmed computer. This apparatus allowed for the translation of dialogue directly onto the film, and permitted the obliteration of the inept dialogue others had imposed on splendid footage.

I had not realized how much dialogue there really is in a screenplay, but I worked long hours. My first film was the classic *Lawrence of Arabia*, which was always popular and ideologically defensible, since it portrayed the cynicism and opportunism with which the British and the French empires fished in alien waters such as ours. The former subtitler had not done too bad a job, but there were occasional howlers. For example, when the American journalist comes ashore and has an interview with Prince Feisal and warns him that General Allenby, the British general in Egypt, is a "slim customer." Instead of being translated as a crafty or devious person, the subtitler had rendered it meaninglessly as "thin shopper." I wondered what our audience had made of that. The truth probably was that they were so frequently amazed by television's irrationalities that they didn't even apply their minds to it. But Allenby *was* a devious man. His part in the slicing up of the region still caused grief and conflict, and he deserved to be called a sly character rather than a thin shopper.

While I was reforming the subtitles of *Lawrence,* Andrew asked me to bend my skills to *Casablanca* as well. The previous subtitling had been done when television began transmission here in the early 1960s. They really didn't make films like this anymore. As a narrative device, I liked the good old-fashioned maps after the credits, upon which the lines by which refugees were escaping the Nazis were marked. I was for a time engrossed in translating the film's opening statement about tortuous, indirect refugee trails—Paris to Marseilles, across the Mediterranean to Oran, then by train or auto or foot across the shoulder of North Africa, to Casablanca in French Morocco. *Here the fortunate ones, through money or influence or luck, might obtain exit visas and scurry to Lisbon, and from Lisbon to the New World. But the others wait in Casablanca, and wait and wait and wait.* Modern directors would consider this too much geographic information for an audience to absorb.

Then the descent of the camera from the minaret of the mosque down into the fascinating squalor of Vichy-run Casablanca. I flew through this film—in one day I got from the start, full of its desperate refugees and the undercurrents of varied allegiance, to the scene where Peter Lorre—Guillermo Ugarte—is defending his practice of selling questionable exit visas, and Rick's line comes up: *I don't mind a parasite, I object to a cut-rate one.* Later in the week, I had to admit that the person who had done the first subtitling had not done a bad job with the comic challenge of the scene in which two potential refugees are practicing the English language. *What watch?* asks the husband. *Ten watch,* says the wife. *Such much?* he responds.

I allowed myself to be taken home each night by Andrew, fed and liquored, and returned to the flat, where I lay imagining myself held and cosseted, at secure anchor with Sarah.

My third film was *North by Northwest.* According to a film theorist I had heard at the university, it displayed the trivial evil which lay behind the classic visages of American presidents on Mount Rushmore. But it also had a remarkable blonde, Eva Marie Saint, and blondes were always very popular with the cabinet and senior bureaucracy; indeed with all our generally swarthy nation.

That editing room, where I sat before the oleaginous Cary Grant and the even more oiled James Mason, with Eva Marie Saint's near-albino beauty as unanswerable as a glacier, sometimes seemed so like my home that it came to me: I could write a screenplay. So many of them had been written in Hollywood by exiles. But since I reminded myself I lacked a future, I began work on my fourth classic, *On the Waterfront,* another Eva Marie Saint vehicle. This one Elia Kazan's work. Eva Marie Saint poignant and maidenly in this, where she had been seductive in *North by Northwest.* She was the face of working-class dignity and innocence, the common woman to Brando's common man. In a way, the same types could have been found in our Eastside markets. I relished the waterfront bar where Big Mac, James Westerfield, the man who makes and destroys waterside workers by hiring one and not another, brings the sinisterly well-tailored Johnny Friendly the rake-off from that day's hiring. *Here's the cut on the shape-up,* he tells Johnny Friendly. I was particularly pleased with the way

I was able to translate the subtext of *A banana boat's in at forty-six tomorrow. If we could pull a walkout, it might mean a few bucks from the shippers. Them bananas go bad in a hurry.* This had been clumsily translated by some English speaker at the *Gazette* office, twenty-five years past, doing a quick job for extra cash with inadequate tools. I concluded there was in fact no need to censor ideas from films in our country, because some scenes that had the strongest political undercurrents were routinely mistranslated. Thus our people, in their living rooms or around the community center's television set, accepted the film and made what they could of its textual mystifications. The speech of Karl Malden's character, the priest or mullah who tells the stevedores that God is with them in the employment melee and in the holds of ships, had been so mangled, no doubt out of fear of outcries from the Intercessionist clergy of the south, that Malden might as well have been reciting a menu.

A frightful demand was about to make its way to me, down the corridors of the National Network, a demand which was the fulcrum of this saddest and silliest story, and so I should at this stage try to tell you what I think was happening in my soul. I believed neither the oaf nor the sage in me—the parts that were below, on the one hand, and above, on the other, the small screen of knowing which was my conscious life—wanted me to take them with me when I went. The sudden fury of energy to produce subtitles before I finished myself was probably the sage doing his best to make a case that there were still worthwhile mental challenges for the bereaved husband to apply himself to. And the brute, from below, screamed, Hear, hear! The beast in his cave liked nothing so much as breathing and an occasional good meal. The sage liked nothing so much as filling the cosmic vacancy with little jobs, such as translating *Such much?* in terms which retained the joke. They were both about to be rescued from my conscious intention to end things. I could hear footsteps in the rather underused corridor which led to my subtitling hutch. There came a polite knock on the door, a knock which acknowledged there was an artist at work within.

When I opened up I saw Andrew Kennedy in slacks and shirt and Mr. Cultural Commissioner Matt McBrien in a gray suit and silk tie and the badge of the Cultural Commission on his lapel. There was a note of deference in the way Andrew stood. He had once told me, It's not necessary to respect the man in power, but essential to respect the power in the man.

Hello, I said. But I did not want them inside the editing room, my refuge.

McBrien asked me how I was and then said, like a man who had acquired new rights to be acquainted with everything others were up to, Andrew's been telling me about the splendid work you've been doing. It sounds as if you're back in creative nick, and we're all pleased for that.

But however transformed by his new economic eminence, he looked a little flushed.

You and I are going to a meeting, Alan, he told me. Do you have a suit?

I have a black suit, I told him. Jimmy Manners had fitted me out with it for the funeral.

Pure black? asked McBrien.

I'm afraid so. This meeting . . . ?

McBrien said, It's nothing to worry about. More a cause for delight. I'm sure you'll be welcome in a black suit. Do you have a subdued tie to wear with it?

I told him that I could find one.

He pulled out a mobile phone, a rare implement still in our society. Excuse me, he said, I'll just tell the Overguard to collect us at your place.

The Overguard?

McBrien assured me, You're about to be introduced to a great opportunity, Alan.

I looked at Andrew Kennedy, who shrugged philosophically while nodding agreement, as if I should take the same attitude. McBrien had stepped aside and was already on his phone. He seemed to be giving the Overguard my address and proposing a pickup there at eleven o'clock, an hour's time.

An anger stirred in me. I didn't want to leave my subtitling room. What if I don't go? I asked.

Don't be a silly bastard, Alan, McBrien urged me. But he looked feverish. Please. You and I don't actually have a choice in this.

The Ministry of Culture, I said as a certainty, and Andrew looked at me dolefully, as if I hadn't guessed high enough. He said, Sorry, Alan, but you can't leave Matt in this situation. He's been ordered to take you somewhere.

To hell with him, I said. I didn't ask him to take his ridiculous job. I didn't ask him to become a junior Old Billy.

McBrien looked frantically at Andrew, who said, Yes, but he does have the job, and he's a friend.

Fuck him, I said.

We don't have a lot of time, pleaded McBrien.

I felt desperate. A quarter of an hour ago I could have finished myself without regard to anyone. Now Andrew and McBrien had sewn me back into the patchwork of responsibility and friendship.

I turned to Matt McBrien. Go and tell them that I'm a man on the edge of nothing.

I gestured to my little subtitling suite. This, I said, is doodling on the edge of the grave. I've got nothing to contribute to anything.

McBrien shook his head and again looked to our mentor, Andrew.

Andrew in turn surveyed me calmly. You can't say that, sorry, Alan. You've been conscripted. I've had the experience, and Matt's just going through it. And now it's your turn. And I'm afraid we're all mutually dependent. Remember Charlie McKay?

I had heard a rumor of the disappearance of Mr. McKay, a longtime Deputy Cultural Commissioner who had had responsibility for Peter Collins's file at the commission, and who had gloried in that association, achieving a celebrity of his own on its basis. Now he was missing. He had not turned up at the office, he had not been seen at home. There were rumors that he might have been obliterated for permitting Collins to defect.

Matt McBrien didn't want McKay used as an argument, and yet the question thoroughly sidetracked us. I don't believe the gossip that he's been punished by someone, said Matt. He had debts and a difficult marriage.

Kennedy said, Perhaps that's so. He's just done a runner. Maybe.

Besides, many a man disappears. That isn't any sort of punishment. It isn't exemplary enough.

I asked McBrien, Exemplary?

Yes, if you want to make an example of a man, you do something that readily becomes known.

Kennedy seemed to agree with this. Like shooting a football manager, he suggested.

That's right, McBrien said, nodding, it seemed to me, to reassure himself as well as us. Look, Alan, we've wasted ten minutes here and you still have to get your suit on.

My shirtsleeves will be good enough for your minister, I asserted, purely bloody-minded, and angry with myself for having lazily lived on long enough to be in this position.

It's not my minister, McBrien assured me in a lowered voice. Please.

His Eminence the Principal Mediator, I suggested, snorting, nominating the elderly primate of Mediationist clergy.

Don't be ridiculous, Alan, McBrien said. Someone else again.

The idea that it might be Great Uncle for the first time brought an absolutely normal pulse of anxiety and even of anticipation.

Come on, Alan! Andrew Kennedy urged me. You must go.

If Andrew Kennedy kept saying these things with such a level-voiced intensity, then I knew I was stuck.

Hell! I said, but I went back into my room, saved my subtitling file, went out to McBrien in the corridor, and walked with him upstairs and out of the building, Kennedy seeing us as far as the door. McBrien had a high-polished black car and a driver. Of course. As we drove off towards my apartment, I noticed Matt exercising his shoulders while breathing deeply, but he seemed to achieve very little muscular ease.

Meanly, I teased him about his earlier remarks. You look like a man going to his executioner, I told him. Are you scared of exemplary or nonexemplary punishment?

I won't dignify that question with an answer, he told me.

A limousine and a Toyota full of Overguard were waiting outside my apartment building. McBrien's vehicle rode past them and parked, and I went upstairs as McBrien went to report to the officer in charge. I ascended the stairs and saw Mrs. Douglas's door, which was open an inch or two, slam shut. I knocked on the door and called, Nothing to worry about, Mrs. Douglas. They're just an escort.

But then, they always were. With the time this took, McBrien and an Overguard officer and two of his men had nearly caught up to me on the stairs, and were able to enter my flat behind me as soon as I unlocked the door. They sought no invitation—they were accustomed to not needing one.

Just get dressed, McBrien said. Better take a shower or a sponge first.

The officer, who was very handsome and square-jawed, laughed. The Boss. Doesn't go for human odor.

Is it true, asked McBrien, that the palace guards shower three times a day and use Tommy Hilfiger cologne?

That's his favorite, the Overguard officer admitted.

Was he talking about Great Uncle? He certainly seemed to tell the story as if it were an illustrative and endearing quirk of someone whose power was godlike and who could make all those Praesidians scrub and sprinkle themselves according to his wishes.

I showered myself more attentively than I had since Sarah's death. I did my best to erase a certain vegetable musk which characterized my armpits—an indelible trace of my imperfect physical being. I used an aromatic stub of a deodorant to try to mask it, and I shaved thoroughly and applied an aftershave—not Tommy Hilfiger, but some birthday present bottle given to me by one of Sarah's aunts. I ensured every inch of skin was dry before I pulled my white shirt on. I had become a subject of the state again, and dressed observantly. Then my black suit, in which I had fled from Mrs. Carter, and my red tie. The red seemed to rescue the rest from seeming odd for the sort of visit McBrien and the Overguard officer were proposing.

When I emerged from the bedroom, McBrien said, Splendid, and the Overguard, who'd been sitting around, reading some of my books—as if in parody of security forces, ones with pictures, historical tracts, and accounts of archaeological digs—stood up. By the way, said the tall Overguard officer, name's Chaddock.

Pleased to meet you, Mr. Chaddock.

Lieutenant. Passport with you?

No, I said. Are we traveling somewhere?

He smiled. No. But passport's needed.

He would always prove a master of telegraphic speech. I fetched my passport from my desk and put it in my breast pocket.

Down the stairs again, past Mrs. Douglas's mute and afflicted door, and into the Overguard limousine. Lieutenant Chaddock took the front seat with the driver, McBrien and I were allotted the midcar one, and two Overguard men took the seat behind us. The officer named Chaddock turned around smiling jovially. Lights out, he announced. With that the two men behind us slung something over our heads, and I thought of the garrotings in the *Godfather* films. I shamed myself with a huge gasp, and then I re-

alized it was not the blackness of asphyxiation but a mere blindfold, which was then tied and adjusted around my head.

McBrien had heard my fearful intake of breath. This is quite
normal, he told me.

The procedure made me sure that we were about to be taken to
one of Great Uncle's twenty palaces, and I became fascinated by
what I might see, feeling all the more sportive since I did not really fear one of Sonny's or the Overguard's bullets, though I preferred that it came notified rather than as suddenly as my eye
mask.

The journey was made faster by the Overguard's absolute right of
passage at intersections. There were three palaces within roughly
half an hour of my flat, but I had no means of telling how much
time had passed, and all conversation had quickly, and perhaps by
design, died in the vehicle. At one stage only did McBrien whisper
to me, Thanks, Alan.

He probably meant, for calming down. For going along.

Our Overguard limousine paused now. I could hear conversa-
tions in remarkably discreet voices. Though Great Uncle came
from a rural family, from hayseeds who liked at weddings or triumphant football matches to stand on a seat and let off celebratory shots at the ceiling or into the sky; though Great Uncle
himself was sometimes known to celebrate in such a manner,
Kalashnikov in one hand, pumping rounds into the ether, he was
also known to like lowered tones from his subordinates, and the
nickname of the palace branch of the Overguard, the Praesidia,
was the Whisperers. This though they were generally recruited
from raucous families, most of them related to him, in his own
northern hills. Hence the hushed dialogue at the gate, and then
our car rolled through, and drove slowly for perhaps half a mile,
the music of fountains and the dominant tenor of the occasional
designed waterfall reaching us from the opened front windows.
Could any of this have been water Mrs. Douglas's nephew failed

adequately to test? The oaf in me, who wanted greater security than this moment provided, had decided my hands would sweat. The sage was full of his normal insistent questions and timidities. Whereas the true "I" awaited events with something like a lively curiosity. I thought that revelation was close.

As the limousine pulled up, the Overguard men removed our blindfolds. We were outside a white-columned building. The back doors of the limo were opened for us and the beaming Chaddock asked, All here? All right. Upstairs.

He led Matt McBrien and myself up the front stairs and past Praesidian guards in glittering white helmets. Inside, however, there were normal-looking office doors, and I saw a Praesidian administration officer walking up the corridor towards us armed only with the revolver at his hip, almost like a normal clerk.

Okay, he murmured, shaking hands with Chaddock and then with McBrien and myself. McBrien's eyes glistened with a touching, edgy fraternity, so that I was tempted to reach out and tell him it was all okay.

Got your passport, Mr. Sheriff? asked the administration man. I presented it and he briefly riffled its pages before clipping it to his other documents.

What if I need it?

You'll get it back in a month or so, he assured me.

He dismissed Chaddock and led McBrien and me to a room with a settee and chairs, and a little table with a bowl of peaches, apples, and oranges.

Help yourself if you get hungry, he said, implying we would be there for a little time yet. But McBrien had barely time to ask me whether I would behave myself when another, more heroic-looking Praesidian officer entered, and asked me to come with him. If I expected revelation soon, however, I was disappointed. I was taken to a bathroom—something akin to a bathroom in a good hospital. I was told to strip down and take a thorough shower. The guards left me alone to shower but asked me to knock on the door when I was finished. I was to wear only the towel they'd provided. They took my clothes out with them, muttering about how I would get them back afterwards.

I showered thoroughly for the second time that day. I dried myself scrupulously with the towel, wrapped it around my loins, and knocked on the door.

I'm ready, I cried. One of the Praesidia came in wearing rubber gloves and handed me a urine sample jar.

Can you manage that? he asked. Or do you need a drink of water?

I moved off towards the urinal.

No, do it here. That's the rule. I have to see you. Don't worry about the floor, we'll wash it.

Naturally, like any man raised in an urban tradition of personal modesty, I tried to piss the exact milliliters needed for the sample, and then to close off the flow. It was not entirely possible, however, and the guard, though he stepped back to avoid urine spots on his glistening boots, nonetheless said, Don't worry, don't worry. Can't be helped. Screw the top on and give it to me.

He accepted my offering in his gloved hand and left. But instantly another man, a white coat over his khakis and gloves on hands, entered and asked me to prepare myself for an examination of my mouth and anus. I passed both tests.

Next, the urine test man was back, wearing gloves still, with the sort of all-in-one sterile suit surgeons wear. I was told to put it on, and adjust the mobcap over my hair. So dressed, I found that my feet did not quite match up with the soles of the thing, which were designed for a bigger man, and escorted out of the shower room and down another corridor, I could only stumble along, a little like a man in chains. Around a corner I encountered uniformed technicians and a metal detection machine, and was asked to go through it, and once that test was passed, I was pointed to a tray with—as I was told—a basin full of permanganate solution on it, and asked to lower my hands into it for thirty seconds. That time up, an orderly actually dried my hands for me with a soft cloth, and when that was done, examined my nails.

Now I was led off further, and entered a plain office door. Was I to be met while still wearing this silly costume? If so, I needn't have worried about my black suit and red tie.

Here there was a desk, a bowl of fruit, a bookshelf largely empty. But on the wall in red was a script page from the Book of Mediation. I had heard that the President-for-Life had written with his own blood and in his own hand a page from that holy book. Through an open door I could see in the next room an edge of an army cot. Immediately I thought, This will not be Great Uncle. I have been dragged in here to see a bureaucrat. Thus, do I have an infectious fever I'm unaware of?

But I heard boots on the parquetry of the room with the army cot, and through the door entered a man in military fatigues and shining boots who bore a potent resemblance to Great Uncle.

There was a large belt around his waist in which was holstered a massive pistol, and he carried a peaked and braided military cap which he placed on the desk. It came to me in a rush, from the individual way he laid down his hat, the way he always laid it down during broadcasts—this *was* Great Uncle. Any rebels, rampaging through a palace, their eyes full of blood, would not look for the President-for-Life in such a humble place as this.

There were so many rumors, reliable and unreliable, about Great Uncle and his mistress, Rhonda Lansdowne, Deputy Head of the National Bank, and Sonny's outrage that his large-boned northern mother, Susan Stark, was demeaned by Great Uncle's association with Dr. Rhonda. Yet Great Uncle seemed to have reduced all this lush gossip to the austerity of an army cot and a banal office. Despite myself, I felt my first surge of admiration. Such humble arrangements as this were never mentioned or praised on the *Hour of Devotion*. Did the peasants who wrote their doggerel for the show sense more about Great Uncle than I ever had? Or was this austerity imposed by some sudden disordered fear about Dr. Rhonda's personal hygiene?

Great Uncle was a darkling fellow from the north. He had profound eyes, a mustache, full lips, the lotion-repaired look of someone who had just shaven. He also seemed a year or so older than the previous image of him in my head. There had been an irregularity in his stride, something to do with his injured back, but it was partially concealed by the vigor of the three steps he took to his desk.

Good morning, Mr. Sheriff, said Great Uncle, as I remained standing rigidly in my strange costume. Sit down, Alan. Sit down.

He sat himself.

I never got a chance, he told me at once, in a voice which remained lowered and as if we were resuming a conversation, to let you know how much I enjoyed your book of short stories. I liked "The Women of Summer Island," and the play your wife made of it. I regret the prudes closed it down after a few days. But the minister got various complaints, and Old Billy had to act on them.

He looked at me with his limpid, dark eyes, hoping I would understand the complications of cultural statecraft.

By the way, he said, I very much regretted for your sake and ours the loss of your exquisite wife. I knew she was not well because she had given up her television role. But I was hoping to see her on the small box at some stage when her health improved. I think that television was her forte, don't you?

Yes, I told him, she liked that medium very much. Thank you, Mr. President. I was actually, and despite myself, flattered for her sake.

Great Uncle joined his hands together and said further, Perhaps there is something you could do for her memory. By the way, have one of these apples. They're from the Piedmont area. Very succulent.

He pushed the bowl of fruit to me. His dark eyes lay on me with the force of command. I picked an apple up. Had he brought me here, in my shroud, to poison me? My paranoia on that issue was on a scale to match his own reported paranoia about germs and assassination.

Eat up, he said. You don't have to worry. They've been screened for radiation, insecticide, and toxins.

I took a mouthful. If it were a poisoned apple, hadn't I been seeking one? But it was succulent, and the juice lay on the tongue more like nectar than acid.

Great Uncle smiled across the desk at my obvious appreciation. You see? You see, Alan? Now, enough about apples! I believe you are contracted to an American publisher?

I told him that it was Random House.

Yes, he said. They were appreciative of us once, the Americans, weren't they? When we were fighting the Others for them. When my friend and cousin General Stark organized the Republican

Guard and we drove our enemy and theirs out of the oil fields and back across the Hordern Straits. An enterprise in which you, Alan, took a brave part as an infantryman, I believe. Our existence as human beings meant something to the West then. Not now. Not with the sanctions. Which unit did you serve in, Alan?

I thought of Mrs. Carter and reddened. In the Fifty-third Infantry, Mr. President. I rose in the end to the grand rank of corporal.

He laughed. A rank not to be despised, he told me. General Stark was once a corporal, in the days when true nationalists were not likely to be promoted in an army full of Western lackeys.

I remembered that General Stark also introduced the summary shooting of soldiers who retreated, and then a return of their bodies home in a black coffin with the word RENEGADE painted on it. But then I found myself close to thinking, in Great Uncle's austere, murmuring presence, that perhaps such thorough methods were needed for the sake of sovereignty, for the survival of the nation with or without Great Uncle. Perhaps I owed my American dollars advance to General Stark's toughening of our army. Power, the sad habituality of it, shone in Great Uncle's eyes, and I was half intoxicated with that. What did one or two black coffins matter in those eyes, their immensity of reach?

And of course the refineries and the Hordern Straits had to be retained. I would like to say, thus the arse-licking sage began to assure me. But no, it was no separate entity, no independent savant who tried to persuade me. It was myself, my reaction to the depth of his eyes, the rustle of his voice, the utter authority of his words. It had taken a mere minute for Great Uncle to enter the room and alter my view of things. This enchantment was, however, about to be challenged.

Great Uncle said, I hear from Commissioner McBrien that your new novel concerns the home front, the impact of sanctions. And brave, ordinary folk.

I must have frowned, for Great Uncle went on in his measured voice, This is purely literary gossip, of course. Forgive me if I have it wrong.

Of course I did not want him to know the way in which the manuscript, virtually complete, had been placed as an offering to Sarah.

I'm afraid, Mr. President, that the novel has been abandoned. It led nowhere—artistically, I mean.

Do you have a typescript?

I knew I must return his stare, but I confess it was hard to do. He was sure he guarded the state. I was convinced I must guard the grave. An image of a desecrating mechanical digger came to my mind.

I burned it, sir, I said. By keeping my eyes directed at him, I hoped it would not seem the barefaced lie it was.

I said, When a book goes bad on you, it seems to be the only thing to do with it. West and East, there are many, many burned manuscripts.

Of course, said Great Uncle. I've read of many such cases myself. The artist wants to obliterate what he sees as his bad work. Sometimes, of course, he's being too hard on himself. Wouldn't you say that? That he's being too hard? Or perhaps too vain?

Not, if I might say so, Mr. President, when the work is in fact really bad.

Do you have any copies on computer disk?

I went to rather silly extremes, Mr. President, and threw them away in the garbage.

I hoped he did not get the idea of setting Overguards to work searching the hectares of waste on the northern edge of the city. My lies made me breathless, but I held the gaze.

Oh, you must have disliked it, Alan. But Andrew Kennedy tells me you've been getting your creative edge back by subtitling films. I believe your subtitling of *Casablanca* is better than the original.

As a mere side issue, I felt angry with Andrew—to know that

such an informal and semiprivate arrangement had been brought to the attention of Great Uncle.

Andrew's too kind, I said formally.

No, Great Uncle insisted. We all have great faith in your talent. We are aware that it was interrupted by a severe trauma. But that it is there—Great Uncle waved his right hand—that it is there, no one doubts.

I despaired of argument. I simply sat still in dreadful anticipation.

Great Uncle said, I ask you to loan the state the great benefit of your talent, Alan.

I was reckless enough to lower my head. These days, you don't find me at my best, Mr. President, I'm afraid.

You simply need a project, he told me, cheerily. You were on the right line. The impact of the sanctions on the people, on the families of war veterans. This is a great story. Men and women who smuggle oil west to the Mediterranean, and down the straits in barges, are the new heroes. The weight of their deeds, Alan, will render the frippery of sanctions irrelevant.

Frippery? I thought.

Great Uncle fixed me with his eyes and told me evenly, I realize my own past novels have been dismissed in the West as pure melodrama. They were fables, of course, and all fables are melodramatic. But because they portrayed the relationship between myself as bridegroom and the state as bride, they were derided by foreigners.

The Americans are not used to fables, I told him.

I really shouldn't have. I knew his books to be utter shit, ghostwritten by hacks at the Cultural Commission. I would have liked to argue that I was being polite for McBrien's sake, and his fashionable wife, Sonia's. On the other hand, I might simply have been genuflecting, despite myself. Most human beings can be brave only in snatches. And nobody knows, unless they have been there, with a god, in his office, within reach of his army cot. No-body can forejudge how they'll behave.

Great Uncle leaned forward, and I heard his boots squeak like those of a recruit.

I have a great favor to ask you.

I knew that he began commands in that fashion.

In four months, he said, the Group of Seven, or so-called G-7, those self-congratulatory controllers of the goods of the earth, those judges of seemly weapons, will meet in Montreal. I have it on some authority that the sanctions which affect your fellow cit-izens will come up for consideration. Some of the G-7 are uneasy about them. Canada, France, Italy.

It does them some honor, I said.

Great Uncle laughed. They are conditioned to think that way. The French helped the Americans found their tiny republic. What do they think now? Now that the Americans so far outstrip the power of Napoleon? What do the Canadians think, living cheek by jowl with the monster? They support the sanctions at least in the sense that they go along with America and give silent assent in spite of moral unease. But they are also willing to believe the worst of them. Pearson Dysart, our PR company, places in the Canadian and European press little items about our people which would make any heart bleed.

Yes, I could but say. But they are right to do so. The sanctions are the main issue.

Exactly, whispered Great Uncle, lightly clapping his hands. A man of such restrained gestures, unlike his coke-inhaling offspring. Now, he confided, our young friend McBrien is a fine fellow, and a splendid writer, but he'd rather write about our past, about intellectuals persecuted by the monarchy in the early 1930s. That's the trouble with our writers. They find it eas-ier, both creatively and, I think, politically, to dwell on historic wrong.

Perhaps so, Mr. President, I conceded with a lackey politeness.

Whereas your stories, Alan, they're always in the present. Real soldiers, womenfolk everyone knows . . .

The serpent of literary vanity, slick and seething, moved within me, as Great Uncle spoke as if the worst that could befall a writer who wrote the wrong things about the present world would be the mildest of rebukes. I thought of Mrs. Douglas's nephew, who had composed the chemical balance of the water wrongly. Had he had his death announced to him in this softness of tone? In this quiet, chiding atmosphere?

Great Uncle said again, I want you to do me a favor, Alan. I want you to do, that is, the state a favor. I don't pretend it won't be demanding. The situation is this. In four months the G-7 meet, as I say, in Montreal. My plan is to release a book in New York at that time, published by a bona fide publisher, bearing my name, which displays to the world the suffering of my people, and their patriotic inventiveness in the face of sanctions. You can put it better than that, I know. I want it to be a subtle novel, with heroes and some villains. I want it to be a book an American would enjoy reading. I want some of the villains—exploitative people—punished in the book, for the punishment they inflict, but I want the central characters to be honest people. Write about what you yourself have seen, Alan. I'm afraid that the deadline is a short one— Pearson Dysart in New York have the publisher primed, but they insist they need three months to get the word of this extraordinary literary coup into the market and to attend to producing the book. And, of course, to let it leak into the market that they have signed a contract with the notorious Great Uncle, and that the manuscript of the novel is very good.

I sat neutralized by conflicting terrors through all this.

Great Uncle began to think. Then he spoke, as he consulted a calendar on his desk. I think we can afford a full calendar month for the task, and this being July 8, you should deliver your book into the hands of Commissioner McBrien and your Overguard escort officer, Chaddock, by close of office hours on August 8. I should tell you Pearson Dysart have an old left-wing publishing house lined up, and they would be delighted to drive a stake through the American administration's embargoes on our oil and the imposed sanctions.

Flabbergasted, I came close, but not close enough, to suggesting he might as well use his pistol on me right now. A masterwork can't be written in a month, sir, I told him.

It's all the timetable permits us, he said with a shrug. Sorry. I know you like to translate your own work, but there won't be time. The top American translator is lined up. He'll work fast too. And the senior editor from the publishing house will work on it in regard to any revisions. You shouldn't let him change anything that's relevant to us, to what we are all going through.

I took yet another profound breath. I could not deal with the thinness of this air.

Mr. President, I said. I am very proud to be asked, of course. But I'm not well, sir. My subtitling was nearly remedial work, therapy. I am a shell. What you suggest is simply beyond my powers.

Great Uncle grasped his upper lip and thought. Then he leaned forward across the desk. You're arguing with destiny, aren't you, Alan? he said. And with so many people depending on you . . . me, Pearson Dysart, the publisher. *And* members of your own race. This is not an instance of vanity on my part. I want the hypocritical sanctions to be shown up, I want our oil without restriction to flow to the world. I want the world's goods to flow to us. I want a book whose humanity will achieve that, and be a reproach to the G-7. In the face of that, Alan, it's no good claiming personal fragility. It must be done. It will mean a great deal to the career of Cultural Commissioner McBrien, also.

So he assumes responsibility for me?

Great Uncle said, I can imagine the two of you swapping ideas in cafés at night. May I suggest you might try dictating? The Ministry of Information has a voice-recognition program on some of its computers, if you wanted to use one of them.

He had managed to make me giddy with a new kind of despair, a kind I never anticipated. I don't know what to say, Great Uncle, I confessed.

And indeed, despite my lapse of protocol, he nodded gently like a generous uncle. Did I mention that advance and royalties will very appropriately be paid by my office to you? You will have security for life, Alan. So get to work. On August 8, I'll accept the typescript from your hand.

There was a long silence in that soundless palace.

Oh, he said suddenly, I understand.

He chuckled—a noise like other men would make if preparing to sneeze.

You ask yourself, once the book is written, why would he not simply bury me away in some prison to make sure rumors of authorship don't start circulating? Or why wouldn't he perhaps be tempted to eliminate me?

There was another stutter of indulgent laughter, in the midst of which he drew a *chardri*, a regulation short bayonet dagger, traditionally curved, from his belt. He laid it on the surface of the table, and looked for something in his desk drawers and found it, a pack of surgical lint impregnated with some chemical or other.

I'll solve it by making you one of my Piedmontese. A kinsman. To show how I value your talent and your happiness. You see!

He extended his own right wrist, fingers upwards. There were five small ridges of scar like a little constellation there.

All right, he said, snapping his shirtsleeves back in place. Everyone knows how I value kinship. This will be a significant day for you and your progeny.

He took a square of lint and cleaned the point of his dagger with it. Surgical alcohol, he said. Give me your right hand.

I pushed forward my fairly effete urban hand and it was suddenly taken in his broad, harsh one. He had worked day after day with farm implements in his childhood. He had strength. With his free hand, he took another alcohol-impregnated cloth and frowned slightly as he reached across the table to wipe the wrist he held.

Many have tried to copy these marks, he told me, but they're like a secret handshake—hard for an outsider to reproduce.

He put the point of the thing deftly under the skin of my wrist, digging at an angle, then flipping the nugget of flesh he had purchase on so that it was doomed to heal in a distinctive nodule of scar. Naturally it hurt. But who was I to scream? In his terms, he was paying me a gesture of intense esteem, guaranteeing my safety, making me a five-dotter. Having produced the effect once, he did it immediately again, on the far side of my wrist.

I was bleeding somewhat by the time he wiped my wrist with yet another square of lint, but not so widely that he would ruin the contours of the curiously raised wounds. The alcohol stung, of course.

He said, Well done! You get the rest of the marks when the novel is delivered. But you are now a tribal Piedmontese, at least of child status. And my word is my bond to me, and vice versa, and cannot be extracted from you even by torture, or by bribe. You and I are in this secret. But so too is Matt McBrien, who will be your mentor. Mr. McBrien has been briefed to a certain extent by my principal personal assistant, a kinsman. He knows there is to be some writing done for me, over a month, and that he is to give you every assistance. But McBrien is no kinsman. I know you are of course a good friend of Andrew Kennedy's. But he is not to know of this. For his own protection, you understand.

Again he emitted the small, half-choking stutter of laughter. He said, The orderlies will put antibiotic powder on those, but best not to cover them too tightly in the first day, or they'll look like a mere imitation of the real thing.

He cleaned his dagger again and put it away, then rose. The matter was settled. I had my task.

God guide your hand, he said.

He rang a bell. The door opened and I was taken out into the corridor. Looking over my shoulder I saw the figure of Great Uncle returning to his spartan bedroom.

Back in the corridors, my wound was sprinkled with antibiotic powder and loosely bound with lint, and my clothes were given back to me.

Dressed normally, I was taken to the waiting room where McBrien remained. He was alone, studying a dossier someone had obviously given him. Instructions for minding me.

How did it go? he muttered. McBrien's eyes were drawn to the injury Great Uncle had inflicted. What happened to your wrist? It's bleeding.

The administrative officer whom we had met in the corridor an age ago arrived and we were led again to the front door and blind-folded by Lieutenant Chaddock and his men. I sat in a daze as we drove, although Chaddock once asked me, How is he? The Man of Men?

I said, He speaks very softly, and Chaddock laughed.

Excuse me, sir. But the wrist. Do you have . . .

Yes, I said.

Put there? By the man himself?

Yes.

Chaddock whistled. Give the world, myself! Congratulations, Mr. Sheriff.

Thank you, Lieutenant.

McBrien asked if he and I could be let off at a particular café, and Lieutenant Chaddock said, Sure. We'll wait for you.

McBrien took me to a private room, where drinks were served. He led me to a booth, asking no further questions, and ordered us both a double Scotch.

When the drinks had been brought McBrien told me the President's principal private secretary had filled him in on the details of the task.

Damn me, McBrien said jovially, if it doesn't all depend on you now, Alan. The big task. A novel. I don't want to know all the details! I don't know what it's for, but I know it has to be done. I'm just to supervise you and supply you with what could be needed. I promise that will be done with a light touch.

What if I do this preposterous thing? I asked him. He could shoot me then, and be secure.

Except, by the look of your wrist, you're on the way to becoming his kinsman. He doesn't shoot kinsmen unless they really screw up. And your kinsmanship makes me confident about myself.

He shot one of his son-in-laws, for God's sake!

But that was for doing unauthorized deals with the Swiss, *and* the fellow was a wife beater, *and* he'd tried to defect. Look, Alan, we'll do it one way or another. Even if I have to write half the thing myself. Our man doesn't want more than about, say, two hundred and fifty print pages. Fewer even. That's about eighty to eighty-five thousand words, tops. That's less than three thousand a day.

I told him he had a strange mind. That he should be selling garden hoses by the length. I drank the double Scotch in two gulps and laughed. Could you do it if it were you? I asked him.

But you have a book nearly written anyhow, he said. You told me at Andrew's place. You can edit that. It will serve our masters. The private secretary said our man would be pleased with something that had the flavor of your short stories. It can be real work. It doesn't need to be as monochrome as a TV soapie.

That book is gone, I told him. I destroyed that book. I destroyed printouts and files and floppies and threw my old laptop in the river. It's gone.

That's a bit extreme, Alan!

It was a creature of my marriage, McBrien, and my marriage has been destroyed.

Did you tell Great Uncle that? That you threw the thing away?

I told him I burned the pages and sent the laptop and tapes away with the garbage.

Look, Alan, I don't know how to say it. Please. *Please!* It's like Toby Garner's wall. It has to be done.

My greatest inventiveness will be dedicated from this point on, I told him, to managing to disappoint the old bastard while saving your bacon. Your suit, your house, your car, your career.

No. You're joking, aren't you? Let me get you another drink.

He began waving like a man drowning.

A waiter came, took the order, and went.

Don't tell me tales, Matt McBrien pleaded. I didn't know it had gone. Your novel . . .

Well, it's gone.

Utterly?

You could send a diver looking for my laptop. Though with the spring current, it's probably down near Summer City by now.

He absorbed this. Well, there's still time.

He grasped for a narrative concept. Why don't you just talk about an oil smuggler and his family? A barge captain? I could set up an interview with one.

Great Uncle mentioned oil bargemen, I said, suspicious that McBrien might have been primed by Great Uncle's office. But he wants someone who's smuggling oil for patriotism, and not for the money.

Well, you could find that patriotism is a motivation. It's a matter of emphasis.

A fictionalizing, story-conferencing light entered his eye. Listen, say a young kid gets involved with a member of an oil barge crew, and say the others mock his patriotism—he keeps on donating his wages to a kids' home. He wants every dollar to flow back into the economy. He's got at home an amputee brother from the war, and that's his motivation. And then maybe one of the tough guys, the skipper say, surprises him with some act of heroism, and he becomes aware that this hard-bitten man is operating from an unexpressed idealism as well.

I could barely contain my anger, but thank God the drinks arrived. Once the waiter had gone off, I said, I can see why you write such shitty novels.

I'm just trying to help you, Alan, to get that side of your brain working. As for my novels, fuck them. This is the job I always wanted. I want to grow to be as aged as Old Billy in it.

A thought had in the meantime struck me.

Do you think this is why Peter Collins cleared out? If Great Uncle asked him to do this and gave him three months, but he wouldn't do it on principle? And then Charlie McKay, his handler, vanishes.

We chewed on this. I don't think so, McBrien said conclusively.

There's nothing for it, Matt. You and Sonia will have to go. I'll stay here and take the medicine. I bet that barge captain of yours could get you onto a Russian freighter.

Yes, and as much as I paid him up front, he'd get double for telling the Overguard.

Well, you might just have to get your nifty suede shoes dirty walking through the mountains.

He said, Can't you understand, Alan? I have my career here. Why can't you just write the damned book? Have an early night! Get up and start! Let's have another drink now. A good night's sleep, and I'll call in on you at eight A.M. Again, any help you need. Only thing: I'm afraid you can't have a secretary. A secretary couldn't be trusted the way Great Uncle trusts us. I'll get a PC delivered to your place, or bring it with me tomorrow. It'll need its

A-drive glued up, because Great Uncle's assistant told me there are to be no possibilities of copies.

Don't bother calling in, I warned McBrien. I'll be out at a restaurant having breakfast. I intend to spend my last thirty-one days in a leisurely manner.

Hell! said McBrien. He ground his brows against the heels of his hands.

On July 9, I did not awake as carefree as I had hoped. With the residual sting of Great Uncle's dagger still at my wrist, I was at once reminded of the weight the tyrant had placed on me. I managed to rise, but did not shave, and sat at a table sipping black tea and eating an apple. As promised, at eight o'clock McBrien was at the door, a new laptop and its cordage in his arms.

I'll install this for you at your desk, he offered. It has a surge protector and a capacity for internal backup. They say you can have voice-recognition software if you like, but it takes at least two weeks to work it into shape before you can start.

He set to work while I watched. The A-drive,

where floppy disks were held, had a plate of metal fixed over it with minute tumblers, such as one saw on those fancy attaché cases with combination locks.

They've kept the code for opening the A-drive to themselves, McBrien told me, sorting out the cords and plugging in the surge protector.

Why are you speaking in whispers? I asked him. Is the apartment wired?

No. They don't do that as much as we citizens think. They're short of resources now, with the sanctions. I was also assured by the principal private secretary that the apartment would not be wired, anyway. That was Great Uncle's own demand. He thinks it's contrary to your dignity as an artist. By the way, Lieutenant Chaddock has been exalted to captain, and will command a day-and-night Overguard detachment, two vehicles, with responsibility for your person.

My God! I said. What a fix! The neighbors will be delighted. Would you like some black tea?

Yes. Just a moment.

He switched the machine on and the screen lit and performed its function. See the symbol there? he said. That brings up your document program. But you know how to word process, don't you?

I told him of course. Sarah had taught me in the university library, and I'd had a word processor myself. Didn't he remember it was flowing down to the gulf?

Oh, I've got a little present for you, he told me. He reached into his breast pocket and extracted a bottle. Tommy Hilfiger cologne. For future visits to . . . to certain people.

I was—as frequently then—touched, yet uncertain. Do you think this will get me a job with the Whisperers?

He smiled. If that's your fancy. I got the last bottle in the markets. Let's have some tea then.

I put the cologne on the shelf above my desk. If the truth were told, I was grateful for his company. We went back to my favorite little living room table, where Sarah and I always drank tea. And then, when he'd finished, I told him, all jokes aside, to go and see a people smuggler.

If I could find one, what about my parents? asked McBrien with some spirit. And my brothers and sisters? Am I to get some damned people smuggler for them too?

He let that sink in. Well, Alan, we know now what our test will be. We get through this, and life is all gravy. I'll probably get an embassy post as cultural attaché in Rome or Paris or Moscow. You . . . the sky's the limit with you.

Thank you, I told him, feeling the drag of the unacceptable and unachievable task within me.

For a second he went pale at my apparent unbiddability. But he gathered all his energy. He had already decided, perhaps uncon- sciously, to go through this trial cheerily, to lift me on his gusts of optimism.

If you're not doing anything this morning, he said, then I have some places to take you. Research. On the way out of the city, we'll remind ourselves how some of our brothers and sisters really live under the sanctions.

Will we, sir? I asked in imitation of a schoolchild. As if I hadn't already been to the Beaumont side and the Eastside markets.

Then we'll talk to a barge captain at Ibis Bay. Should be back in time for a late lunch if we start now.

I think I want to get on with *On the Waterfront*, I told him.

He said ironically, That'd be a brilliant idea! Absolutely bril- liant! Listen, if you're doing nothing in the next thirty days, you might as well come driving with me. Come on!

He had a black car with his own driver and there were no blindfolds for us today. And it was true that once we crossed the ridge of Beaumont and descended into the poorer townships in the southeast of the city, one became aware again of the fearful terms on which many of our fellow citizens lived. The West had come to an arrangement that they would take a billion of our barrels a year, but the money for them would not come directly to us but to the United Nations, which would then decide how to filter it through to ameliorate the condition of such suburbs as these, and hungry townships in the countryside. The last time I'd been here it had been to look at a rally, research for the book I had given over to Sarah, and all the speakers had complained of the indignity of this arrangement. One man had said, They make us not earners but beggars. By now though, there was probably more doubt in the ordinary people. In the hearts of the women who queued at the end of crumbling streets, drawing up risky water from the city's ancient and part-destroyed conduits, Great Uncle might be blamed with an equivalent sense of fury as was earlier directed against the U.N. sanctions.

From my last visit here I had learned of a popular illegal newspaper, produced by a young mother of the Beaumont townships. She complained that on the broad river ordinary people saw the parvenus to whom Great Uncle and the Overguard had entrusted both the smuggling of oil above the one-billion-barrel limit and a share as well of the U.N.'s largesse given in exchange for the modest legal quantity of our national output. This new class could be seen luxuriating at sunset on glittering cruise vessels. Rowboats on the river, manned by fathers and sons trying to catch a little protein for their shanty kitchens, were swamped by the cokehead skippers of cruisers. Busloads of the dispossessed lower middle class and workers, moving about the city, were likely to be overtaken by fast cars, with scant regard for pedestrians, driven by Sonny's ugly circle of friends. Situations of poverty and degradation unknown at the time Great Uncle's forces secured our borders, to the joy, at that time, of the West, were now appallingly commonplace. In Market Street, child prostitutes ran after McBrien's vehicle yelling, A dollar! A dollar! These offers were made within the potential hearing of parents. When I had been writing my book, someone told me, You can tell the child prostitutes. They're not as skinny as the others.

Their suffering and indigence were futile, as any of the children, any of the parents, could have told us. The sanctions, which bit into living flesh, and the aid-for-oil arrangement were absurd, because soft-voiced, fragrant Great Uncle and a thousand other powerful people not only subverted what came the country's way but tried with some success to bring the people to the conclusion that only Great Uncle's ménage could rescue them from the silliness and malice of the West. My book's purpose—in Great Uncle's mind—might have been more to discomfort the U.N. than actually to end these arrangements.

Even now, revisiting, I found these suburbs as shocking as McBrien, for his own purposes, would have wanted me to find them. Someone should write a book about it, I thought, and of course I had. But it belonged to Sarah and could not be retrieved in honor either by memory or by hand.

We descended through hilly streets towards Ibis Bay and its storage tanks, an occasional legally moored tanker, its mission recognized by the international community, and the hosts of barges and lighters. They did the real work of breaking the sanctions, of getting out into the straits to find the numerous waiting tankers that ran our oil for profit, illegally, to the world.

We stopped near the Ibis Bay wharves. Across the street from a seamen's café stood a vacant soccer ground, and there oil trucks released the dregs of what had been delivered to the barges, to make a black, slicked, inhuman, and inflammable acre.

Come on, said McBrien.

I simply went along with him. A dock supervisor led us across decks of barges, over great black pythons of hosing. The air was full of the smell of crude oil. At last we stopped on one squalid, oil-slicked deck. Under the serial number on the barge wheelhouse was painted a grimy name—*Joanna.*

The skipper of the barge was working with a large spanner and brass coupling behind the wheelhouse. He saw us coming but did not utter a greeting. He yelled down the little companionway. Hey, Bernie, get up here and try to loosen this.

Bernie came up. He, like the skipper, had a darkness to his skin, as if he'd been marinated in sump oil.

Mr. McCauley? asked McBrien.

Stocky McCauley inclined his head. Come and have some coffee, he yelled over the noise of engines and other busy sounds.

In the little cockpit we entered I grew nervous as he lit up a small spirit stove to make coffee. It seemed to me that the air was pregnant with oil fumes, but no explosion occurred.

So you found me all right, eh? he said. Lovely conditions we work in, we crudies. But it's a sort of living.

So, when's your next trip? McBrien asked him.

McCauley laughed at the innocent eagerness of McBrien.

Don't know, he said, with a noise that implied, Silly question! We get a signal. Then we go down the river and out into the straits.

McBrien said, Great Uncle raised a group named the Sanction Breakers. Are you one of them?

Mate, I wish I were. Some of them are rich bastards now.

But many of them were sincere?

Yeah, and dead too, or given up. Oh, they were great kids.

McCauley began closing down now, in case he'd said the wrong thing.

I mean, they were real patriots.

The coffee was ready and he filled three small cups and offered cubed sugar around.

Thanks, said McBrien. You know, there's no reason to be shy, Mr. McCauley. We're involved in a project. It's a film project. But a feature film, not a documentary. We want to know what it's really like. No one knows we've come here. You'd be doing us a favor if you just told us what it's all been like.

Easy for you to say, McCauley commented.

Yes, I said, a little amazed with myself for playing along. It's easy. But we've got to make this film.

McCauley looked at me. Maybe it was the lack of engagement in my eyes that got him talking.

Well, said McCauley, for a start, the Sanction Breakers were a total farce. Why wouldn't they be? They come on as volunteers, saving people from the sanctions, and so on. Then they find that most of the people they're working with are in it for the money. And they know where the real cream goes—into buying Daimlers for the men in charge of the organization. They think they're going to be earning aspirin for the poor, and they're earning computer-driven automobile transmissions for the rich. Now you can go and report me if you like. I don't give a fuck. I'm earning twenty times what a fishing skipper earns, and even if we bargemen don't have a protected life, I still know a lawyer who gets us all off. You guys might get to the Overguard, but we've got our own network down here, and the Overalls are on our side.

We aren't going to bring a whiff of authority your way, McBrien assured him. This seemed merely to increase McCauley's defiance.

Well, that's okay, he told us, because I ought to warn you. It's freedom of speech and freedom of assembly down here in Ibis Bay. It's not as easy as you think to run past coastal shelling and patrol boats from the other side, and even though the Americans are way out in the gulf, they still send the occasional rocket our way, too.

He was now fairly launched on his view of the world. I mean, he continued, why should a young kid believe in giving his life to get oil down the straits when you're actually doing America a favor in any case? It's a charade. They need us too. What we smuggle out there keeps oil prices stable. And the American warship skippers know this. They were put there to stop us, but they know with half their brains their country needs us. God bless America!

Why do *you* do it? asked McBrien, no threat at all in his voice. We just want to know for the film. Why does your kind of man, and the men round you, do it? One well-aimed shot from the Others across the straits and you're obliterated. A flame.

Okay, said McCauley. I do it for my family. And for myself, I suppose. I like filtered coffee and the occasional drink. And presents for the missus. I like a bit of space in my life. The poor bastards of Beaumont, they have no leeway in their lives at all.

I knew from earlier research that this was true—that even men and women with jobs had to resort to the black market to make a living.

There are rumors, I surprised myself by commenting idly (I certainly heard such rumors), that officers on the other side are bribed to let people through.

Finishing his coffee, McCauley considered this. I'd say that's probably true. Otherwise, it must be that they're shithouse shots over there, or half blind. I wouldn't be surprised if some of the Others were bribed. But for their own sake they have to fire off a few shots, and make an occasional kill.

You've lost friends? asked McBrien eagerly.

A few. But it's usually the novices that get blown up. I had one of those Sanction Breakers on board, and he picks up an AK-47 and starts firing back at the shore batteries. A kid of seventeen! Willing to be martyred and have his balls fried. I still don't believe we got away. Me and the deckhand, we took him ashore, filled him with vodka, and beat the crap out of him.

Have you ever been approached to get people out? I asked, my eyes on McBrien.

McBrien put his forehead in his hands and McCauley looked at me lividly, but with a certain whimsy. Then he began to laugh. Go to buggery, he said. If you're going to ask questions like that, you can just piss off.

I'm sorry, I said, but I had some friends . . .

What do you think I do? Hide people in oil drums? Wouldn't do it to my worst enemies. Tell your friends to catch a plane. There's no room for anything but oil barrels and an engine on this barge. Even Bernie and I sleep in the wheelhouse.

For whatever reason, I didn't fully believe him. There must be a way. McBrien and Sonia must be got out within the month. Down the straits some benign tanker, Panamanian or Norwegian, Liberian or Russian or Colombian, must be able to receive them. There had to be a way—some way which wasn't immediately apparent from this cockpit.

Anyhow, I gave it up for the moment. I felt tired, and realized there was no need for me to deny myself sleep during this ridiculous month.

Mr. McCauley, I said, wanting to close the field trip down, I'm grateful to you for giving us your time.

Not at all, gentlemen, he said. A sly grin overtook his features. He believed, wrongly in fact, that as individuals we were immune from that edge of danger at which he worked continually.

As we left McCauley and made our way back towards shore over the slippery and chaotic decks of other barges, McBrien said hopefully, There you are. The man is a living character—the likable rogue. Construct a family history for him. Until he took this job, was his kid one of the kids running after our car, offering himself for a dollar? Did his wife carry skin ulcers for which there weren't any antibiotics? My understanding is Great Uncle wants social realism, but with the sort of subtlety you had in your stories. That man, McCauley, was social realism in spades. The rough-diamond hero. Hemingway would love him. And his file says he's a veteran of the wars too. Maybe you can throw in a bit of magic realism. His dead friend stepping in through the window to talk with him. I don't see how you can pass it up.

The way he delivered this apparently informal but well-rehearsed scenario made me think that he was somehow operating according to a fixed bureaucratic scenario, on a path he or someone else at the Cultural Commission had already trod. I began therefore to achieve something like certainty that the national poet, songster, teller of narratives, Peter Collins, had been choice number one, had heard this spiel from *his* minder, but had fled the task.

We reached the pier again, and could see Chaddock, who had followed us in his limousine, looking benignly from his car window and allowing us civilized movement. The earth of the plaza and side streets seemed a combustible amalgam of oil and dirt.

Would you like tea? asked McBrien, pointing to a teahouse whose awning itself seemed impregnated with oil. We went to a table half in shade, half in sun. McBrien took the sunny chair, offering me the seat of lesser glare. A young waitress who seemed unsullied by the air of Ibis Bay came and took our order. As we waited for the tea, I told him that I didn't want to be a bastard—I'd write it if I could. But a month isn't time enough for a sustained literary effort, I told him. I don't care how good those PR people are. They can't make a success out of shit.

You'd be surprised, McBrien assured me. And people will buy this book for its curiosity value.

But I'm brain-dead, I told him. The idea of writing makes me ill. Physically. And in other ways.

Come on, I know you lost Sarah. I know you feel half dead. But this is the act by which you prove yourself living again. You'll be kind of subtitling our state. Is subtitling other people's films any better?

With the privacy screen of his limo drawn, he continued to talk to me thus all the way back to the city. Obviously, he took comfort from the fact that I seemed more submissive than I had been. He became quite light-headed with his conviction, or the intensity of his desire, that I would prove amenable to the task. We'd lost a good part of the day, he said, but he was sure I could get a few thousand words written by evening.

Do you need a bottle of vodka to get you going? he asked.

It seemed true that McCauley was a great character incarnated. One could at least think that someone else, a healthier man than me, a young literary tiger, could make something of him. That much I could agree with. What if I organized to take a trip with McCauley, and then simply boarded a ship, one hoped a Norwegian ship, and claimed asylum? But for what good purpose would I seek asylum and leave Sarah's remains behind? And how could such a journey be undertaken under the surveillance of Captain Chaddock's Overguard escort? I could see the Overguard limo behind us as we pulled over the crest of Beaumont and looked down on the city, fraught, beautiful, squalid, exposed on the banks of its great river.

A sort of love for it all possessed me and a little nostalgia arose for the book which lay beside Sarah in the grave, merely because it had encapsulated this city as it was in its pain and vulnerability. Of course I did not regret the work's present destiny. What sort of husband would take it back, when it had already been consecrated to her, just to feed the G-7 fantasies of the President-for-Life?

This book had gone well enough until Sarah's fatal episode. Towards finishing it I had felt some disappointment that technically it did not seem to be much advanced upon my much lauded book of short stories. It would, that is, be a reasonable follow-up. It would not quite make the West step back, or evoke comparisons to Gabriel García Márquez or Vargas Llosa. But it had been intimately crafted and imbued with all my passion. As for its significance as a gesture towards Sarah, my offering to my dead wife was an absolute one, even if my talent had limits. I did not give it to her as a means of opting out of the task of making it better. It was what it was. I gave it to her because it was the best I had to give, and was a sign that any idea of future literary excellence was rendered fatuous by her destruction. Or to put it in another way: there was really no sense to those or any other words I wanted to place on paper, in a world from which she had been removed.

But a phantom literary impulse began to itch in my mind. If I had the manuscript with me, if all were normal, I could edit it in a few days, hand it to the tyrant, confirm McBrien in his career and sweet Sonia in her smile, and then vanish from the earth.

Sometimes it seemed that some malign force had deprived me of Sarah precisely because I concentrated so much on women, even in the short stories—their vulnerability, and their risky hold on their lives. Their loves so thoroughgoing, whether it be for their husbands or their children. Yet all hope was so frequently thwarted by chance and politics and little invisible bugs in water or the air, or in the blood of friends. I had that sense of fragility from the death of my mother, I suppose, when I was sixteen. But as I've already said, I saw it too in Mrs. Carter.

My novel had thus concerned, in some part, two women. You are good at women, my wife told me, flattering me. You can convey the sense of the sword above their heads.

I shouldn't imply my book was exclusively about women—it wasn't. Though it had its beginning in the present miseries, it also described the period of the early military governments, which rose on nationalist rhetoric, but secretly assured the British, French, and Americans that that was all it was, hot air, and that it would be business on the normal preferential terms if only they would equip the national army. (Great Uncle, as a young Fusion Party apparatchik, had hated the shallowness of such governments, and disrupted their public events with demonstrations of dissent. But that's another story.)

There are, in the novel's prologue, two lovely girls, educated by doting parents, both members of all-girl families. That is, what the Intercessionist peasantry and their clergy would consider a catastrophe of values—women of independent minds. (This was close to my mother's story too—she had only one brother, and she was adored and given a thorough education in music and the humanities by rather Anglophile parents.) So, these two girls from all-girl families. One marries a senior bureaucrat—the Mrs. Carter story again. The other marries a naval officer, and both of them bear sons, which bonds them even more. The bureaucrat's wife lives in a spacious, middle-class apartment by the river; the naval officer and his wife live in a smaller flat but well located to all the joys of a civilized life—the cafés and bookshops, the boutiques, the river restaurants which served our delicious, pink-fleshed river perch.

The first woman's husband is killed along with his crooked minister by well-meaning but overly zealous agents of the Fusion Party. Friends of the dead husband in the department, however, out of a sense that an injustice has been done, maintain the widow's pension under the new regime. The pension is considerable and permits her to live in comfort. But her son is killed in the battles for the refineries, and she is rendered a scarecrow, confined to her apartment, barely going out, barely using the generous pension which inflation gradually erodes. This was ominously close to Mrs. Carter's story, but these considerations don't necessarily prevent a writer from exploiting people he knows, and I had put in sufficient points of difference between my character's tale and Mrs. Carter's life to mount a plausible defense that this character was not her.

The husband of the other educated woman, the woman who is actually central to the story, Rose Clancy, is captured early in the war by the Others when his patrol boat is sunk in the straits, and he receives a shrapnel wound in his hip. Due to his capture, his rank remains fixed at a junior level. When repatriated he accuses a well-connected senior officer of having collaborated. Though the senior officer is ultimately imprisoned on his return home, Clancy is maneuvered into retiring and taking his pension.

It is through the decline of the Clancys that the reader encounters the increasingly cruel terms of existence under which our people live.

It sounds vain for me to say it, but I was working on more than the old Dickens proposition that a modest sufficiency is happiness, and a sufficiency that just fails to pay the bills is tragedy. I was trying to work with much more even than the idea that those rewarded with affluence often are not as noble as those who aren't. The book was, in its way, overtly political, insofar as all my characters were aware of being held in a vise of politics.

Clancy, the man! I loved him authorially as much as the women characters, and he was based explicitly on a man I met three years ago on one of my visits to the Eastside markets. For the writing of the book I had in mind, the Eastside markets were essential research. The man was in early middle age, selling black-market

European and American cigarettes. He approached me and said, Sir, I have Virginia and Turkish cigarettes. Would you care for one at a mere thirty U?

He made this offer in the remains of a good serge suit, and though when he walked he did so crookedly, he had the unsurrendered remnants of an old-fashioned bearing, military or bureaucratic.

Like any bourgeois in territory difficult to understand as a mere visitor, I grasped onto him as my guide and mediator, and spent two afternoons with him in the markets. He did not work there in the mornings, since he had to put in time at the water plant. I bought all his cigarettes for 850 U, the equivalent of fourteen dollars, nearly five times what he made a week as a water engineer. He had not been a naval man, as Clancy was in the novel, but a former sapper lieutenant who had spent time under the care of the Others, and his military pension of twenty U, set in more plenteous times, was now, through inflation, the equivalent of sixteen American cents.

I was very conscious that without my inheritance from both parents and a deceased uncle, and without the added good fortune of my U.S. dollar advance, I would become this man. And what also stood between us were Sarah's considerable earnings from television residuals and—sometimes in foreign exchange—film royalties, either from Europe or from countries of our region. Even so, in the company of this urbane man, the filament of chance seemed as thin as silk between us.

So he agreed to walk me around the markets. He told me incidentally that he was his street leader, and that he intended to spend the largesse I'd brought his way on the neighboring school, which had nothing, not even chalk. It was easy to believe him, with his canting walk and air of uprightness.

We visited the furniture stalls. There was, of course, rubbish—vinyl-covered lounges in garish colors. But one could see excellent pieces—ageless paintings of ideal riverbank gardens, or of ancestors in procession or engaged in battle with swords and shields, and the *chardri*, the sort of knife-cum-bayonet with which Great Uncle had operated on me. Presses hundreds of years old, carrying the intense demeanor of retained clan history, stood in an extraordinary jumble and under a coating of dust with pieces that looked Victorian or Sheratonesque. Under the monarchy, such pieces had been much prized by the ruling and middle classes. People of some quality had in recent times, impoverished by inflation, given up these pieces cheaply, and someone with a sudden windfall like the one I'd paid the water engineer could similarly buy them for a song. What every dealer hoped for, my friend told me, was that one of the parvenus and big-time black marketeers would drive over from town and buy a good piece at close to its true value. By and large, my friend said, the furniture of the nation, like its citizens, had been deflated by sanctions.

And by Great Uncle and his friends too? I asked.

Yes. But best not to talk of that. Otherwise despair could begin.

Where do you get the time to be a street leader? As well as the waterworks and this . . . ?

He looked straight at me, a no-nonsense look. I'll tell you the truth. I'm attracted by the endurance of people there. They're a mixed bag, of course; I don't pretend otherwise. But my God, they endure perfectly! They bury too many of their kids. My fault. I'm supposed to be a water engineer. But they have the grace never to point a finger at me.

He led me on to a large tent with open sides. A sign on its front pole said *The Art Exchange*, so I thought there would be paintings piled up inside. Instead, at long tables sat a number of artists of the capital, smoking butts and drinking their tea ration. They had little signs in front of them, offering art equipment for exchange. One had a huge, pristine tube of chrome yellow, a standby hue for traditional paintings, to exchange with anyone who had a spare six-feet-by-three-feet canvas. Another offered a palette knife. Having moved on from impasto work, he sought a thin brush.

They might sit thus for some days, before the implement or paint they needed came in. I got talking to one artist, a man about my age, and of some reputation. He was the sort of fellow to whom the Cultural Commission, before we were declared a pariah state, gave free paints and equipment, and probably paid him a wage as well—possibly still did, but one which could not match inflation. I, not he, was the one who kept damning the limitations on his art. He persisted in remarks such as, Well, it makes the artist less precious. You value every line. And the finished painting—it means so much!

The cigarette seller and I went for tea ourselves. What did you mean earlier? I asked him. About water engineers being to blame?

Well, metaphorically, he told me.

He savored the tea.

What I can't get over, he said, is that one day soon the West will invade us over our chemical and germ weapons, and the sins of certain of our people. In the meantime we can't make enough chlorine to treat our drinking water. The sewerage works don't get any at all. All the chlorine we have goes to treat our reservoirs. They in turn are drawn from the river, where the unchlorinated sewage has already been dumped. The system's failing, our pumps are kept together with bits of wire, and there's very little to do, really, at the waterworks. All my fellow engineers put in an hour or two in the mornings and then sell black-market tobacco in the afternoons. And the children, thirsty from their play, drink the water direct from the pipe at the end of the street—even though we've told everyone to boil it before taking a sip.

He shrugged. Typhoid, cholera, dysentery, he recited, ticking off the fingers of his left hand. What do children think of any of that? They know only about thirst.

Sitting back in his chair, rubbing his jaws as if he had toothache, he answered my question about where vendors got their black-market cigarettes. A massive warehouse in Beaumont, it seemed.

We check them out by the packet, and return what we don't sell. The warehouse management gets fifty percent of what we sell. God knows who's at the apex of it all, of all the warehouses in all the cities. Some friend of Sonny's, I'd imagine.

I returned him all the cigarettes I had already bought. Look, I said, sell them again. You can realize a full hundred percent on them.

He looked me in the eye. There was some reluctance there. Thank you, he said at last.

I remember going home to Sarah, creatively excited by what I had seen, a typical scavenging writer. I relayed the sights, smell, dust, and tragedies of the Eastside markets. I took my contact with the cigarette vendor seriously: he was my guide in the netherworld where most of our people lived.

But any illusion that he would continue in the role was destroyed on my next visit to the markets. I found him walking in the long broadway between the tents. I offered to buy his cigarettes in exchange for his guidance.

He said, I'm sorry. I can't.

I'm sorry too.

He explained it to me. The thing about windfalls is that they're no solution. You go and write your book. It might do more good than a windfall. I don't look to chance to save me for a day or two. Actually, I deserve better than that.

He was very pleasant about it, considering my earlier patronizing manner. He became, of course, my model for Clancy. You can see how much more noble a character he was than McCauley the oil smuggler.

In a sense he remained my validation as I then sought out teachers in schools without books and chalk. Bare spaces. And their eleven-year-old students would tell them: I can earn more on the black market than you earn for trying to teach me.

I met the shoe-shine children who shared half their fifteen-hour-a-day earnings at the bus terminal with café loungers who rented them their shoe-shine boxes. I saw the swollen-gutted children in hospitals I was admitted to by doctors for whom I'd bought coffee. The physicians told stories about grandfathers who died for lack of spare parts for the defibrillator equipment. There was a pact amongst all physicians to share the available pharmaceuticals equally amongst all admitted children, as diminished an impact as that would have. The doctors and nurses I invited to coffeehouses for interviews gave me a potent sense of the pyramid of infant corpses our nation had become.

One woman said, Our society is meant to be more than a refugee camp. In a refugee camp people eat aid food, and sleep. But what about visions and science? What about clean water, for that matter? What about the arts?

She told me her boyfriend, an aficionado of the piano, had to go to the university, to one of the country's rare pianos, and line up behind others to practice.

And so I had my Clancy, and I thus imagined Mrs. Clancy, who is the core of the novel, living in a tumbledown house in Beaumont, having been a young woman of hope and cafés, with her daughter, son-in-law, and their three children, and with her son, one of war's many amputees.

As the widow Mrs. Clancy knew in adolescence and early marriage shrinks—in the manner of Mrs. Carter—to a wraith behind the shuttered windows of her apartment, venturing forth to spend her money only if someone who served with her son deigns to visit, Mrs. Clancy fights a truer battle. She stands up to the black marketeers who adulterate pharmaceuticals in a manner likely to create damage to the brain and other organs, tries to save her grandchildren from prostitution, and—a vital woman still—is pursued by a whimsical black-market trader, a brave McCauley type. The book was intended as a paean and an elegy for the valor of those who maintain the dignity of their hunger in the face of crazy international measures, aimed to undermine Great Uncle, but cutting like a buzz saw through less elevated people, whose chief politics were—as the water engineer told me—endurance.

That was my book, now in Sarah's hands. It had taken me three years. It could not be pressed into ready service on the tyrant's behalf.

Poor Matt McBrien, who was now the chief matter for my concern, kindly dropped by later with a bottle of vodka, and I set to work on it. He refused to understand that the problem really was my mental capacity—I did not have the sinew to write a book even if I could think of one. For McBrien to suggest material to me was a little like a healthy man rallying a starving one by himself devouring a meal.

I woke late next day, and with a headache, but got up to go to a café. I had in my mind the sole concept of a large glass of iced orange juice. I saw the postman at the letterboxes though, and with a smile which I later thought might have been prescient, he placed an air letter in my hands. It had German stamps, and a Frankfurt postmark. I put it in my jacket pocket, for I did not necessarily want to be seen reading it by those who might be observing my movements on the street. From the doorstep I surveyed the pavements and the narrow string of traffic, and could see the limousine and white Toyota of the Overguard. When I got to my regular café down the street and ordered my orange juice, my coffee, my boiled eggs, I opened the letter. I had already half recognized the writing on the envelope—I had suspected it was Peter Collins's writing from Frankfurt, and it proved to be.

Dear Alan,
  I hope you're in a good state to receive these greetings from Frankfurt. From the heart of my winter of exile.

That was typical of him ... *winter of exile* ... He'd heard that Sarah had died unexpectedly and he sent the normal commiserations. In a sane country, he said, she would never have lacked fulfillment or employment. He almost implied that Great Uncle's unconscious thwarting of her acting career had somehow brought on her death—a suspicion I found unwelcome, since there might be truth to it. He hoped that I was as well as I could be in the circumstances.

I should tell you what we have heard through the ages, from the famous exiles of the Roman Empire onwards. Exile is not a happy condition, whether chosen or imposed.

But he had done, he told me, a few feature articles for *Frankfurter Zeitung*. He was singing songs in a Tuesday evening cabaret each week, and had done a little television, and some radio interviews. But he feared his career would be limited chiefly to that of an academic, almost anthropological curiosity. He'd always liked the fact that his songs and tales were organic to the people, his people. He had never wanted them to be museum pieces. But if you chose exile, you had to expect that, he said.

He told me then that there were other prices, too, not as apparent. He had fled for good cause, he said. He had been given an impossible task to perform. A task of such a massive nature that he had for some days considered suicide before his wife and German editor persuaded him to escape with her. And he couldn't complain. For Frankfurt was full of our fled compatriots, academics, scientists, whose arrival had gone utterly unnoted by anyone but immigration bureaucrats, and who now worked as parking attendants.

But now he got to the point. I should, he urged, let my friends know that they should not lightly go into exile. After all, in retrospect he wasn't certain that if he had summoned up all his powers he could not have attended to the demands, however ridiculous, which caused him to flee! *This morning,* wrote Collins,

> *I walked out of my door to get a newspaper, and found a box there, addressed to me, and delivered by a courier. The courier's sticker gave it legitimacy in my eyes, so I took it in, checked on its provenance—it claimed to come from the University Press, hence its heaviness. I cut the adhesive tape with a knife, and took the lid off. There was something indistinct encased in bubble wrap. I undid the bubble wrap with some disquiet, because the object within seemed messy. It was the head of Charlie McKay, my former file manager from the Cultural Commission. The poor bastard! You can imagine how I reacted to the horror—I dropped it on the floor. Freda screamed. I'd read that the Overguard had an international presence, but I had never believed it. Charlie's head! I took it to the* Polizei, *who seemed very calm about it all. Oh yes, they*

said. It had happened to Ted Bowers in Paris. The head of his liaison officer in the Department of Science and Technology had been served up to him this way.

Freda and I are artists, not warriors. That's a nice way of saying we're neurotics. I wondered if one of our heads would turn up at the door of some other émigré soon. No, said the police. That would make too much news.

Please, Alan, I tell you this with great anguish. Because if any of my friends need to escape, then they must do so, but there is a price, and they need to know. I thought you were a good man to tell.

I gulped my orange juice. Was this really Collins's signature? Could it have been created electronically? I looked at the paper carefully. Collins had made an indentation when writing the *P* and added a flamboyant tail to the *r.* The more authentic it looked, the more suspect. And the more suspect, the more authentic.

I went straight home, my brain itching, and compared the letter's signature with one of Collins's signed books from my shelf. It certainly seemed exact. I called McBrien. Come right away, I told him, and my urgency seemed to cheer him up.

While he was on his way, I drank vodka and tried to put the horror that Collins had passed on to me beside the image of Great Uncle, so calm, so full of cultivated concern, so confident in public relations rather than the axe, so willing to let me have the royalties.

There had been at least a display of some sort of equity behind what he proposed to me. But there was nothing equitable about Charlie McKay's head delivered in bubble wrap.

McBrien arrived promptly. He placed a file on my living room table. He told me, Captain Chaddock said that file comes to you from high sources. You'll find some loose-leaf notes from me as well. Just some narrative ideas I wrote down. You don't have to take any notice of them. But there might be a catalyst there.

In that instant I found myself not annoyed but liking him more again, in the old way I did before he became a Cultural Commissioner. His willingness, his faith, his naïve but powerful hope.

I'm sorry, Matt. I have something to show you.

I gave him Collins's letter to read, and he attacked it with the slight frown of the speed reader. He looked up at me once, after, I guess, he had read the bit about Charlie McKay's head. When he was finished he set it aside and expelled air through his teeth. God Almighty! he said.

Is it Collins's handwriting? I asked.

Looks like it. How would we know? What motive would anyone have to fake a letter like this, anyhow?

Oh, I said, I can imagine motivation. To get me to work.

I suppose you think I might share that motivation too?

No. I've decided you're not malicious, Matt. We're friends. Besides, you seemed to think Charlie had run away with a woman. You see now, though, that you and Sonia have to clear out.

Or else you could finish the damned novel that's there to write!

I am incapable, I pleaded again.

No, said McBrien. I want to see this through. I want to see how it works out. And I'm just well known enough that if I go, someone will suffer in my place. You, for example.

I won't suffer. The evening of August seventh, I shall drink red wine and open my veins in the bath.

And what if you don't? What if Chaddock comes rampaging in? Come on, Alan! You've been talking suicide for two months. There's something in you that doesn't want to take that route. So just get to work, like a good lad. It's only an exercise after all. And we still have loads of time. Another ten days and nothing done and I'd start to panic a little. But settle to it, that's a good boy. By the way, Captain Chaddock wants to come up and have coffee with you at seven. He might make it a regular thing. He's not a bad fellow.

McBrien went. I picked up his notes and gave them a quick reading, sighing. Then I picked up the file, and saw that it carried the presidential seal. Within was a moderately thick sheaf of pages, of the computer printout variety. I hoped for a moment that Great Uncle was writing my book for me. The title on the first page read: SOME USEFUL PLOT POINTS FROM THE LIFE OF HIS EXCELLENCY THE PRESIDENT-FOR-LIFE, NATIONAL CHIEF-TAIN, COMMANDER-IN-CHIEF, AND GREAT UNCLE OF THE PEOPLE.

I flipped at once to the back page to look for a signature or a covering letter. Nothing. The document's authorship went un-claimed.

The document began:

1. The President was born on April 27, 1939, in the small village of Lower Piedmont, west of Scarpdale. His 22-year-old mother was Sophie Stark, whose husband, Henry, was killed in a truck smash on the winding roads of the area. A maternal uncle, Fred Simmons, raised him with a loving strictness, but like most of the poorer Mediationists who occupied that arid hills district, Sophie, her brother, and her first child lived in dusty poverty.

I liked that term—"dusty poverty." I could perhaps use it as a grace note in the fraudulent book.

The boy's mother remarried to Ron Jenkins, a watermelon farmer, through which alliance the future President acquired three stepbrothers, including Reginald Jenkins, the future General Jenkins, General-in-Charge of Military Research. In their small adobe house, the family lacked all plumbing and sanitary arrangements, and had no electricity. Sophie Stark-Jenkins frequently cooked the family rice on an outside fire. It is believed that one day this one-room ruin of a house will be restored as a national monument as famous in our nation as Abraham Lincoln's Kentucky birthplace is in the American firmament.

Thus it was that from an early age the future President experienced some of the pain—the lack of protein from red meat and fowl—which his people now suffer as they cook their lentils in the streets. The President-for-Life sees them from his car and feels for them. Many of them grew up like him, and now in middle age feel that same bite of want and hunger again.

The boy also knew the oppression of labor, working in his stepfather's fields. He was the lowest of the low, and felt it, as his people feel the bite of sanctions now. He was required to take the sheep for grazing into those stony hills, and did so without shoes, his parents not having the money for them and he, though the eldest of Sophie's children, being considered— according to country custom—lower in the family pecking order than the Jenkins sons.

His hero had always been his uncle Richard Stark, a Scarpdale schoolteacher who had spent many years in prison for his part in the 1941 army rebellion against the Anglophile government of the time. Uncle Richard, like other patriots, did not wish to succumb to Churchill's demands that our government and soldiers become involved in a European war. Uncle Richard, a lieutenant in the army, was discharged for his part in this patriotic endeavor, and his years in prison enhanced his convictions. National policy should favor not the interests of the great powers but the interests of the people! It is because, however unlettered, the future President-for-Life admired the values of his uncle that he wanted to live with him, and when he was ten, with the blessing of his mother and stepfather, he went to reside in Richard Stark's household in Scarpdale.

*2. There he met his cousin Adrian, the future Minister for
Defense, who though a year younger than the future President
was already reading. Though teased at school for his late start
on literacy, for an ignorance that was none of his fault and
characteristic of such villages as Lower Piedmont, the future
President-for-Life struggled for a scholarship and suffered
the pangs of inadequacy which are characteristic of the
dispossessed of the earth.*

Oh, Great Uncle, I thought, you certainly know how to swamp a
tale with bathos! It was as if he thought I was writing a biography.

*In 1953, Richard Stark, his family, and his nephew moved to
the capital and settled in the southwestern suburbs, a poor-to-
middling area where many Intercessionists from the south had
settled.*

For *many Intercessionists from the south,* one read: *many bump-
kins without trades or literacy.*

*After school, the future President worked at finding passengers
for a particular taxi driver, and sold cigarettes around the
coffeehouses. He found the clients of the coffeehouses self-
indulgent and in some cases corrupt....*

I shook my head, and turned again to the rear of the document,
being relieved to read there:

*These ideas are in no sense to be interpreted as prescriptive,
but are merely offered as possible help.*

As the sun vanished from the river, I found Captain Chaddock
knocking on my door. I surveyed him through the peephole in his

impeccably snappy uniform, his red beret at the right angle to convey esprit and rigor. He was so large too. Coffee time.

I opened up.

Convenient? he asked.

Definitely, I said.

Just a chat, he assured me. Won't be on your doorstep all the time.

I led him in and he sat near my worktable by the partially disabled laptop as I went to make the coffee. I had already noticed that the prescriptive cologne the Overguard wore had turned stale on him. This distance from the palaces gave him that much latitude.

Going well? he called to me while I was out of the room.

So far, I lied.

Get the envelope this morning?

Yes. Thanks.

I put a few pastries on a plate and brought the coffee into him on a tray. He took a lot of sugar.

Don't want to dent your rations.

No, please. I've got plenty.

For a long time, and in silence, he stirred the sweetness in. I considered him, his large, masculine features which might balloon in later life. I asked, You're not outside twenty-four hours a day, are you?

He said, My men are when I'm not. You're safe. Every hour.

I tried to humanize this lummox. You must have a family though?

Not a question to answer, he told me. Could put them in harm's way.

Of course, I said. But that's not the reason I'm asking.

All right, he conceded. Wife. Three kids. No more questions.

Okay. I just wanted to achieve human contact.

You've got it. With me.

As you say, with you. Want a pastry?

Okay.

He crushed it into his huge warrior mouth, and chewed it slowly. There was a passing delicacy of pleasure on his face. When he had finished he reflected on the aftertaste. Quite good, he told me. Then he drank the hot coffee, pretty much in a single draught, and sat back to consider me.

He said, My unit's got a specialty, Mr. Sheriff. Watch and guard without interfering. Don't know what you're doing for the state. You're doing something. That's good enough. If you don't see us all the time, doesn't mean we've stopped. We pick up subtle things. Visitors. Your mood. The light in your windows. Yes, even though you're at the back of the building. The light. Maybe, means you're wrestling with the task. Can tell if you're drinking. Best to cut down.

My face flushed. I'll drink if I damn well choose.

Long as no rashness, he conceded. Have ladies if you want. We'll know who they are before they turn up. If a risk, they *won't* turn up.

I won't be having any women in, I assured him.

Might change your mind. A man's a man.

Sometimes, I told him, with futile acidity.

He stood up. Thanks, Mr. Sheriff. A few words now and then, that's all. Won't see us.

The neighbors will.

They'll get used to it. Good night.

My regards to the wife and kids, I said with unfair sarcasm.

He saluted. I let him out. I paused a little after the door had shut. Could this man have ordered things on the scale of the shooting and exposure of Mrs. Douglas's nephew? Could he have said, Just a bit of juice, as he applied the electrodes to the vagina of a female prisoner? These were all within the Overguard's repertoire, after all. And how did you go home and be tender with a wife and three kids after such exercises in state security?

Or maybe he had always been what he was in my case. Mere surveillance. I desired, for his sake and mine, that that was the case.

Just to cheer myself up, I began to make notes on a special file named in ironic honor as TASK1.doc. A McCauley-like barge skipper named, for the moment, A, was an oil smuggler, getting oil out of the country and thus creating more wealth than the West permitted us to have. A1, one of his sons, was an idealistic blockade runner who brought pharmaceuticals in by truck from Istria in the northwest. The second son, A2, was an accountant used by a black-market mogul, a friend of Sonny. No, I can't say that. Scratch A2. Press the delete button and expunge it before Chaddock notices the faintest fragrance of such sedition and knocks on the door with his respectful absolutism. No,

don't scratch A2 entirely. There were Istrian black-market opera-
tors who lived opportunistically amongst us, and when they were
caught, Sonny was ruthless with them, because they were competition for his friends. There had been, three months before, outside Wolfmount prison, a public hanging of two Istrians who had
tried to profiteer out of car parts they'd brought in. So I could have
an Istrian gangster, Z. Bring back A2, but portray him as having
lost his job due to the sanctions and succumbed to temptation for
the sake of real but corrupt wages.

It was good to be working, even on shit. The idea that such a
character as the Istrian, Z, might spark anti-Istrian feelings did
not, under the pressure, mean much. Get the damn thing written
and then give it manners!

Creating even these few bad ideas evoked the forgotten pleasure of imagination fast and fertile. Now the barge skipper A's
teenage daughter, F1, becomes involved with the Istrian, Z. A2,
the accountant, has to suffer the sting of seeing his boss flaunt
his sister round the warehouses of Beaumont. Z wants a piece
of A1's, the pharmaceutical smuggler's, action. The accountant
brother knows that Z will adulterate the pharmaceuticals and
cause death.

I made a note not to make Z too much of a villain, since the
West and the sanctions were to be the chief miscreants. The point
of the book was to be that few are able to escape the harshness of
Beaumont, the sharp edge of the sanctions. Blah, blah, blah!

The problem now was I had actually to write this soap opera in
such a way that it had the plausibility of a real book. Nonetheless,
I turned out the lights at two A.M., strangely contented at having
made a plan.

Next morning I began writing this melodrama. It limped for
days, but I always told McBrien, when he called in, how well it was
going. If the tale should die on its feet at two weeks, I would still
have time to persuade Matt to flee. I operated on the principle now
that if one could write one letter after another to people one had

no fundamental liking or respect for, one could also write a plausible novel, a few thousand words at a time.

About the fourth day, I went back to drinking McBrien's vodka, and it put me into a sort of subtranscendent lather of creativity. About then, McBrien asked could he read some of the pages of this melodrama, and I let him since it might fuel him towards becoming a refugee. But he made applauding noises as he read and seemed to find the material quite acceptable. When, despite myself, I felt flattered by his approval, I produced twenty thousand words in eight days.

And you'll speed up, said McBrien, joyfully. Because both of us knew the second half of a book is always faster than the first.

But then a possibly fatal thing happened. I got involved in A2's, the accountant's, experience as a soldier. It was then that Hugo Carter, my military comrade, asserted himself for two days while I wrote in clearheaded fervor the short story I should have long since attended to. This tale I had been waiting to tell began to insinuate itself into the soap opera narrative I was writing. It waited for the point where my feeble, fatuous tale put the McCauley figure's son at Summer Island during the war. And here Hugo Carter had appeared, choosing to disgorge himself into the sluggish waters of my Great Uncle—ordered narrative.

The story I wrote was along these lines:

On Summer Island we conscripts were required, when stood-to, to wear both our oppressive gas masks and rubberized gloves. Summer, normally a time for heroic dives into rivers, for folly and ice cream and plaintive evening songs of longing, was a harsh season on Summer Island for the conscripts in this oppressive wear, but they made us wear the mask and gloves long enough so that we became accustomed to them. For there was no guarantee the Others would not try to gas us or drop a biological bomb amongst us. After the day's reconnaissance planes instructed the command that there were no signs of attack, we were allowed to take everything off but keep it within reach.

Young Hugo Carter, who had frankly disliked the long claustrophobic crawl along a thousand-meter L-shaped pipe when we were in training, was also honest with me about how he hated the mask and gloves. They added to his feelings of being forgotten by God, by all but his indulgent mother back in the city. Besides, he murmured to me, we're the ones who use the damned gas. They use mass immolation.

Carter and I provided a seasoning of city Mediationist boys to ranks considered too heavily Intercessionist. The southern Intercessionists were popularly looked on as hayseeds and cannon fodder. They came from a background of folk superstition and religious fundamentalism. Many were only chancily literate. But they deserved—in my experience of them—a little more respect. They had kept solidarity with us in our struggle against the Others, even though there were a majority of Intercessionists across the straits as well, in the opposing army—indeed, among the officer corps.

Southerners had, however, begun to complain, as taxis from the front delivered their dead young men in coffins, octopus-strapped to the vehicles' roofs, that we secular, urban, take-it-or-leave-it Mediationists were letting them carry the burden of casualties. It had until then been very easy for people like Carter and myself to become officers or to get exemptions. We could plead a special area of expertise, or say that our studies added to the strength of the state. In a sense it was more important than anything we could do militarily. But because of all this Intercessionist complaint, in the year Hugo Carter and I were conscripted, no excuses were accepted, no commissions were available. We were two students of humanities. What did we have to offer a state with such an ancient and complex culture except our lives?

Carter and I, with the same birthday, and from the same faculty at the university, stuck together, but we rather got to like the southerners, with their casual, earthy humor which escaped the net of orthodoxy. They were brave and practical young men. On good evenings, drinking coffee round the campfire, we felt the normal solidarity of untried troops. Our training was the usual banal stuff, relayed in a thousand tales of a thousand wars—crawling, lunging, presenting weapons for inspection, throwing one grenade to find out what the experience was like, counting one-two-three until the NCO told you to duck down behind the wall of stone. Such technicians of death were we! Considerable esprit. Considerable amounts of banter. You city types aren't such bastards as we thought. And, You pig-fucking hicks aren't so bad either. The army is an education, if only you survive it.

We stood on disputed ground—these oil well regions and islands had been ceded by an earlier government to the Others, but we had no doubt that this earlier accommodation had been nothing but that, an adjustment made under superior political, diplomatic, and military force. Thus, between the redneck Intercessionists and the most religiously casual Mediationists, we had no doubt that this country of tall reeds, sand dunes, eroding granite, and oil wells was our inheritance, to be retained.

Carter and I had arrived on the Summer Island front in time to be put to work on the latest national triumph—a thirty-mile canal which ran through the sand dunes and reed beds right across the island, a mile wide. Though mere infantrymen trained in the use of the trench mortar, we were put to work on placing steel reinforcements along the banks, and then carrying stones from a nearby hill to make the bottom of this vast ditch uneven for a potential, wading enemy. At the southern end of the island, many of the reed beds which had been studiously drained during the days of the British Mandate after World War I were now flooded to make similar barriers—wide, shallow pools, requiring attackers to wade towards the assault.

After our work on the canal, we went to defend the southern marshes, living in superbly crafted bunkers amidst the dunes and the scattered granite outcrops. Between us, Carter and I made up a trench mortar team led by an Intercessionist corporal who had been in the army for years and who rather loved having two city boys at his mercy.

The bunkers we lived in behind the trench lines were a physical sign of the contact between Great Uncle and his soldiers. Many were equipped with bunks, and they were sturdy since, comfortingly, Great Uncle did not want casualties. Heavy casualties might yet win him the war but lose him the peace. That was one of the reasons our French-built Gazelle helicopters were sometimes seen to drop over the marshes, on the other side of the straits, five-gallon drums which we knew to be mustard gas cocktails fitted with a burster charge.

More interestingly we sometimes saw professional-looking, more shapely bombs descending from the bays of our aircraft. To save our lives, Great Uncle was dropping gas and nerve agents and committing a war crime against the Others. We were forbidden to speak about this knowledge, and everywhere we went we were meant to have gas mask at hip in case the dosage accidentally came our way. But the weak prevailing wind of the straits, generally from the west, favored us when it came to mustard gas. That didn't mean the Others could not, if they chose to, destroy a battalion of us with a little canister of tabin nerve gas, if they had it in stock. Tabin tended to be denser, so the gossip had it, and to stick more to the place where it was dropped, penetrating even the ground on which the Others lay.

Every late afternoon we were shelled from across the straits—again dependent on the stocks of shells and missiles the Others had to hand. Most of us sheltered in the bunkers at these times. Hugo Carter and I surprised ourselves by our calmness under these projectiles as large as 122 millimeters. We believed in our cement roofs in the same way we believed in our mothers, even allowing for the fact mine was dead. We were ready at our officers' commands to emerge and take up position by our dug-in guns and tanks should the shelling be harbinger to an assault. We got quite used to this thunder—again, I amazed myself in that regard.

Generally, the Others left the oil wells to the north of the island alone—for they hoped, by defeating us here, to inherit them.

It was the first assault which was a great shock to Hugo and me. They came in small dinghies and were seen in the first light of day crossing a broad swath of shallows in breathtaking numbers. By not preparing us with cannon, they had nearly stolen a march. Carter and I were in our trench and by our mortar within seconds, hauling the tarpaulin off, and calibrating its trajectory at the corporal's orders. The zealous Intercessionist youths whom the Others chose to breed came rabidly ashore, purple bands around their foreheads, immolating themselves willingly on our mines. This was, in its way, an astonishing savagery they imposed on their own. They allowed young bodies to be torn to gobbets of flesh on the promise the heavenly and perfected body would be divinely reassembled in the world after death. The better trained regular army came on behind, walking in the path made by the martyrs. They knew the low granite island top behind our trenches would give access to the oil well roads, and so they came en masse at our positions. Carter and I were relieved to be able mindlessly to keep feeding the trench mortar, but then, because it was not a sophisticated instrument, our corporal told us to cease, the enemy was too close, and to grab our weapons. I closed my eyes as I fired at the lines of men sixty yards away, not wanting to know anything. I continued thus for ten minutes, concentrating on my task, reloading magazines with eyes open, shooting blind. Many others, I'm sure, did the same, yet some good fortune attended our blinkered firing, because it became apparent we had beaten the Others back. God help them, said the corporal, showing fraternal feeling for a moment. It's just a pause, someone said. It's just a pause.

Next morning, about the same hour, they came back in apparently bigger numbers. We emerged from our bunkers wearing our gas masks. Gradually, because of heat, most of our fellow soldiers took them off, given that the Others were not wearing them in the first place.

Their martyrs were pathetically willing again, and Hugo began weeping for them as we served the trench mortar. But we could not make their regulars depart as they had on their previous attack. They captured a section of trench on the flank of the granite hill, so that all of us had to withdraw to the secondary line of fortifications. I could tell that our officers considered this serious. In the afternoon they were able to land their artillery, which fired all that following night. It was a scale of fire I had never heard before, and we huddled now in our mothering cement, pitying the men on watch in the trenches.

Deprived of rest, I felt mad, deranged, jangled. As Carter and I, the night having turned cold, huddled against the jolting wall of a bunker, I asked, Did the air force drop gas today?

If they hadn't, we both wished they had. We knew that if they kept on firing and sent their men in under the protection of the guns, we would be forced out of our hole to face it all.

We were all in our positions by four-thirty in the morning, an august and terrifying moment in which the sun rose before the straits, blinding us with glory and terror. A heavy artillery exchange began, during which we were required to remain in the trenches, all our senses ringing and juddering inhumanly. The tanks from both sides joined in the orchestra. Though both our French and Russian suppliers had equipped them with sophisticated land-computing sights, these were beyond the understanding of most of our tank men, who simply surrounded their vehicle with a bunker and fired away like fixed artillery pieces. Yes, yes. I could rave along about such subtleties of our conflict, the Others and us, the southern Intercessionist yahoos incompetent with their tanks, but Carter and I, city-slicker nominal Mediationists, were no better anyhow, timorously feeding our trench mortar and hoping that it was an instrument of sufficient death. Our bombers were all at once there, no more than a few hundred feet above us, dominant as the artillery eased and as the Others came roaring forward. As Carter and I and the corporal took our positions, I saw the steel canisters descend from the bellies of the bombers. They might have been smoke bombs to obscure the battlefield—though I knew they were not that, for what was the purpose?

The use of gas is a crime against the conventions of war. And yet some of my fellow citizens had taken the risk of removing one dangerous commodity, phosphorus, from these bombs, and replacing it with another volatile entity, mustard or nerve gas, or a blessed cocktail of both.

Our corporal called to Carter and me as we fed the mortar, Your masks! Put on your masks, for God's sake! The wind was sluggish from the west that dawn, but the profile of the granite mound behind us caused it to skitter in a little eddy there. Our corporal knew this. Intercessionists, being chiefly country people, understood these subtleties of breeze.

Get your masks on!

I put mine on. Mine's in the bunker, Hugo yelled—rather I half read his lips as saying that. Yet he could not go for it. An officer would see him as fleeing and would put a bullet in his head. Whatever was in the canisters our planes had dropped, it seemed to barely add to the weight of the air. There was screaming all over the battlefield, but that is quite normal. The corporal and I wore our gas masks, and I looked through the lenses at barefaced Carter and envied him the clearer air he breathed, the lack of obstruction.

It became apparent that the Others were withdrawing to the positions they had left that morning. What I was aware of was a curious noise in the new, hollow silence; human animals, having tested the M16 against the AK-47, the American 122-millimeter howitzer against the entrenched Russian T65 cannon, were now filling the sky with the same orphaned howl. My hands burned, and I lifted them to the eyepieces of my mask and saw that they were red and blistering, exactly as they felt. I saw then as I swept my masked head to left and right that our trench was an abattoir. There were dead and living horrors, the disemboweled complaining about the spillage of their organs, or reconciling themselves to it; the beheaded and delimbed who made no further complaint, and the defaced, a man whose visage was now bleeding steak containing perhaps one horrific amazed eye. Everywhere in the trench and for hundreds of miles beyond it, mewling and calls for rebirth were heard, screams and invocations to a God who had been asked for something cleaner and swifter than had been given.

My hands, I said. They itched crazily and I waved them in air to cool them.

What? asked Carter. He could not hear me distinctly through my mask. He was, however, distracted by the state of his own hands. He sat red-faced at the bottom of our trench, and began sneezing. He drew a bunched hand down the length of his nose, as if to clear the nostrils. Then he dragged the hand into the shadow of his left shoulder and hunched forward, shivering. Officers and NCOs ran along the trench telling those of us who had masks to keep them on. I saw a blister forming on Carter's cheek. I stopped rubbing my hands since it made skin come away. I got permission to go to the bunker a hundred yards back and fetch Carter's mask. I ran, cursing away at my hands, and looked in a pile of military gear for his mask.

When I skittered back with it in my smarting hands, the masked corporal was leaning over Hugo, swearing at him tenderly. Private Carter raised his welted face to me. His eyes had swollen closed. Flesh had begun to fall away like a beard from his blistered cheeks. I tried to put the mask on him but he shook his head with what I thought of as the irritable stubbornness of a man in temporary pain. When he persisted a while I realized he was not only blinded but had lost all reason. The corporal hammered me on the shoulder. Give it up, he told me. Carter vomited and began to convulse. An officer came up to me and said through his mouthpiece, Shoot him! I looked stupidly at the officer, mask to mask. Isn't he your friend? I heard the officer ask. It's a cocktail this time. Indeed, Carter seemed to be choking. Froth had formed on his lips. The officer leveled his pistol and thunderously shot Carter dead. The air was punctuated now with similar mercy shots, both sides of the line exercising the same compassion, though *they* would no doubt spare some of their treatable cases to ship them to hospital in Switzerland, and show the world how Great Uncle violated international agreements.

We were stood-to throughout the day, but there were no further attacks by the Others. In our section of line we treated our hands with soothing blister cream, donned white gloves, helped the wounded back to ambulances, buried the dead, and in a gully behind the line, beneath the small scarp for which the Others had been trying, we made a pile of the unsightly and unlucky dead whose nervous systems had been attacked by the nerve agent which had accidentally fallen amongst our regiment. The bodies we had removed to the gully, some seventy, were—and this was thoroughly understood—not to go home. A special team wearing white clothing appeared to attend to the ultimate total consumption of Carter's and the other bodies, burning them in a white-limed communal grave.

That night the enemy withdrew, in boats small and large, across the straits. We did not at once occupy the wing of the island they left vacant—it was vastly contaminated with mustard and tabin. The officers moved us to a safer part of the line, where, maskless and gloveless, we sat at ease, disbelieving all that had happened and still full of a grief which had not yet come to focus itself. Gentlemen, a colonel told us as we sat on the ground in a mass, we have survived, and not without the great help of certain agents dropped from planes. We have sustained lower casualties than the enemy. You have seen some of your more negligent comrades perish accidentally. You are, let me make it absolutely clear, to deny all knowledge of this. You did not see it happen. If you say otherwise, you will pay the penalty and your unpensioned body will be sent home in a black coffin. Be aware—you did not need to suffer death yourselves, but all because a merciful regime has separated you from it by the special application of these chemicals and other agents.

It has to be said that this point seemed perfectly reasonable to the regiment in the midst of which I sat, and to me as part of that multicelled unit.

So, said the colonel, your friends are all officially not dead but taken prisoner. You will comfort the parents of the men you were friendly with. Any mother or wife who turns up at the Ministry of Defense with a complaint that her missing son is dead will be traced straight back to the one who said so. You've been blessed, boys, under God. Stay blessed. I will interview you individually over the coming week and ensure you are willing to keep this compact.

Why would I not be willing, Mrs. Carter, to tell you that your son was a prisoner? What would you rather I had told you? That his flesh melted before my eyes?

It was as this true tale burst forth from me in what I saw as the last month of my life that I perceived the answer, there in the colonel's speech.

I had only to tell the truth to that serial nuisance of my life, Mrs. Carter, I had only to ask her pardon for the long, well-meaning, state-advised deceit. And it seemed so easy to say what had not been said before, and so wholesome not to take this pretense to the grave. A mercy to me, a mercy to her. The colonel had said it would take only a mother or a wife turning up at the Ministry of War, asking was the story true, to ensure that the source would be traced back, and the former soldier punished. It could not be counted McBrien's fault, or his wife's, that I became suddenly reckless with Mrs. Carter, loading her with the real news, saving the remnant of her life from the vigil she'd been keeping for the better part of six years.

I called Mrs. Carter, and she was so grateful and excited I almost hung up.

I'm so sorry I didn't get a chance to offer my condolences personally at the funeral of your dear wife, she said. I was waiting to do so, but they told me you had been overcome. I can understand that.

I told her I wanted to come and see her now. It was the first approach I had made since the one following my return home from the front, during which I told my consoling lie. I could hear the mounting excitement in her voice. I, the bereaved, who had survived the battle of Summer Island but had lost a wife, was coming as a peer to compare grief with her whose son was amongst the great unnamed of the POW camps over there. I, who had had all the luck and the beautiful actress wife and a fledgling repute, would now approach her as an equal in loss. I feared, of course, that I would be greeted with a table groaning with pastries and biscotti. We would eat the feast of grief together—worse still, she would see me gorging myself for no purpose, the pain still there whatever the skill of the patissier.

I said to her, Please, no coffee, no cake. I'll be right over.

When I left the building—why should I not visit the mother of an army friend?—I saw the Toyota and limo in their usual place across the street. Though they no doubt wrote down the time of my exit, and the limo would probably follow me at a funeral-pace distance, there was no frantic reaction to my emergence.

I knew I would suffer a retribution from the old lady. She was not an old lady, of course, but had condemned herself to be one. She seemed to be bent on proving that the truest love is the love between mothers and sons. I remembered my mother, holding my hand and weeping, in her last week in the Republic Hospital. A mother who had been restrained and now, lucky enough to be a patient in a time of plenty before the sanctions, primed with the sort of painkillers that made one weak rather than kill the truest pain. She said, You were always my joy.

Had she lived, she would have been saying it when I was sixty. Partway to Mrs. Carter's, I felt an urge to get things over and hailed a taxi. The limo easefully increased its pace as I made good speed towards the apartment of a woman whom half this city in my father's day had gasped for and declared unapproachable, but who had now become a hag for her son's sake.

My descriptions of her were, of course, cast up by my sense of being hunted by her. Now I was to liberate her back into the stream of womanhood, and liberate myself as well. I would hear the army's knock at my door and I would rejoice as I was taken away before the startled gaze of Captain Chaddock. After all, the Overguard was the Overguard, but the army was the army!

When Mrs. Carter opened the door, I could see she had not been able to help herself. There was not a set table of goodies, but there was coffee on the coffee table, and three or so plates full of various delicacies. She admitted me with a slight frown, in response to my own.

Dear Mrs. Carter, I said, finding the nearest chair to the door and sitting as soon as I could. You should sit down too.

She obeyed me, placing herself crookedly on a chair by the corner of the table. She was agog.

All right, I said. I have to tell you at last that you have been misled. The government version of what befell your son is not the truth of it. I regret the part I have had in sustaining the deception.

I told the story, a fraught smile appearing on her face each time I mentioned her son early in the tale. Whenever I paused, her coffeepot made a metallic ticking sound, as if to warn us it was getting cold, growing less and less drinkable. She listened with a careful, stricken quality, massaging the corners of her mouth with thumb and forefinger. When I had finished, she seemed very controlled. She leaned on her fist and released a few tears, and I rose from my seat and caressed her shoulders. For the first time, I was not frightened of her, and thought of all the times Sarah had helped nurse me towards meetings with this woman.

Sit down, she told me in a minute voice.

I sat again, like a man expecting punishment, my fists, indifferent to defense, spread on my knees. I heard her gasp once, silent tears fell from her eyes, and she straightened herself in the chair. Then she put her head back and emitted the most ghastly, high-pitched wail. I stood again, whimpering, spreading my hands like a man letting go of deceit. She rose too with a plate of honey pastry in her hands, and hurled it against the wall behind my head. It did not matter now, she clearly thought. She was not preserving a home decor for someone. She walked to me and drew back her hand and slapped me across the face, stingingly, twice. For the first time since the funeral I began to cry. Poor Hugo, poor Hugo! I howled. She returned to the coffee table and upended it. I could see in her stride some of her legendary force, revived.

She yelled, You say he did not have his gas mask?

I said, He was not good at all that stuff. He always left one or two items behind. He had a gift for poetic approximation.

This isn't the truth, she asserted, wild-eyed. I did not raise him that he'd vanish through a simple accident like that.

Did you notice how I came to your afternoon teas? Like a sullen teenager. That was because I was lying. Now . . .

Why didn't you stop him? Why didn't you stop that officer?

I knew I would have to do it if he didn't.

Why didn't you run with him, out of that trench? Out of that poisoned air? You stood and watched him vomit and froth?

Then a thought struck her. I know, she went on. You're punishing me for the death of your wife. You're punishing *me*. I was once as beautiful as your wife, and now she's gone, and you're punishing *me*.

I saw your son die. Why would I tell you that if it were not true?

She fumbled in her mind awhile for possible reasons. Because you are a fabulist, she hissed, splendid and electric in fury, wanting to provoke me, wanting, and I swear to it, a blow so she could hit back.

I loved your son, Mrs. Carter. It was a heinous waste. There's no justice in these things. I wish he were here and bringing your grandchildren to visit you in some cranky old Saab.

Now she leveled a finger at me. I am going straight to the Ministry of War. I will tell them what you say, and they will tell me whether it is true or malicious.

It's true, I told her, though they'll tell you it isn't. They initiated the lie.

I watched her as she struggled to believe or disprove me. I meanly thought, I don't need to drink your coffee anymore.

I rose and went to the door. Is there a friend I can call to come and sit with you? I asked.

Where are my friends? she howled. They have all fallen away.

Call one of them, though, I advised her.

I opened the door and heard her say, Wait a second there! But I passed through. She signified that she would really speak to the Ministry of War by throwing something solid against the door I had just closed.

This method of letting myself and the McBriens off the hook had proved painful beyond belief, and there was no sign at all that it would save Mrs. Carter from her obsessions.

Are you well? McBrien asked me by telephone.

Yes. I've written a lot in the last three days.

Good. Why did you go and see Mrs. Carter?

You're not supposed to know that I went and saw Mrs. Carter.

Don't be ridiculous, said McBrien. I get the reports. You're the artist, I'm the bureaucrat.

I explained, I was writing the war scenes. They put me in mind of her son. Her son was with me on Summer Island.

I suppose you have to have a break, McBrien admitted.

Believe me, I said.

Two mornings after my painful scene with Mrs. Carter, I was limping on anyhow with my melodrama when I heard an insistent knocking and answered the door to Captain Chaddock and an army officer who held a pistol in his hand. Both their faces were somewhat flushed, and Chaddock made fraternal eye contact with me over the shoulder of the army officer. The latter asked me my name, while Chaddock muttered, Come on! You know!

The officer told me I was under arrest. My plan for deliverance had come to fruition, and suddenly it did not seem to be the shining scheme I had at first thought it. Chaddock clearly lacked the authority to oppose my arrest, and the officer called down the stairs a little way where two of his men waited to handle me on the way to street level. I was permitted to grab my coat from its hook.

Chaddock said, I called division, Mr. Sheriff. They said they'd sort this out.

I began to feel half pleased at the prospect.

Under the eyes of the Overguard, whom Chaddock had clearly ordered to show jurisdictional restraint, the soldiers loaded me into the back of a military police wagon from the Army Historical Corps—believe me, they called it that, and possessed their own police—drawn up outside my apartment block. I could see through a grille at the back of the small truck Chaddock standing exasperated on the pavement. The guardians of history drove off with me to an army barracks in the suburbs, and my heart leapt ambiguously, with welcome and terror, when we entered the gate and I could see the barbed wire atop the walls. I was given a cell—plain but ample. Two young officers visited me, files in their hands, and sat me down at a table. They did not seem as angry as, in my original plan, I imagined they would be. But then, I had always desired an exit, not necessarily bruises.

One said, You claimed in a conversation with the mother of one of our heroes that he had been gassed by projectiles dropped by our own bombers.

I saw it, I told them, my voice quaking, but partly with pride. I told them I was there, at the northern end of the line with the Fifty-third Battalion. I was fortunate in that I had my mask with me.

The younger of the two officers said, You must be driven by seditious intent to claim that. We don't use chemical or biological agents. The idea that we do has been promoted by our enemies. Our records show that your friend, Private Hugo Carter, was captured during the battle.

And you told Mrs. Carter that, I suppose?

Of course.

How could he be captured, I asked with some sort of delight, when the military historians show that our line was not breached by the opposition? To be captured he would have needed to stand up and present himself to the enemy. But they were already dealt with when it happened. I can assure you, I saw him buried in a pit, in mounds of white chemical. He was not taken prisoner.

The officers communed and the elder one told me, I'm afraid I must give you some time to reconsider your position, Mr. Sheriff. It's a matter of fixed principle. We know and you know that our state does not use biological and chemical weapons, and we would not like to have one of the heroes of Summer Island, as you appear to be, spread a slander against our state. The official military history shows that the Others were very successful at your end of the line, and penetrated many of your battalion trenches.

Triumphant in my expectation of punishment, I declared, I was in those same trenches as Carter. If he was a prisoner, I was a prisoner. In fact, I saw him slump at the bottom of the trench. I had a mask, he didn't. Even so, my hands were blistered.

I showed them my furrowed and unaesthetic hands, given to redness and scaling. This is the result of mustard gas, I told them.

Surely you are mistaken, the second young officer suggested, giving me every chance to recant.

I refused every proffered lifeline. No, I insisted, an officer told me that the way Carter and the others convulsed meant it wasn't only mustard gas, but nerve gas mixed in. Everyone in the front line knew we could depend on such aid against the invaders. We were grateful, don't you see? Except the lines were so cramped at our end of the battle that our forces were stricken too. We absorbed the mustard gas and tabin intended for the enemy. It was proximity, and bad luck with geography—the escarpment made the wind whirl a little. That's what killed Private Carter.

We can't let you go, said the more junior of the two. You seem to be a buffoon. Think about it! The state does not use biological or chemical weapons. This is one of the principles of the state. We suffer under the sanctions of those who think we do. Did you think we would let you go around backing up what liars like CNN and the BBC say? I don't know what's got into you.

There was a notable lack of remonstration from them as they left the cell, leaving the table there but taking their chairs with them.

Left to myself, I came to terms with my yellow-walled cell, its low cot with a blanket and a pillow, and the lidded bucket for my waste. I did not expect to be permitted to sleep and had a fear of some episode of degradation of the kind prisoners were subjected to, yet in some ways I felt happier than on any day since Sarah's death. I was tenuously proud of my heresy, for I fancied I felt her pride in me like an acute presence in the cell. I'd unburdened myself to Mrs. Carter, and altered her from a timid widow into a plate thrower. I had committed an ecstatic apostasy. I had said mustard gas. I had said tabin. I'd really put myself in it, and I felt both proud and terrified.

Sometime later an orderly slid some stew and a jug of water under the flap by the base of the door. I ate it, but remained full of the anticipation of torture, or of its helpmeets, men with heavy fists and hobnailed boots. Yet I drifted off. About midnight, my cell door was opened with a vigorous gesture and I sat up, ready for an end. It was McBrien, wearing an evening suit, accompanied by Chaddock, and now it was the army officers' turn to be in the background.

Alan, McBrien called pleasantly. What are you doing? Are you trying to kill yourself?

It was too weighty a question for me to answer.

I said to him, I was present at Summer Island at the sector held by the Fifty-third Battalion. A comrade of mine named Private Carter died from the effects of mustard and nerve gas.

McBrien shook his head, half amused, in the direction of Chaddock and the officers in camouflage. He said, Not only is he a veteran, but he's a renowned writer and he's cracked up with overwork.

An officer said, Can you get him to shut up though?

Every time, said McBrien with practiced ease. He had become an accomplished bureaucrat already. He must have been shitting himself, but it did not seem so.

I'll bend every endeavor, he announced. So will Captain Chaddock. But as serious an accusation as my friend here has made, I must remind you he has presidential immunity. Show them your wrist scars for a start, Alan.

I refused to, but McBrien and Chaddock remained the authorities at the scene. You must let him go, McBrien told the officers, and we'll manage him our own way.

It's all very well for you, said an officer. But what do we do with the crazy old woman?

Chaddock groaned. Don't have to tell *you*. Next time shipments of dead POWs come back, give her a corpse to mourn over.

We don't do that sort of thing, said the officer. We don't fake records.

Well, said McBrien, at his best now. He's a novelist. You gentlemen can be novelists too, can't you?

A senior officer kneaded his face. You can take him, he said at last. But we don't want to hear any more of this gas shit.

I burst into laughter at the puniness of this threat. It was in such contrast with their martial bearing, their campaign ribbons, the glitter of their caps.

McBrien would not let it go at that. He said like an advocate, Isn't it possible for a friend of Great Uncle's to have suffered from war trauma? But we can get him treatment.

Mr. Sheriff, Chaddock invited me.

Come on, Alan, McBrien ordered me, so smoothly that by now he had my admiration.

I will die for my belief, I said, keeping my backside solidly on the cot.

No stupid stuff, Alan, McBrien said, entering and wrestling me to my feet, with the sudden clattering help of many warders in ringing boots. Please, he said, looking in my eyes with such insistence. The situation's changed. Please.

I retrieved my shoes and socks, and was frog-marched into the corridor even before I could get my jacket on. I shouted and wrestled but someone bludgeoned me, I suppose expertly, near my right ear.

In McBrien's car, I revived and found myself sickened, as well as by the blow, with self-reproach of the bitterest and most deathly kind. I didn't think it would be so bad, since part of my being dreaded the punishment the history cops could have inflicted on me. But I was disappointed I had managed to make the whole incident into a comedic episode. I looked out the back window and could see Chaddock behind us in his limo. I was thus uninhibited in telling McBrien, That story came from me. The only decent thing I've written in the whole process. I can write and not write, and I don't give a damn anymore.

McBrien gave me a soft answer, just to frustrate me. We have more than two and a half weeks, he said. Now that you know you are immune, doesn't that give you wings?

Fuck you, I told him.

By which, McBrien replied, I believe you mean: To hell with me! Does that mean into the pit with Sonia? Would you condemn her too?

She's the normal bureaucrat's popsy, I said in concussed petulance. To hell with her too!

McBrien said, shaking his head, Does that include her unborn child also?

He picked up an envelope from the backseat.

Open it! he commanded me.

He switched on the reading light behind my head.

The envelope was unsealed and held two large sheets of film. It looked at first like an X ray of the brain or heart—a layman can never tell—and I wanted to peevishly demand he explain what these films were. When one examined them further, there were many images on each of a sac, and in some of them the darker image of a bean-shaped organ. Looking closely, I saw the bean shape had a head. These were ultrasound images, provided in the National Republic Hospital, one of two hospitals that held the necessary machine and open to senior bureaucrats and military officers and their spouses and children.

Yes, Alan, said McBrien. She's pregnant. The newest citizen of our state lies under her heart, my dear friend. But also in your hands.

I looked away from him and rubbed my ear and groaned.

Would you condemn that along with me and my . . . what did you say? . . . popsy? I don't think so, Alan.

Great Uncle might finish me anyhow, I argued. After tonight.

Well, he seems omniscient but he's not quite. He doesn't know. Chaddock reported it as a case of mistaken identity. So Chaddock's in your hands, too.

I hated these extensions of responsibility. Chaddock did it to cover his own backside, I claimed.

But the unborn, who had earned no malice and whose snubbed features were visible on the film, who had planned no artillery strikes, who entered the world with an avid but innocent little mouth!

What's its sex? I asked McBrien.

They don't quite know yet. Next ultrasound they can tell us.

I want to see an obstetrician's report, I said.

McBrien said, All right. I'll bring it round by coffee time tomorrow morning. But get it clear, Alan. Until the eighth of next month, you are condemned to live a charmed life. Not even the military can touch you.

The next morning, McBrien was at my apartment by eight-thirty, carrying a detailed obstetrical report declaring that the child, possibly female, was well advanced on its second trimester, and signed by a Dr. D. J. Wharton. McBrien was insistent that I read it, and call the doctor if I must. But by the morning's painfully clear light, I accepted the existence of the unborn McBrien. It struck me wearily that I now possessed more lives dependent on me than if I'd begotten a family of ten. So nature blindly extended the lines of responsibility. So the mute egg collaborated with light and tyranny both. Our lies, timidity, and vanity might have earned us Great Uncle. But no one could wish him on the McBrien unborn.

So why don't you just give in and tell a story? he asked me. Without rogue sections like the one you wrote on Carter.

I said to him, Because there is a way out for you via the mountains.

McBrien laughed, magisterial in fatherhood, it seemed. And will my child appropriately stay fixed in Sonia's womb? While we hide in caves and travel over stony tracks in trucks with no damn suspension? Settle to it now, Alan. You thought there were exits, but there aren't.

He pointed to the computer with the maimed A-drive on. Very authoritatively, he said, Save us, Alan!

I went back to the tale of the McCauley-style barge skipper. The melodrama—up to the point where I had lost my management of myself and began writing the story of Carter—occupied three large computer files, TASK1, TASK2, TASK3. The character A1, the blockade-running son, was bringing in a specific shipment of antibiotics and narcotics for the administrator of East Bay Hospital. But the minions of the Istrian black marketeer hijacked the truck in the mountains beyond Scarpdale, using their boss's hold over A1's sister and brother, bimbo and accountant in turn to the black-market mogul, and nominated in the text as F1 and A2, as leverage over brave A1. And so on. I took up the thread determinedly. There is a simple comfort in work, even if it was a debased task I was at. Its necessity helped me for some thousands of words. But I couldn't bring myself to give the buggers names.

Thus my task limped along for two days—I wish I still possessed a copy, to show you how deplorable it was. For the fact that I knew it was to take Great Uncle's name helped to make it, more and more, assume the character of his florid prose. I was able to creak out the required two or three thousand words a day, though, at least until I got a phone call from Mrs. Carter. This was a forgotten consequence of my earlier actions—the fact that Mrs. Carter had always had my telephone number and could call at will.

Alan, she said.

Yes, Mrs. Carter.

I felt confident with her, poor woman. I had in my way also released myself from her power over me.

I've been to the Ministry of War, she told me.

They told me that, I said.

I demanded information on Hugo. Like reasonable men, they asked me why the government would go on paying Hugo's wages if he had in fact been deceased all these years. They pointed out that they went on paying wages into the bank account only of men who had a homecoming somewhere in their future. They said you were a novelist, and your fiction making got away with you.

That's a reasonable argument, I said, not quite knowing whether to hope as energetically as the Historical Corps that she would accept it.

Yes, she conceded. But for some reason, when they said that, I knew they were lying, and you were telling me the truth now at last. And that you had lied to me year by year, season by season.

I could find nothing to say to that.

She went on, As soon as the weather gets cooler, you are to drive me to the place. We are to make every effort to exhume his body.

No, I said. I can't help you with that, Mrs. Carter. The place is unmarked. There are too many . . . well, it's complicated. It's beyond our means, and it would only distress you further.

All right, she said. Then I will do it myself. You will see what an *old lady* can do! And please accept this call as a curse upon your entire life.

She slammed the phone down.

A ridiculous threat perhaps. Except that now it was harder to grind forth the melodrama. To ease it out of me, contrary to Captain Chaddock's instructions I drank two-thirds of a bottle of vodka one day and a little more the next. On the third day, McBrien, during his daily visit, said, You look frightful, Alan.

He took off his suit coat and scrambled eggs for me, and made me herbal tea. It's the least I can do, he told me cheerily, for a man who's making my career.

He had not mentioned the child, but it remained our most serious motivation. And in the last week he had been reading some of the material on-screen.

This is good, he boomed, as he read the more recent output. This is right up the big man's alley. Less social realist than I thought. He'll like it. It reads like a fable. The American lefty reviewers will see it in those terms. They mightn't say you're the new Steinbeck, but they'll call you the new Chinua Achebe.

It's absolute diarrhea, I told him.

That's probably what we need for a success then, said McBrien. We want a devastating and sudden success. We don't want *Ulysses*. We don't care if people are reading it in fifty years. Plausibility is all the big man asks of us.

He finished reading and looked up.

Look, I know you can write differently from this. In the Western manner. But you'll have leisure to do that. And the critics will be disposed to see any broad strokes, any primitivism, as a postcolonial legacy.

I shook my head and laughed.

You talk such utter balls! I assured him, with the acids of last night's liquor still tugging at my throat.

My old friend Andrew Kennedy called to say he had missed me from recent Thursday parties, but of course he understood that I might be hard at some special work, and still grieving.

You're allowed to go out, aren't you? he asked.

I believe so, I said.

I'll pick you up this Thursday from your place.

I said, I'll come with McBrien.

Let him come on here with Sonia. I'll collect you from home at five-thirty, Thursday.

I felt grateful, yet needed a further quarter of an illicit bottle of vodka just to prepare myself. Besides, the text had now become a mere dribble of words. It was particularly on it that Mrs. Carter's idiotic curse seemed to have fallen. As for the rest, vodka ran in my veins like boiling mercury these days. My blood crepitated. I would wake at two and then at three in the morning, my brain weeping, irked at some small noise.

My God, said Andrew, chirpy at the door on Thursday. You've got two carloads of Overguard down there. A man of some importance.

Oh yes, I assured him. Every citizen should have such luck.

You're letting your beard grow.

Sorry, I didn't get round to shaving.

You're forgiven.

I grabbed a jacket and we descended to his Mercedes. His driver, having held the back door for me, ran around the outside of the vehicle to take his seat. We moved out into light traffic, the white Toyota of the Overguard traveling behind us. The other, the limo, would obviously keep watch over the apartment block. Such was the division of Overguard duties for the evening, as far as I could perceive them.

I have a bit of news, Andrew told me. Louise James is back. She's got a bit of a grant from somewhere to do some research here. She's staying with us. You remember her?

Yes, I admitted, uncomfortable at once.

She had once been the young radio broadcaster I had come close to being entangled with. Her father had run a TV current affairs program for Andrew's network, in the days when we were permitted to have current affairs in this country. As well as being threatened by the way our friendship had ended, I began to tremble with an angry suspicion that I'd been brought out to make up some silly gender equivalence at Andrew's party. He could sense as much.

Come on, Alan, he pleaded. We're all friends. No scenes.

That made my anger mount.

To hell with you, Andrew. Am I supposed to see Louise James's tits and be consoled? Is that how you think things work?

And do you think I flew her from America just for this party? For God's sake, Alan!

But she and I will round out the couples.

He shook his head and asked softly, Where does all this irritability come from, Alan? Can I do the right thing by you, whatever I do? I know and respect the scale of your pain. Don't doubt that for a moment.

You know damn all, I asserted. You're just a habitual stooge, a lackey, a purveyor of sitcoms.

Fortunately, the driver's window prevented my outbursts from reaching the front seat. I was still controlled enough to be careful that the man at the wheel did not hear. For even I knew, as did Andrew, that this was something other than me talking, an evil spirit compounded of vodka, loss, and a duty at whose nature he could merely guess.

I think I should go back home, I told Andrew, as close to apologetic as I could manage.

He said, Shut up, Alan, and enjoy yourself! I'll get you a drink as soon as we arrive. And don't say anything else until it's safely inside you.

We traveled on another three minutes in silence, and then, like a child, I began to feel carsick. I swallowed and sweated. At last I said, Andrew, please, could we pull over? I'm not so well.

The car parked on the edge of a riverside park, a strand of threadbare lawns out of which two palm trees rose. I left the car and leaned against the knobbly hide of one of them, examining its surface intimately with that acidic clarity of a man about to be ill. I saw an Overguard driver watching me from the open door of his drawn-in white Toyota. Fluid and bile and alcohol tore its way out of me. Two or three retches, and then I gasped and gasped, my throat burning. I looked to the green relief of the nearby canal. Andrew had his hand sturdily on my shoulder as my breath returned. When I remembered to look at the Overguard vehicle, Captain Chaddock was making his way towards me, but tentatively, as if he thought this was perhaps too direct an approach, a betrayal of his philosophy of nonovert surveillance.

Andrew whispered, Poor old Alan!

Wiping my mouth, I broke from Andrew and walked up to Captain Chaddock to forestall him.

All right, Mr. Sheriff? he asked.

Thanks, I told him.

All right in all senses? he persisted.

Yes, I said.

He nodded. That McBrien! A bootlegger!

It's a tummy infection.

Chaddock smiled in polite disbelief.

I'll watch it, I told him.

You must, said Chaddock, and he gave me a minimal salute and returned to his vehicle.

I turned back to Andrew. My step faltered but he supported me. He was trying to shorten the delay as well, for everyone's sake.

I got a letter from Collins, I told him. Must show it to you.

Yes, maybe later.

As we walked, my back was to Chaddock's white vehicle.

Don't show any surprise, I said. Great Uncle's given me the job of writing a book to be published in his name. McBrien and Sonia are hostages to it, of course. Now Sonia's pregnant, so there's a little McBrien also a hostage. Isn't that a bastard of a setup?

Andrew's eyes narrowed as he directed me along. I don't want to know any of this, he insisted. It's not good to blurt things out like that. Come back to the car.

He seemed very worried, for my own sake as much as anything. It was one of those rare occasions when I saw his sweat show through the well-shaven, blue-pink cheek, and thought, So, you live in fear too.

They won't let me kill myself, I told him, perhaps too self-indulgently. I've already tried to do it. I wonder could I get an oil smuggler I know to put me in contact with someone who'd shoot me. If I was murdered, they couldn't blame McBrien, could they?

Andrew did what was necessary, delivering a brisk cuff to the back of my neck. He said, like some old colonel from Summer Island, Pull yourself together, Alan. You're a danger to shipping.

Leading me to the car and manhandling me in, he gave the order to the driver to proceed. And so, in silence, we reached his house. Grace herself was at the door, since Andrew had had the driver call ahead to her. At seeing me, there was a genuine delight in her face which took all my residual sneers away. At the back of the house, the company around the pool, the McBriens, the Garners, the proudly independent filmmaker Wilf Apple, and his boyfriend, Paul, subsumed me effortlessly. They all spoke to me normally, without an undue or lumbering air of condolence. This was because they were true friends. I accepted a glass of fruit juice spiked with vodka, drank it, and reflected that liquor drunk in company by afternoon light was somehow chemically more benign than the stuff one bolted oneself, in secret desperation, at a sink.

Nor did Andrew and Grace try to introduce Louise James to me—it was Sonia McBrien who eventually did that, informally, approaching me from the flank. I saw her coming, this woman I had cold-shouldered years ago. I saw her well-coifed black hair, and her jawline that, with maturity, had taken on the look of her father's interrogatory jaw. She looked very American. She could be imagined in one of those shopping malls, inspecting fabrics or testing the consistency of face cream along with the most consummate of American consumers. Yet there were also banked questions in her, and I could sense with panic that she was anxious to raise some with me. To delay her, I congratulated Sonia McBrien on the conception of her child and she smiled with that hapless smile of motherhood and its ruthless process before she drifted away.

I was hoping to meet you, Mr. Sheriff, Louise James said, smiling in an all-forgiven manner.

It's good to see you, Louise, I told her.

I loved that book of yours. Even in the West it's considered kind of groundbreaking . . .

You don't need to say that stuff.

She lowered her voice. No, it had all those qualities that attracted me. And, all right, you brushed me off.

The memory of that day returned to her in the form of an ironic smile.

Do you know, she asked, that you're the only man who's ever done that?

It's a wonder you talk to me, I said.

Well, I need to, she said, lowering her voice. I heard about your wife. I am sorry, Alan.

Yes. Better not probe too deeply into all that. It's all a raw mess.

I understand. That's not what I wanted to talk to you about. I have a friend at the University of Texas, in the Institute of Regional Studies. That's where my father worked until his death.

Your father's dead?

Eighteen months ago.

Did Andrew know?

No, we didn't write. And there was no mention in the press. In Texas, he was just another obscure adjunct professor in media studies. In any case, the institute's well endowed with research money. Some of our fellow countrymen and -women have done quite well in Texas, and are anxious to put something back.

Her vast eyes on me, she lowered her voice further. Is there any chance of your going there? They would make a position for you. They wanted you to know.

I stared at her incredulously and she became embarrassed, shaking her head.

Forgive me if this is inappropriate, but I didn't know when I'd get a chance. I think they would simply want you to be a kind of guru in residence.

I should have been grateful that people in other places were drafting a possible career for me. But I was in my own hopeless bubble of *the task,* and the idea taunted rather than soothed me.

And I suppose, I suggested, I would do an occasional commentary spot on CNN, attacking sanctions and being written up as a friend of Great Uncle's?

She shook her head but took no offense. In fact she seemed to perceive what I had said as a comprehensive argument against taking up such a post.

It's always fascinating, she said. The reasons people go, and the reasons they stay.

It's more than fascinating, I told her. I can't leave the land where my wife is buried.

She bowed her head. Then you do her great honor, Alan Sheriff.

I thought I began now to see her instinctive method, a good

one. To answer, in each case, in a manner some degrees removed from the expected answer. I'd been half hoping she would utter a banal *How romantic!* so that I could be chagrined at her and thus get her off my back. But she had not permitted me that. Perhaps it was a trick she had learned on the Public Broadcasting Service.

You're not here, are you, I asked, to look over the National Broadcasting Network for the CIA? For the day they come?

She laughed shortly. What a cynic you are. I don't deny that I could quickly get a travel grant and money to do just that, even though the job's already done by absolute experts over and over. But I've paid my way here.

Andrew says you had a grant.

I don't know where he got that from. I'm on PBS wages while I'm here. That's all. Paid leave.

She looked at me from under her well-plucked eyebrows. Do you think it will be a terrible thing? she asked. The day the Americans come?

Great Uncle is a frightful fellow, I whispered. Fabulously horrible. But the Americans are not his cure.

Who is? she asked. It's funny that when you live there you begin to see the American point of view. Not in any way that I would like to be an out-and-out apologist for them. But they restored Europe after World War II. Europe itself wouldn't do it. They feed the Third World, or try to. Would others? Would Great Uncle? They don't get credit for what they call *the good stuff.*

Come over to Beaumont, and I can show you some good stuff. Courtesy of the sanctions.

Oh sure, she conceded. But can you say that Great Uncle doesn't want his people to be hungry?

I waved my hand. This sort of wave was a national habit. It meant to say, We can't get anywhere by comparing evils.

I said in fact, I'm sure the Americans will enjoy the programs you make here.

But she was determined not to be condescended to. She smiled again at me. There was actually an old-fashioned maidenly component in the smile that came more from us than from the Americans.

The Americans enjoy what they enjoy and believe what they believe, she said. Valiant little PBS cuts a very small quantity of ice.

Andrew could see that my conversation with Louise James was edgy, and he came up with a bottle of wine to restore her drink and give me a genial promise that he would soon attend to mine. She accepted a further measure of wine, told him what a wonderful party it was and how superb it was for her to see old faces again, to see faces which had meant so much to her late father. Then she went across the patio to reencounter them. Andrew called the housekeeper and whispered my drink order in her ear—the equivalent of, Make it a strong one!

He approached me. An impressive young woman, he remarked.

I said, I knew her at university. She offered me a job at some Texas college.

He looked at me dolefully.

We all get those offers.

Circus work, I said.

Well-intended gestures, he murmured. He shrugged. One day we might all go off together. But there's something to be said for staying here. In the end, you know what really happened. The expatriate merely thinks he does.

Our voices were descending further and further. We were becoming more and more discreet. Andrew whispered, I shouldn't even refer to what you said earlier. But, I thought you had a book as good as finished.

As good as, I said.

Then . . . ? he asked.

I wouldn't give it to Great Uncle.

Why not? It would get everyone out of trouble.

It doesn't belong to me. It certainly doesn't belong to him.

How so?

I put it in the grave with Sarah.

At this admission, alcoholic tears came unbidden and stung my eyes.

My God, he said. Don't you have a copy?

I buried the disks and printout with her. I deleted it from the hard disk. Then I took a walk over the Republic Bridge and gave my laptop to the river as a propitiation. These are excellent funerary rites.

Hell! said Andrew. Forgive me, but given this is such a desperate time . . . could you perhaps exhume the novel?

I treated the idea with silence and contempt.

Come on, said Andrew. Sarah wouldn't want to see you in this mess.

Sarah is entitled to the gifts I gave her, I told him. Sarah thought it wasn't bad.

Andrew murmured, You're destroying yourself.

I won't give that bastard Sarah's book.

That bastard? asked Andrew. McBrien?

No. I shook my head in irritation. *That* bastard! I won't give him Sarah's book. It would be . . . I gestured helplessly with a hand to indicate the enormity of such a choice.

Will you finish in time, though? asked Andrew.

I shrugged. I think the thing is finishing me, I admitted.

Andrew said, That's not good enough. Sarah would say that that's not good enough.

I shook my head.

He said, You don't make a habit of telling people this story you've told me, do you?

I only told you because you're my father figure.

You'd better give up the booze. Have another drink tonight. But I mean from now on. Next time you feel the appetite, think that the bastard has driven you to this. Then you'll stay dry out of pure bloody-mindedness.

A good suggestion, I drunkenly told him.

And be nice to Louise, he advised me. Nothing is her fault. Let me take you to breakfast tomorrow. I won't take up much of your time.

When I woke next morning, the first message from my stinging brain was that indeed I was not to drink again. I dressed hurriedly and went to meet Andrew at a café on the corner. He already had a half-empty cup of coffee before him, and gestured me crisply to the seat not opposite but beside him.

I can't stay long, he told me. How far are you along with your melodrama?

I told him thirty-seven thousand desperate words.

You see, you and McBrien have made a mistake. You think Great Uncle wants something like he would write. He wants something like you would write. Didn't he make that clear?

I shook my head.

He spoke in mysteries, I told Andrew. He spoke like an oracle. Maybe he made that clear. But he says the PR company in New York can make a success of anything.

By the light of the morning, is there any room for sentimentality, Alan? I can get an exhumation order, very easily.

I was appalled, but later I would remember that my first words were, On what grounds? That I might have poisoned her?

And then I thought further and asked, What would my Overguard companions think of that?

I know a pathologist who did a television series for us. Dr. Prentice. You probably remember him. He studies sudden death in healthy young people, and he could make some reason . . . he might mistrust the coroner's finding. We could have people in white coats there. They might just take a fragment of flesh, and then she could be put to rest again, forever.

Naturally enough, I began to shudder and weep. I could have tried to reproduce the material, perhaps, I pleaded, if I wanted to do what you say. But I don't want this story to end in the bastard's hands. It's too good for that.

Look, Alan, said Andrew. Great Uncle never makes an amendment to the clock. As his TV man I know that better than most. It's July twenty-seventh now. Less than two weeks left.

He paused. It's a horrifying period, Alan. But you'll have peace at the end of it.

The idea he had suggested terrified me, making me question my profoundly placed markers as to who I was in the first place. Yet, because Andrew had raised it and even given me a doctor's name, it seemed apparent, too, as the very best solution. If only it were not sacrilege.

I can't do it, Andrew. I can't give the tyrant anything so important. All I can do is hack out this soap opera. If it's not good enough, he and his PR people mightn't have the taste to know.

Think about it, though! urged Andrew. More than think about it! Get the damned thing back!

Like a sage uncle who had taught me the squalor of the earth, he walked me back to the apartment so that I could resume the dreary task.

And there, about noon, was McBrien calling. How's it going, comrade? he asked.

I had polished off fifteen hundred words, and—with Andrew's alternative in mind—had found it as close to painless as one possibly could. How is Sonia? I asked.

She's vomiting quite a bit, he declared proudly. This child is going to give us a lot of trouble! Now, Louise James has applied to the Ministry of Culture to interview you. They spoke to Chaddock. There's a consensus a refusal might create a level of suspicion, but you know how to answer most public questions. Do you think you could do it? I'll be present.

I was a rude bastard to her last night, I told him. I think I could manage it.

Without, of course, telling her your secrets? he asked.

I'd be too ashamed to tell her those, I said.

All right. Keep working, for God's sake. I'll bring her round about four o'clock.

I found the idea of visitors superficially attractive, and I resolved to be less aggressive this time. All her questions would be irrelevant to our situation, but I could answer them automatically, as if I were my own agent. I even ground out another thousand words of my soap opera before the hour arrived, and McBrien appeared at my door accompanied by an unexpectedly tentative Louise James.

Occasionally during that afternoon, I had, despite my anticipation, found myself rehearsing angry speeches I might make if she asked the wrong question. At Andrew and Grace Kennedy's party she had behaved, I thought, like Lady Bountiful, holding out the chimera of a scholarly or creative post. Yet something, some stimulus connected with Louise, caused me to take down McBrien's gift, the bottle of Great Uncle–approved Tommy Hilfiger cologne, off the shelf where I had put it. I comforted my face and throat and temples with it before I sensed the obscenity of my behavior. Instantly, impatient for the scent to die away, I poured the stuff down the bathroom sink and emphatically hurled the bottle and its spray apparatus into the garbage.

But when Louise arrived in McBrien's company, an impression of timidity was increased by the fact that since it was such a dusty day, with the wind flattening the river to a metallic sheen, and atoms of desert and the crumbling northeast suburbs filling the air, she was heavily shawled and thus, apart from a few telltale signs—a fine watch, a Dior scarf—might have been a woman visiting from the country.

I invited them in, and where yesterday I might have offered them a drink so that I could stupefy myself along with them, I asked a cheery McBrien to put the kettle on.

Thank you for seeing me, said Louise James as she unwound the shawl and then the scarf, and shook out her hair. There was something unwelcome in this, because it was a gesture not exactly like, but too close to, a remembered gesture of my wife. It seemed a usurpation. Fortunately, the mannerism was restrained and of a momentary nature. When it was over she stood still, definitely herself. I wondered why the blood ran so merrily and orderly in her head when it had been unable to achieve the same daily and ordinary marvel beneath Sarah's skull.

Please, I said. Take a seat. I gestured towards a chair near my desk. I moved to take a straight-backed one facing her.

Okay if I set up the mike just here on the corner of your desk?

Certainly, I said.

As she worked and muttered into the mike and replayed the mutter on the tape recorder to ensure that it was working, she seemed edgy still, remarking that she had no interest in creating trouble by anything she ultimately broadcast, and so she would stop the tape whenever I said to. She wanted to talk about cultural matters, matters to do with society. She wanted to make an interesting program. But not at anyone's cost. The restrictions people were under in speaking on matters of politics had been well canvassed amongst her audience, and she did not want to endanger any old friend just for the sake of creating what she called a *frisson* amongst the motorists who listened to PBS current affairs broadcasts as they drove to and from work.

Not that I don't believe in freedom of speech, she assured me with a frown, her huge dark eyes gleaming with conviction. But I know I'm treading a fine line here that I wouldn't have to tread anywhere else. If I were interviewing government ministers, of course, or Great Uncle, I wouldn't feel as constrained.

Okay, I said.

By now, McBrien, who knew my kitchen well, had emerged with a tray of pastries—he had brought it with him from a patisserie—and tea.

As he placed these nearby, Louise James lowered her voice as if she did not want him to hear the next few words. We got off to a bad start, I feel. Like all those years ago. My fault.

Rubbish, I told her. Mine. I'm guilty about Sarah, I'm guilty about you. It'd be pitiful if it weren't all so damned ridiculous.

The tea was poured and after one more inquiry, we began. She read an introduction about my somewhat sketchy but fortunate literary career, and spoke of the extraordinary impact my debut had had in my country. I had recently lost my wife, she said, who had been a famous, classically trained stage, film, and television actress.

We began talking about the tradition of the theater in the country, the fact that peasant theater had been common for fifteen hundred years or more amongst the Intercessionists, while a more stylized tradition was practiced in the old royal courts, just as in European countries. Only the most literally devout people had a bad opinion of it. Though Sarah had been trained as a small girl in ornate traditional costumes, there had been a flowering of cinema in our country from the 1920s onward, and we exported silent and then talking pictures throughout our region. Sarah had made her first film, *Amongst the Clouds,* about an orphaned city girl looking for her grandparents in the mountainous north, when she was thirteen.

I found it delightful to speak of Sarah. I was lost in her career for a time. I brought out albums full of her pictures in the parts she had played: orphans, maidens—the latter especially. Only once a lover. Pictures of the production of *The Women of Summer Island.* I explained that she had the seriousness that sometimes accompanied great beauty. Of all her gifts as a person, her renowned capacity to allure the camera was the one she considered her least. She would have continued in film ultimately, I said, for she wanted to be a director.

We can edit this question, said Louise James, but let's ask it first. Is it true that your wife refused to act in a soap opera devoted to propaganda?

Oh, I asked, is there no propaganda in American soap operas?

Well, yes, I admit, the soap opera can be a vehicle for prevailing attitudes and even for prevailing hysteria. But, if I dare say so, you didn't quite answer the question.

I thought this interview was to be sensitive?

Everything in it is up for revision at your wish, Alan, she reminded me. I said that and I meant it.

I think that I can put it like this, I told her. That my wife was not entirely happy with the direction some of the programming had taken. But then you have to realize that we have been subject to these terrible sanctions, which do not affect me directly because I'm one of the privileged. But they affect many ordinary people ruinously. The city is in ruins because of them, and the people live among the ruins, among the busted pipes, and the broken taps, the shattered curbs, the whole sad landscape. It's understandable enough that under those circumstances drama would be enlisted in an attempt, however naïve it might seem to the outsider, to help the people.

I can see that, conceded Louise quite graciously.

My wife suffered from acute migraines. If there had been replacements for the CT scan machine in city hospitals, her problem might have been picked up earlier. But of course, the policy of the West in taking hardly any of our oil means that even for the privileged, whom I've confessed to being—even for us, there is no adequate imaging service.

But isn't it also true that the government makes the most of the sanctions, using them as an excuse for corruption?

Corruption? I asked. She was turning into the woman of the cocktail party again. I wouldn't know about that, but surely you're not arguing that one evil justifies another? Indeed, if what you say were true, it would add to the reasons for ending sanctions.

She switched off briefly. Very good answer, Mr. Sheriff.

A very safe answer, I told her.

She smiled.

No one requires that someone of your talent should offer up his life for a radio station in Texas—mind you, syndicated through half the nation, including Washington.

Then she switched on and resumed. Let's talk now about your book of short stories, which the *New York Times* called "a huge event. The emergence of a new Salinger!"

In answer I found it easiest to talk about the famous production of *The Women of Summer Island.*

She asked, How did you feel as a private soldier in a war largely about stretches of river and sandbanks and little rocky outcrops and oil wells?

Do they fight about better things than that in the West? I inquired. Wasn't World War I about rivers and mud and outcrops?

Okay, taking all that as read, how did you feel about the war?

I explained that our soldiers were not as anxious to be killed as some of the other side seemed to be—it was a cultural difference. Because the other side had a very profound tradition of fundamentalism, they sent youths forward wearing purple bandannas to shatter themselves to meat on minefields. Again, the same thing happened in European wars, with the Russians. Hadn't these things happened, in effect, at the battle of the Somme?

What made you willing to fight for *that* particular country down there in the south, then?

I was conscripted. In any case, Louise, that area was part of our state from ancient times, and defined as such from the very first monarchy. Troops on the other side obviously believed the opposite.

Now she raised the issue that some of my compatriots, notably Peter Collins, had gone to other countries. Was I ever tempted? I raised my eyebrows at that, and she bowed her head and smiled in a way that said, Do your best with it.

Before my wife's death, I told her, I had felt bound to my community because they were, insofar as I have written anything, my brothers and sisters *and* my material. I'd had a curious vanity: to see how things turned out, and to be here when they turned out as they did. After my wife's death, I was bound here by the fact that it was *this* earth which accommodated her body.

At last she turned off her machine. Gosh, she said. She looked at me, full gaze. Everything you said about staying. You actually mean it. She seemed, in a peculiar way, moved.

I shrugged. Yes, I confirmed, checking what my real soul would have been had I not been under Great Uncle's edict. Yes.

I went so far as to grin at her. I think I mean it. Especially about Sarah's burial place. I definitely mean that.

She said, You'd lose that, that clarity, in the States. That would be the price.

Perhaps, I told her. By the way, I hope I've made up for my gaucheries, both those long past and those committed at Andrew's.

There were no gaucheries, she insisted.

No, I said. I've been one of those mourners who think their grief exempts them from normal courtesy. I've been a pain in the arse, haven't I, McBrien?

You've been a monumental pain in the exact center of the cosmic anus, affirmed McBrien.

We smiled at each other.

When I say I enjoyed her company, I mean just that. For an hour or so I had been lifted back into larger questions, into my life before Sarah died and before the task descended upon me. Everyone knows that the hunger for contact sometimes becomes greater than the hunger for love itself, and I had fraternally enjoyed the discussion I had had with this woman arisen both from our ancient river—as dark-eyed women of mythology did—and from Houston, Texas.

I would love to know why you are so protected, she murmured, as she packed up her gear.

Protected?

Well, you have Mr. McBrien, my classmate from the university, to make your tea. And the Overguard. And then, the older woman who sits on the bench along the river looking at the apartment door while pretending to read a novel—I bet she's part of the setup too.

Louise James raised both her hands. Fear not, I don't want to be told now. But perhaps, one day, one day . . .

McBrien frowned. Older woman?

Yes, said Louise James. But it doesn't matter, please!

My apartment was at the back of the building, and lacked a view of the riverside park. Mrs. Douglas's flat faced the river, however.

I suggested, Perhaps you could point her out, if we can find the right window.

McBrien and I led Louise downstairs, and I knocked on Mrs. Douglas's door.

Opening it, she blinked, of course, seeing the strangers, and having grown in mistrust of me since I began to receive special care from the Overguard.

Mr. Sheriff, she said.

I'm sorry to intrude on you, Mrs. Douglas. I wondered if I could make use of your living room window, just to look at something?

She uttered a cold "Certainly!" as she admitted the three of us grudgingly. We stood like uncertain guests by a table on which there was a great deal of cut glass—it always seemed to me that china and cut glass were a comfort to women, stable elements in a world of flux, of limbs exposed on ramparts. I felt an impulse to tell Mrs. Douglas that I too felt as if my tyrannized limbs had been hung on ramparts, but that was somewhat excessive, and she would not have understood.

I won't be a moment, I assured her, and I walked across the floor and looked out through the curtains of the front window. It was Mrs. Carter, seated on a bench along the riverbank, watching the entrance of my building.

Who is it? asked McBrien.

The mother of an army friend of mine. I turned back from the pane and looked meaningfully at McBrien. Mrs. Carter. Remember her?

McBrien said, We'll tell the boys to get rid of her.

No, I insisted. Look, she's harmless.

He frowned and shook his head, casting his eyes ceilingward. Louise James, of course, was mystified but too discreet to inquire.

I told McBrien, Tell them to tolerate her, but keep an eye out.

A day later, as I came back from breakfast, I saw Mrs. Carter by the white Toyota, offering coffee from a thermos to the Overguard. It was so strange to see her in that mode, cozying up to my guards. I knew then that she would be troublesome. But, one hoped, as a mere nuisance rather than a cataclysm.

From SOME USEFUL PLOT POINTS FROM THE LIFE
OF HIS EXCELLENCY THE PRESIDENT-FOR-LIFE,
NATIONAL CHIEFTAIN, COMMANDER-IN-CHIEF,
AND GREAT UNCLE OF THE PEOPLE.

*3. As he reached adolescence, the future
President-for-Life developed an innocent
affection for his cousin Susan, but he also
began to participate with his male cousin
Adrian in street marches protesting against
the slavish regimes of the day, which were
nothing more than clients of London and
Washington. Because of his involvement in*

*these national activities, when he applied for
military college at the age of sixteen, he was
refused admission....*

This two-dimensional tale wearied and distressed me, and I felt
bound to put it aside and take tea. Irony is the lifeblood of good
writing, and there was a melancholy lack of irony in this document.
How I wanted to be back with the comfort of subtitling American
and British films. It was then, in sudden insight, for the first time I
imagined Sarah's survival—*really* imagined it, that is, like a scene
from a film, from *On the Waterfront*, except more really. No Eva
Marie Saint. Sarah. I could see her, by my desk, with her steadfast
frown, her positive presence going along with the negative presence
of my trashy novel. It was as if, for a moment, I had created a pat-
tern in all the chaotic iron filings of this miserable existence. I
imagined her repeating her slogan: You must not serve.

And I said, But I have to.

Death is better.

But the McBriens, I replied. And the McBriens' baby.

Death is preferable. You must not serve.

I tried to get out, I told the vacant air. I tried that.

An entire dialogue was in progress. I uttered the last sentence
aloud. The adored wraith was gone.

Was it true that in Great Uncle's prison, politically sensitive as-
sassinations were achieved by injecting a bubble of air into a vein,
or else an overdose of insulin, which is said not to be traceable
even by a pathologist? I wondered how I could research this question. And then I despised the thought. Research. As Sarah would
have said, Determined people find a way.

I had tried my little stunt, I had tried to find my way out, but a
comfortable one and one which allowed even in the act the chance
of stepping back from the brink.

I can't imagine what my death will be like after it's happened,
I said to an empty room. It was the abiding problem of my life.

I returned to USEFUL PLOT POINTS.

When the monarchy fell in 1958, the future President was amongst those who led heroic Nationals into the Sunrise Palace.

Translation: He ran a gang of thugs who hacked the twenty-three-year-old king to death, dismembered the king's uncle, McCloud, and hanged his remains in front of the Ministry for War as McCloud had done with the senior rebels of Uncle Richard Stark's adventure in 1941. The prime minister got away and headed for Scarpdale dressed as a woman, but Great Uncle's gang of boys had been amongst those who tracked him down in the outer suburbs, killed him, drove vehicles across his body, buried him, and, not satisfied, disinterred him, applied their *chardris*, and ran through the streets displaying fingers, toes, fragments of scalp.

After the first President, Robert Dunstan, despite earlier promises to the people, made a further secret deal with the British, the future President-for-Life again led a band of patriots whose job was to oppose the new and treacherous president's Minutemen. The future President-for-Life and his uncle Stark tracked a Scarpdale presidential informer to the outer suburbs of the capital and had no compunction in shooting him dead. They were detained in the Palace of Disappearance, Wolfmount Prison, but let go for lack of proof. In prison the future President acquired a sense of the hardihood needed by ordinary citizens in their struggle for a genuine nation, in their losses from the war, in their want and neediness. Released, the future President-for-Life was involved with other young men in an attack on the motorcade of the treacherous President Dunstan. A number of the young conspirators were on the pavement along the route of the

presidential procession, armed with weapons provided by
people of similar mind in the officer corps. The future
President-for-Life took up a position in a nearby building to
provide covering fire for his operatives on the ground.

Translation: Even the Fusion Party and the officer corps didn't think he was up to the primary job of performing the assassination, and gave him the number-two job of creating confusion in the wake of the shooting.

When the presidential motorcade came along, some of the
younger members of the assassination group panicked and
fired prematurely.

Translation: And the future President joined in the general panic.

A number of officials fell, but the false President was merely
wounded. In covering the withdrawal of the assassination
party, the future President-for-Life was injured, but skillfully
evaded capture.

All that was true, though what it had to do with my (his) proposed book, I could not guess.

So the "plot points" continued, following Great Uncle into exile, where he was separated from Susan Stark, his cousin, to whom he became betrothed in absentia. Loneliness, deprivation of love, plotting—even talking to the CIA—all in exile, in Egypt.

The return occurred only when Uncle Stark and his old friend, one General Ian Baker, helped in those days by the CIA, brought a crucial number of tanks and an essential wing of Hawker Hunter aircraft to bear on the presidential palace. The treacherous president was shot against the wall of the Palace of Government. So the future President-for-Life came home and married, and Uncle Stark's influence got him a post on the bureau of the new President, Ian Baker, in which (according to popular rumor) he imitated his idol, Stalin—a rough and only partially educated boy from the country, despised by the intelligentsia of the Fusion Party, and given a special portfolio in relation to farmers' affairs. He also molded the gangs he had led as a youth into the Office of Reconciliation, whose military wing would become, after Ian Baker died, the potent Overguard.

In all this there was a passage which meant something to me:

In the Palace of Disappearance, a prisoner must distance himself from the clammy walls, the cockroaches, the lice in the bedding pallet, and the stench of one's own waste from the bucket. Here there is no light but the light a man creates for himself. To discuss anything with common criminals, amongst whom politicals are often placed, is an indignity, weakens the soul, and reduces its status. The Great Uncle of the Nation, being so profoundly influenced by the experience of imprisonment on two occasions, one short, one much longer, appreciates the horror of the Palace of Disappearance and thus, when he came to his present eminence, decided that this sanction should be used only sparingly, and solely against those individuals who had seriously violated the trust of the people.

I wondered did he thus sometimes undertake summary justice, as it happened with Mrs. Douglas's nephew, to save the prisoner from the memory of seepage, stench, and itch.

———————

Reading those notes, for reasons I cannot gauge, finished me. Maybe it was that their spirit approximated to the spirit of my awful melodrama. I surrendered. I could not go further. I had come to an end. Trembling, I called Andrew and asked him could he enlist Dr. Prentice.

I'll speak to him, said Andrew, and later rang me back.

Okay, the situation is that he's researching the DNA of sudden adult death syndrome sufferers. The deaths, as I told you, of apparently fit young people. Two days' time, Alan. I'll take you to the cemetery nine o'clock Thursday.

The flow of the melodrama immediately shut off. I resorted again to McBrien's liquor.

The day it was done, there was an evil wind out of the desert and the light turned the river the color of ink. Andrew remarked that he had never known an early August day to be as bad as this; the cold was of a clammy febrile quality, and smears of black grit blew across the face of a dim sun. We parked, as is the national custom, and as we had done at the burial, outside the cemetery gates—the pathologist must have taken a truck in, but it was so normal for the living to approach the dead on foot that we could not break the tradition, especially since we were both, to varying degrees, consumed by guilt.

I did not let myself think at all. I was numb as we found our way amongst the monuments towards a small marquee where men in white coats waited, their gloved hands folded in front of them. In contrast to their professionally hygienic demeanor, I noticed the rough clothing and lustily unsterile air of the two grave diggers who had prised the marble slabs aside and already dug out the grave. They had erected a creaky-looking windlass of thin iron uprights near the head of the grave. I was in near and indefinable panic as Andrew nudged me forward.

There's Dr. Prentice, said Andrew, almost cheerily, as he edged me on amongst the monumental columns of mourning and across the arid gravel between graves.

I stood at the graveside, and like a man with vertigo risking a cliff edge, forced my eyes down. There was the sullied, earth-stained white coffin, immaculate on the day of burial, as sturdy still as a reproach in the disturbed earth.

One of the grave diggers gave a dry cough to advise me not to fall in. I staggered and Andrew caught me.

How will they get it out? I asked.

With ropes, he said, nodding to the dusty grave attendants. They're used to it.

I saw a tall, soapy-featured man in a white coat approach me. His eyes were full of a doglike melancholy. Come with me aside for a moment, Mr. Sheriff, he said.

He took me away towards a bare patch amidst the graves. He asked for permission to smoke and took off one glove and hitched up his white coat and extracted cigarettes from a crushed pack taken from his pants pocket. Lighting one, he pushed the pack back again.

I see you're distressed, he asserted. It is, of course, natural enough. But I believe you need something extracted from your wife's grave.

A manuscript and some disks, I told him and began sobbing.

I'll sterilize the pages for you. We have an autoclave for that purpose still working at the lab. The disks I'll need to disinfect by hand. I'll have all of it delivered to you later today.

Let me see her, though, I demanded.

He clamped his cigarette in his lips and held up a hand, counseling me against that. He said, It seems from her certificate the cause of her death was a cerebral aneurysm. But maybe that sub-arachnoid hemorrhage wasn't severe enough on its own. Maybe she was susceptible to this sudden adult death syndrome in which apparently healthy young people drop dead leaving very little trace of the cause—their hearts look perfectly healthy to a medical examiner, but even so their hearts, not their brains, are the cause.

I felt very much at sea to hear him ring the changes on causes of death, and he could perceive that.

Look, he said, it probably was the severe aneurysm, but SADS, the syndrome I'm working on, is also marked by occasional predeath migraine episodes or dizziness. Do you understand? That's why I'm doing this.

Of course, I said.

Nothing gross will occur, he assured me. We will open the coffin, unwrap the funeral bindings. And I must take a scrape of flesh from the arm or thigh to justify the exhumation. We have no sophisticated testing here. I have to send my samples to England for testing in a lab in Exeter already dedicated to researching the syndrome. We'll have the results in about six weeks.

I must see her, I persisted.

You can't be dissuaded. He sighed. It isn't her.

I owe it.

But it really isn't her. The cells that were her have ruptured. Autolysis has taken place. Self-digestion of the body. It is now a matter of bacteria and fungi and protozoa. It's hydrogen sulphide, carbon dioxide, methane, ammonia, sulphur dioxide. It is fatty acids. It is nothing to do with you or any humane obligations.

I grabbed his free, gloved hand like a pleading infant.

He said, You're very affected, young man. Then if you must. But briefly, I counsel.

He finished his cigarette. He nodded towards the grave, into which one of the workers had descended carrying a rope.

What's he doing? I asked like a panicked child.

He's putting a rope around one end of the coffin, then he'll do the other end and . . . I'll go back to the tent, if you'll excuse me.

I walked back to the grave and stood beside Andrew. The busy grave diggers connected all the ropes they had placed beneath

Sarah's coffin to a single cable attached to their rickety windlass, itself powered by a small petrol motor. One of them, tugging at a lever, started it into chugging life, and they both steadied the coffin as it rose, jettisoning clods of earth. When it was clear, one of them altered a primitive gear on the machine, and swung the windlass on its base and delicately lowered the coffin to solid ground. The engine was cut, and in the silence, somewhere over the river, beyond neem trees, a lonely bird called some loveless *too-wheet* to the vacant day. The men functionally detached the rope and carried the coffin to the tent, where Dr. Prentice held the flap open for them. The weight of the coffin and Sarah did not seem to strain them.

Andrew saw my tear-smudged face.

Don't say anything, I ordered him.

But all at once his shoulders were shuddering. He, Andrew, the steady man, raised a tear-drenched face to me. I loved her, he said. I don't know how. As a father, an uncle. Maybe in my mind as a lover, but I was always confused about that. You behave like you have a monopoly, Alan. But *I* loved her.

I was appalled by this display. It was like watching a father confess his sins and his hopelessness. But then I embraced him and felt his body quaking within my arms.

We waited together ten minutes, through unutterable phases of tears, numbness, and panic. But Andrew's collapse had tipped some courage my way—the sense that I was not isolated in my bell jar of torment. I bravely made conversation. I talked to him about this sudden adult death syndrome theory of Dr. Prentice. Andrew could sense it was something I found hard to adapt to. The tragedy which had had only one awful name now potentially had two. Uncertainty had entered.

Don't worry, whispered Andrew, cleaning up his face with a handkerchief. Prentice's critics say he thinks anyone under forty who drops dead has died of that syndrome. In fact, some doctors doubt whether it can properly be called a syndrome.

The grave diggers came out of the marquee early, nodded, and went off to smoke by their windlass. Andrew put his arm around me.

Dr. Prentice emerged from the tent, gloveless now. He whacked his pants pockets again, yearning for a smoke, but thinking better.

Do you want to come now, Mr. Sheriff?

I'll come too, said Andrew.

The doctor held back the marquee flap and we entered the enclosed air. I was well used to the smell of death from all those zealots who trod on mines on Summer Island, and something in my brain had already prepared me to accept that, though the smell of corruption seemed discreet, focused, almost delicate in here, sharing little with the vaster, generic stench of the battlefield. I saw my manuscript and disks, wrapped in plastic, on a side table. The portable steel table on which she had lain for Prentice's test was being sprayed and swabbed by a lab assistant. And so I gathered myself, my nostrils pinched, and regarded the open coffin.

There are no words for what one sees of the beloved months after death. She was tucked back into her winding sheet, so that we could see only the face, the temples, the ruin of her hair. I looked of course on the putrefaction of all love. It was not her, as Dr. Prentice had said, and yet it was. It was on one hand the parody of a bride. The features were sunken and patchily protected by areas of leather or parchment. The veins at the temples and forehead were a black tracery, as if a malign, skeletal plant had overgrown her brow. But she was above all something pitiful and violated, which should never have been exposed again to air for the convenience of the living.

I heard Dr. Prentice muttering to Andrew Kennedy, These high-priced coffins! Don't do as much for the corpse as the undertakers say.

What was worse was that having seen this beloved victim, I did not want to join her yet in this state, in the journey her flesh was making. I had had that option once, but now not only had it somehow been taken from me, but I would not have chosen it. I had become a normal coward again. I stood there in such a quandary and state of shame that my legs gave way, and Andrew and the doctor helped me out into the air.

You'll get the items this afternoon, Dr. Prentice whispered to me.

Andrew took me to a café where he was known, for he wanted them to put cognac in my coffee.

I never said an improper word to her, he told me, staring into his own coffee.

I know, I said. I knew the nation loved her.

Even Great Uncle, said Andrew with stricken eyes. He knew the score. But he wouldn't punish her.

Soon McBrien turned up, father-to-be, splendid looking in his suit. Andrew and I gathered ourselves together to face him. It occurred to me he had often been edgy when a writer, but he was smooth now. In my shock, he looked to me like a visitor from a remote place—the morning's experiences had driven him out of mind. Not even when grave robbing had I remembered his unborn child. Now he would need to be informed about the morning's dark work.

To my vast relief, Andrew said, I've filled Matt in. On this morning. You don't have to explain anything to him.

McBrien touched my arm. A good idea, he said, nodding a lot. Now you have a choice of texts, don't you?

Yes.

Steinbeck or Achebe. Hemingway or Ben Okri.

I believe that at Kennedy's instructions the waiter was being more generous with me in pouring our laced coffee than he was with the others. I receded from my friends, swept away from them, a little bit like a passenger on a train, listening to the diminishing and less and less comprehensible best wishes of those on the platform. I was already dense-headed and neutralized by liquor when Louise James entered in her good American weeds. Some of the older men in the place, I could tell even tipsy, disapproved of her on principle, but their disapproval had an erotic edge to it as well. It was the willingness of women of her class to drink coffee on equal terms with men in such places as this which gave coffeehouses a bad name with plain folk and rural Intercessionists.

Alan, she said. I hope you're feeling well.

Kennedy's got me half drunk, I said, but with a smile.

Why not? asked Andrew. The boy has had an awful morning. Let's get something to eat. Some kabobs or something.

I barely participated in the conversation after Louise James sat down. It was a little like listening to clever people on the far side of a wall. Sometimes, out of reflex comradeship, I smiled when they laughed.

The food came, and tea. At some stage Andrew Kennedy asked us to excuse him—he obviously intended to visit the lavatory.

I'll join you, said McBrien, his tie undone.

Suddenly Louise James's large eyes were upon me and she

spoke like a doctor diagnosing a case. I have the cure, she promised. I've thought about it at some length. For years in fact. Why don't we go ahead with marriage, Alan?

Why would you want to? I asked, frowning in distaste.

We would be a good alliance. I am now a New World woman. I am permitted to make the first move.

She beamed at that idea. We choose our husbands, and I have chosen you. I will save you from grief.

Grief? I asked, uncomprehending.

Yes. Of course, only in so far as I can. But I'll make you a happy home. Did you think you were never going to marry again?

Yes.

Well, she said. Perhaps you could expand your thoughts.

Do you know what happened this morning?

She frowned now. No.

I've just robbed my wife's grave.

Robbed?

I shook my head, knowing that of course I could not tell more. Let it go, I urged her. The thing is, you don't know anything about me.

I read your stories. They are classics. De Maupassant, Katherine Mansfield, Alice Munro, Grace Paley. You're everything they are.

You can't tell a man by his short stories, I warned her. That's a stupid mistake. That's the sort of mistake undergraduates make.

But then, what other criteria should I apply? Are you attracted to me at all? You seemed to be when we were younger.

No. I'm sorry, but I'm not attracted to anyone.

But you could be. It's only natural. I will take you out to America in the end. Because this is barren.

You won't take me to America. I don't want you to say anything else.

I love you, she assured me. I know you from your noble stories,

I saw the way you operate. You saved me a lot of embarrassment by being brave enough to confront me back then.

Brave. I spoke the word only to mock it. You're interested in me because I'm a hapless figure. You think I can be made less sullen, that I'll be improved in your golden aura.

Ah, she said. I have an aura, do I? That's something.

She considered this issue for a while. I'm certainly impressed by the depth of your mourning. That's characteristic of you. But it's a price Sarah wouldn't want you to pay.

My mourning had now become so complicated by the day's treachery that I couldn't contest or debate that.

I said, I won't be marrying again soon, if ever. And I won't be leaving here.

Your grief is really like a pure flame, she told me.

Don't say that, I warned her. It isn't true. Besides, it sounds so American.

Oh no, she said. It is precisely from here, from the fourteenth-century love poets. You're mourning in the national spirit.

She thought about this, and added, I doubt I could ever marry an American. She shrugged. I tried. I was once engaged to one.

You should have pressed on with it, I told her.

No, no. It was silliness on both our parts.

I had a chance to laugh. And this isn't, I suppose?

I'll stay here if you insist on it. In this country. By your side. I'm just warning you of genuine intentions. I just want you to know that there's a life ahead of you.

By now, I was in closer touch to what I thought of as the real world—it was at least twenty minutes since my last cognac. Three or four meetings when I was young, I commented. And three meetings this time. That's all we've had. Fast work even for a New World woman, Ms. James.

She smiled, full-lipped, and I could see in an abstract way that the smile had all the right ingredients for wifedom.

Kennedy and McBrien came back full of joviality from the men's lavatory.

We'll get you home, Alan, said Andrew. A last order?

I demanded one more coffee, and McBrien joined me in it, as Andrew and Louise James discussed John Updike's *Rabbit* trilogy. Andrew argued it was overrated by the standards of world literature—couldn't, for example, hold a candle to Márquez.

That's comparing apples with pears, Louise James argued. I don't want to pull the *I've-been-there* trick, but if you live in the United States, it's astonishing how those books of Updike's get the essence of the experience, all the desperation beneath the gestures of affluence. And all the sexual despair. I don't think your average Mediationist farmer or Intercessionist peasant feels any such thing. Yet all of America seems to. It's as if they believe what is normal and human are all some unachievable magic.

Intercessionist peasants prey on their own nieces, said Andrew with a smile. And then, with an onset of gentlemanly coyness, revised what he had said. No, I know that's our stereotype of them. I get your point. If you don't have to despair about your life, if the refrigerator's full of food and you're going to live to seventy or more, I suppose there's leisure to think about these things. Would you say, he pursued, that in our world survival is the difficult achievement, and in America human intimacy is?

That's exactly what I'd say.

McBrien and Andrew, progressives though they might be, were slightly shocked by her explicitness about what was eating America. For me, of course, the main issue remained the parched and hollowed visage of my dead wife, whose muteness said, What you give, you take back. She had gone back into the earth, I imagined, as the thwarted bride who merely wants to turn her face to nothingness. That could never be forgotten by me. To hell with whether Updike was up to strength with Márquez! To hell with whether Americans had leisure to spend their conscious

hours on their own loneliness! To hell with Louise James's senti-
mental intentions! McBrien and I said good-bye to her, and to
Andrew. Andrew told me to call him at any hour if I wanted anything.

When I was driven home, I saw the familiar Toyota. So habituated had I become to the Overguard, and they to me, that they
waved as I went inside, helped by McBrien.

On the stairs McBrien murmured, I'll stay with you till Prentice sends the manuscript. Let me make you tea.

Yes, but I'll need someone to come in and download the disk on
my hard drive. They'll have to unglue the A-drive for once.

Sure, he said.

Once it's been done, they can glue it up again.

Sure, he said appeasingly. We're going to make it, aren't we?

Yes, I said. Three or four days' revision.

You need vodka?

No.

We reached the door, and he helped me with the key. He said,
It mightn't be the right thing to say, given the day it is. But Louise
James adores you. When this is over, we wouldn't feel badly if . . .

If what?

Well, he said. As they say in American novels—*consenting
adults*.

I said, It isn't the day to say so, Matt. I've just robbed my wife's
grave.

Nonsense, said McBrien. Sarah would have been happy.

Oh yes? She was an honorable woman in a way you wouldn't
begin to guess, Matt. And the dead are stricter than the living.

At three o'clock, while both of us were dozing, an Overguard
technician arrived. McBrien explained to him as I roused myself,
Mr. Sheriff needs to use the A-drive for a second or two to transfer
material.

That was all right, the technician answered, but he would have to stay here and take away with him any disks I used in the process.

Have some tea, McBrien told him and settled him in a seat by my desk.

The package was delivered late in the afternoon. McBrien took delivery of it at the door and brought it to me at my desk. Wait, he told the messenger. We've got to make sure it's all here.

I opened the envelope and there, wrapped in plastic stamped with the word AUTOCLAVED, were the pages and the disks.

I opened them in turn with a deliberate briskness and callowness. They felt drier than the leaves of a dead tree. The business had been done, title to the work had been exchanged if not stolen. I owed it to her to be functional now. I had seen her mute and decayed reproach, but having done my worst, I pressed on matter-of-factly with the minor features of the crime.

Will you go into another room, please? the technician asked. Clearly there must have been some program hidden deep in the computer with a code which he must now use. When he called us back, he had removed the metallic gag from the mouth of the A-drive. A metal tongue the same size as a disk was also extracted.

Do your download, he told me.

I transferred the files of my novel, which had survived all that they had been subjected to, onto the hard drive. As each one came up I got the crazed idea I should write to the disk manufacturer. Their product had endured a lonely and buried test.

Finished doing it and checking the results, I thanked the technician, and McBrien and I returned to the kitchen while he reapplied the gag.

Then he said good-bye and was gone.

I opened up the pages, to compare with the computer text.

You can go now, Matt, I told him. After a small and somehow mutually reassuring argument, he did.

I rose, drank tea, then returned to the screen and brought up the first twenty-page file. Then I took up the manuscript, from which I would work, entering changes onto the laptop. So I re-asserted myself, with a strange ease and lack of nostalgia, into the pages written in a golden time. I barely adjusted the more notable attacks the book made on the regime, so taken with the sanctions was this material. Suffering, in the eyes of those who go through it, is often an apolitical experience. It debases subtlety of thought, and I talked at least in part about the sort of people to whom suffering came not so much as a result of policy but from the hand of God, as something to be accepted. My central characters, the Clancys, however, understood the politics thoroughly, and that made their survival, at least through most of the book's pages, more admirable.

There was enough of my old self left to enjoy the final gloss of my lost book, to make my work quick, and to cause me to re-nounce drunkenness. With my dear book back, grief was forgotten for at least ninety seconds at a time. In a curious way I felt a species of relief at having decided the issue. I was done in five days.

The last paragraphs read:

Having said good-bye to the last funeral guest, old Mr. Sayers, who still hankered for the monarchy but loved Clancy, Rose Clancy walked back into the room empty except for the presence of her husband, the being designated to occupy this day in this century with a death more inflicted than natural. She reentered like a visitor the room where he lay and took a seat in a corner chair, not in any of the chairs of honor overlooking the head of his ceremonial bier, the white satin with which his past life was honored. I'll have to get all these borrowed-in chairs returned to the neighbors tomorrow, she reminded herself, and wondered how she could manage it.

He'd have it done in half an hour, of course. He'd organize the street kids. Such energy, she said aloud. Such energy!

All expended too. He had been one of the officers brave

enough to demonstrate against the king and his ignorant and sybaritic son. He had door-knocked to motivate people to be on the streets in protest against the unexpected cowardice of presidents tamed by the CIA and the British Foreign Office. Then war and imprisonment, and more door knocking. At a humble level, on a level so low that politicians might need a microscope to see him, Clancy had summoned up the people's unease, leaving her side after the evening meal, leaving his children with stories unread and untold. Knocking on the wooden doors of poor adobe houses whose wiring was risky and whose walls eroded, saying, Come! Speak! Be heard!

But those forty years of urgings had swallowed him. The West had decreed that for his cough he should not have antibiotics; for the pounding of his aged blood, he could not have beta blockers; the world had punished him for every rat-tat-tat. His arteries contracted, the wheeze deepened and became systemic, the blood grew too weighty for his veins. Hardening to a pebble, it blocked the traffic between heart and brain.

She stood up. He who had been so particular and natty in youth had become a stubbly corpse. In the week before his death, he had not been able to acquire a razor blade or afford a barber. Not only had the world cut off from Clancy his panaceas, but the means to make himself an acceptable corpse as well. So Mrs. Clancy sat like a late caller by her husband's corpse, weighed by the mystery of why the world had punished her honest, earnest husband.

I called in McBrien, and he turned up with a printer and read the material as the pages came off it. Oh Alan! he'd say occasionally. And sometimes he'd say, Implied criticism of government here. He'll just have to live with that, I would reply airily.

McBrien had tears in his eyes when he finished. This is good, he said. This is the book we wanted.

You mean it gets us out of the crisis.

He laughed. That's exactly what I mean. But this is a really good book.

By the standards of Márquez?

Fuck Márquez! said McBrien. He never got me out of hot water. There are a few literals.

I told him to mark them up and I'd fix them. I spent the afternoon and evening doing that, while he took the printer away. I felt no acute discomfort anymore. I watched television. I hoped they would let me go back to subtitling now.

I slept like a child, but not an innocent one.

In the morning I heard McBrien and Captain Chaddock ascending the stairs, chatting like normal citizens. The tension had eased. You could tell from their voices. They were near a fair end to an assignment. Chaddock followed McBrien into the apartment. He carried a steel box. Won't keep you, he said. A pickup. How are you, sir?

One day, it was rumored, the Overguard would rise and slaughter Great Uncle in the manner in which Praetorians had slaughtered Roman emperors. Once more, it was hard to imagine Chaddock in such a role. He packed the manuscript into the steel box and made me sign a receipt.

McBrien also had something for me to sign.

I've been in contact with Great Uncle's office, he told me quietly. They're delighted, particularly since you're two days early. I'm told Great Uncle himself has set aside a day to read it and have it read to him by relays of men, and read by Pearson Dysart. I wonder would you mind signing this, all three copies?

He had taken from an envelope three typed pages.

He told me, They're all the same.

Each of them had at the top of the page the word DISAVOWAL. The text read:

I have heard with some shock the rumor that the book published in the United States as_____has been attributed to myself instead of its true author, President Stark. I seek in the most emphatic terms to disavow any association with this well-known book. As happy as I would be to claim any part of its authorship, I find the denial of credit to President Stark to be malicious, and obviously politically motivated.

In case of any future controversy, McBrien told me.

I signed all three. And why not? The exhumation of Sarah had rendered me amoral. An Overguard came in and took away my computer. Then Chaddock chatted to me as his men gently searched my apartment for any form of facsimile. When I say *gently,* I mean that they opened drawers soundlessly, they sifted through them with their fingers, they flung nothing upon the floor. Chaddock told me, Something we've got to do. Won't be a moment. We'll be round for the next few days but be off your back soon!

For the next day and a half, apart of course from sleeping hours, I sat in a café overdosing on foreign newspapers. On the second evening, looking out across the river, I was working my way through an amusingly Tory article in the *Spectator.* It was one of those British magazines which makes a reader forget where they are, and positions them very solidly in a certain procrustean version of London. When I was finished, I put the magazine back in its rack for the next coffee-drinker-cum-reader and went out into the night. I have to confess that, in a reduced way, I felt very much alive. A cleansing wind from the east had taken the dust and pollution back towards the desert, and the stars which had always shone over our ancient river, over emperors and kings and presidents with roughly the same result, were sharply delineated. They seemed to reassure me in the idea that I'd got the worst out of the way, as had they. The big bang was over for both of us. We knew all about the violent universe. Now we glimmered in our cold isolation.

As I neared my door, I saw Captain Chaddock standing by his men's white Toyota. He crossed the road and met me near the door of the apartments, where he saluted and said to me, That woman. With the eyes. Waiting in the lobby for you. Curfew's two hours off.

The old woman? I asked.

Young one, he insisted. With the eyes. And he joined his hands, fingers splayed across his forehead and nose to indicate something more striking than Mrs. Carter. He must mean Louise James. The eyes.

Not my business, said Chaddock. Maybe she needn't leave at curfew.

I stared at him. He seemed embarrassed, and cast his eyes about. Been a hard time for you, Mr. Sheriff.

Yes. Particularly with you fellows all over the street.

He grinned and wagged his head about, to show he could take a joke.

She's from America, I said.

She's been checked out. Relatives here. He shrugged. None of my business, but . . .

The lady will be gone before curfew, I told him.

Your choice.

Yet again, was it possible to believe that in the right circumstances he would put a bullet in a head while a family watched, howling? Or was he used only to softer jobs? Was I a soft job? I said good night and went in the door.

Louise James was sitting on the old settee at the bottom of the steps. I hadn't seen anyone sitting there in my entire residency. She stood up, the dim lobby light on her. Yes, *the eyes*, as Chaddock had remarked. Interestingly, I found I was pleased for her company.

Good evening, Alan, she said. Pardon the intrusion. But I'm flying home—I mean, *back*—tomorrow.

I said that I hoped the journey was a happy one.

I made a bit of a fool of myself, didn't I, the other day? I'd say it was the sip or two of brandy that did it.

I raised my hands to appease and reassure her.

But I meant it. Let me be your wife and look after you.

I smiled. I'd been humanized a little by finishing my task. I asked gently, In Texas?

Or here, she said. I don't care.

No, I'm sorry, I told her. This gets more and more ridiculous.

No, it's less and less so.

I pleaded, There are other matters . . .

She sat on the settee again.

For God's sake, I told her, Come upstairs and have a drink.

I wondered if anyone saw us rising up the stairs, and reached the same facile conclusions as Captain Chaddock. With the furtiveness of a student, I let her into the flat. I took her light jacket, went to fold it on a lounge chair, then took it to the bedroom where lay the spectral residue of both the Sarahs, the living and dead. I did not put her jacket on the bed. I hung it on a hook behind the door.

Outside again, I offered Louise James a drink, but she said she would just like tea. It was a long flight back to the United States, she explained, virtually twenty hours, since she had to change planes in Paris.

This university post for you, she said. It's got nothing to do with my other . . . my other proposal. Do you want me to initiate it?

Thank you, I said with my newfound manners. But no.

I could not really imagine any future at all. Perhaps Great Uncle would imagine one for me, by being discontented with my prose. Perhaps he would send Sonny to chastise me.

Then I will have to come back here, she said. I'm sorry to be importunate. But I see it as a matter of destiny, my coming back.

How would you make a living here?

Well, I'll make a living being a stringer to, say, the *Washington Post* or the *Atlanta Constitution*.

That's a perfectly good way of getting into prison, I told her.

I could also be the servant of your international voice. She said this without irony, with her huge dark eyes upon me.

I laughed. That should take at least two hours every week, I said. I have no international voice. I intend to be a film subtitler, if anything.

She leaned forward and touched my wrist. Her hands were not thin—they were more sumptuous, a substance to them. My observation in this matter had more to do with comparative anatomy rather than any rediscovery of desire.

Why don't I make us both tea? asked Louise James.

No, I said, in a sudden panic. I was suddenly willing to block her access to the kitchen by force.

She stood. Come on, she said, I know poor Sarah died making tea. But that doesn't put the kitchen out of bounds forever, does it?

The question, asked at any other time of the lunatic that I'd become, might have caused fury and blows. Asked tonight, it had a curious effect. The skin on my arms felt astringent—a particular kind of grief was exiting by my pores. It was like the casting out of a spirit of sorrow. My neck crept, and I was taken from below by the idea that it was all right to have tea made in the kitchen by someone other than myself, McBrien, and Sarah. More than that, I half liked the idea of a woman making tea for me.

All right then, I told her. You'll find the tea on the shelf beside the refrigerator.

I'll attend to it, she said.

Yes, I told her. You can go to make tea. But I still don't intend to marry you.

I sat drowsing, and after about five minutes was awoken by the caterwaul of the kettle. She emerged with the teapot on a tray, and two cups and saucers. I had got out of the way of trays and saucers, and found them strangely touching, the way a child might who has returned to a normal living room after time in an orphanage. She set the tray down and stood pouring. Like an anxious mother waiting for a son to approve a recipe, her vast eyes lay on me. Delightful, I said, after mixing in sugar and taking the first scalding mouthful.

Very well, she said, smiling broadly. That much is established! I can make tea!

We drank our tea in silence.

I made some banal remark when I finished—very refreshing.

She stood up. Stand up, Alan! she told me.

No, I said. I was actually amused.

Stand up! she said. It was as if she were proposing a parlor game. Naturally I asked her why. Sometimes, she told me, it's best for big boys not to ask questions.

That's silly talk, I said. But I stood up.

She grasped me—it was like a wrestling hold. Her eyes glittered powerfully and seemed to take up most of my vision. She was not as surpassingly beautiful as Sarah, but she had a handsomeness and a lot of physical strength. Her breath felt hot yet fragrant. Now, she said like a girl, I've got you wrapped up. You see? It's not so hard to be held by a woman, is it?

Against my will it is, I told her. Where in God's name did you learn to behave like this?

Ah, she said, winking. You think it must be the hedonist influence of America, don't you? Because everyone agrees America's hopelessly decadent, don't they? Not our society though. Not Sonny and his cohorts.

Her voice took on a hoarseness, exciting and, as I told myself, foreign. Foreign to me, that is. I had forgotten that it was one of the gifts of women. Stimulating in particular to the oaf in me, and not offensive to the sage either.

You see? she said. You see? And, by the way, the United States, along with places like Canada and Australia, has passed the Benthamite test of providing the greatest happiness to the greatest number.

And bad luck for those who miss out, I argued, feeling I and my argument would be choked.

Don't be such a spoilsport, she advised me.

To be held so fiercely had its attractions. Perhaps disgracefully, absorbing and consenting, I began to hold her. I can't blame it on my lower impulses. It was the total I who kissed the side of her neck, in sudden hunger for companionable flesh. It was I who held her with a kind of need, which I did not see as erotic at all but as an even profounder appetite, very simple, nearly infantile. I could discern in the reactions of her body a marvelous willingness to satisfy me.

She said the one word, Quick! Thus, it was apparent that she did not wish to satisfy the prurient Overguard by overstaying the curfew. Or else, of course, she had other urgencies.

There is no need to go into the disrobings, the clothing one loosened oneself or had loosened by the lover. Louise James had a succulent, broad, muscular, full-breasted body. In fact, as I remembered later, she represented very accurately the national ideal of womanhood, the ample seductress and the mother of the tribe. She lay back on the floor, smiling and happily dazed, ready to accept me. There were no complaints about the discomfort of this. It was too serious a battle of the senses for that sort of thing. Ever a lusty child, I drew on the imagined milk of her wide breasts. Maybe, I thought in my heat, maybe she will become my wife, and I can be here, in the shelter of her broad shoulders, for a lifetime of nights. But first, this evening's discourse of flesh! After I had explored her with more patience than I felt, the antique manuals of love at work even in my haste, I felt that supreme homecoming of berthing my penis in her. I was sure I wanted to stay in this mode of freshness and discovery eternally, but the pressure of the blood, so ordinary and so laughable in retrospect, was driving me. In my certainty of my own power, the only question for the moment was how long I could withhold.

I had read in the past that impotence can strike at the height of passion, though I had never believed it. Erection is not always the fundamental problem. That pressure and frenzy to pour all your substance in the one direction itself requires that all one's life be encapsulated in a second of giving. All ghosts are summoned up in that second. All lost battles. Forgotten doubt can rise and powerfully mist the veins.

Predictably, I saw again Sarah's transformed face, the leather of it, the filaments, its sunken and vacated features, and across the brow and temples and cheeks, veins once submerged by her beauty now demarcated by the evil, clogging ink which her blood had become. Desire for Louise James was closed off as suddenly as a door shut by a gale. What I was engaged at seemed what it was. Child's play.

I rolled away from Louise James, I was on my back beside her, and there were tears on my face. She put her arm around me, but it felt different, less essential than it had been.

Is there something I can do? she asked.

No. I'm impotent.

I knew that specter would always be waiting for me, just below the summit of desire. I knew it.

It doesn't matter, she told me. You've had a cruel time. I understand. It's not important to me.

I said nothing to her. She got up and on her wide, spatulate feet with painted toenails, she went and got a towel from the bathroom, and began cleaning up my tear-besmirched face. Hush, she said. I'm not as shallow a woman as that.

I told her she was far too good a woman for me, and I could see that though she felt flattered at that, there was sorrow in her eyes. I admired the way she had descended from her desire to turn so quickly into a nurse.

She smiled. I shall keep contact. I have not necessarily finished with you yet. But I won't push as much now.

She spread her arms, bare-chested, kneeling beside me. You know where rescue lies.

We put on our clothes like two members of a beaten football team, although I the one who had very little faith in our future competition chances, and she retaining too much. It was a little before nine o'clock. There was plenty of time to escort her home or call her a cab before curfew. We walked down the stairs together. She retained a certain smile as we descended in the dim light—it was the sort of smile an aunt would have for an eccentric nephew. I could see Captain Chaddock's dark staff car and white Toyota. I knew him nearly so well, I felt now, that I could ask him to give Louise a lift home. But I decided that might seem strange, and an uncomfortable experience to subject my friend Louise James to. The street was empty of cabs, and so I began walking with her along the boulevard.

From the corner nearest to our door emerged a bustling Mrs. Carter. I stopped in my tracks, but Louise James had gone a step or two ahead before she realized I had halted.

Mrs. Carter was wearing a shawl against the night chill. It was tied under her chin. She said, So, Alan! Do you think you can walk this street and pluck whatever beauty you want? In my boy's place?

I shook my head.

She said, You won't have beauty after beauty.

She produced a long knife that looked almost surgical in its contours. She drove it upwards into Louise James's sternum.

I heard Louise utter a fearful cough. She stepped back and leaned against me. Blood ran between her lips; she turned her enormous eyes upwards to me. Within seconds, however, the leaning became a collapse. I sank down with her.

Captain Chaddock and his men were all round us.

Mrs. Carter, said Chaddock. What have you done now?

He won't possess beauty, she said, as if that were an argument that would hold up in a murder court.

I was kneeling by Louise James, whose eyes, lit by the torches of the Overguard, retained only the briefest pleading and disbelief. An Overguard removed Mrs. Carter's exorbitantly long knife from her hand. Chaddock was calling instructions into the radio by his chin. So were various of his officers. It all looked so practiced, as if they were used to murders of this kind committed by the bereaved mothers of soldiers. Chaddock went down on one knee and faced me over Louise James's body, which had now begun to shudder furiously. I had in part lifted her and held her tightly by the shoulders, a man promising to hold her together. She urinated on the pavement, the first indignity of her death.

Chaddock said, Don't get too messy, Alan. We've just had a call for you.

A call for me? I asked, unbelieving.

Yes, you know, a call. And he pointed his index finger towards heaven. I'm sure it's good news. But you can't linger.

He yelled to his subordinates. Where are those fucking lazy Overalls?

He meant the Metropolitan Police in their blue overalls, who would eventually come to take Mrs. Carter away. Crimes of such passion as Mrs. Carter had just committed were not within the purview of the Overguard. Their tasks were both subtler at one extreme, and more Gothic at the other.

Chaddock returned his gaze to Louise. We both saw her eyes roll up in a strange way. An ambulance wailed into the curb, and Overguards lifted me away so that the ambulance men could deal, kneeling, with the victim. It seemed that within seconds a creaky old Fiat of the Metropolitan Police rolled up too, and a man in a suit and three Overalls got out.

One of the ambulance men tried to pump Louise James's heart, but deep veinous blood emerged instead of breath. The ambulance man looked up to the plainclothed Overall and Captain Chaddock. No, he said. Sorry, he told me, as if I were James's husband.

Chaddock said to me, Sorry Alan, but you've been called away.

Not now, I told him.

He pulled my elbow.

Not now, I yelled.

Calm yourself, Alan.

Curse you, Mrs. Carter, I yelled stupidly as Overalls pushed her into the Fiat. She looked at me with purest hatred. Now two Overguards took me, for the first time in our association, firmly and fiercely by the arms, and dragged me off.

You see! yelled Mrs. Carter through her window. Perhaps in her mind, the Overguard were taking me to be punished for long-established lies. I was thrown, rather than aided, into the back of the car. Someone opened a flask and brandy went willy-nilly down my throat. By the time I had stopped choking on it, and its artificial comfort entered my veins, the car was rolling, leaving behind the Overalls and the ambulance men and ranting Mrs. Carter, and the limbs of Louise James.

As the limo rolled, the blindfold was applied again, and in the darkness I began the futile yet disabling business of absorbing all that had happened to me and to others. I mentioned to the darkness of the limo that I had blood on my shirt—I could feel it.

Don't worry, Chaddock told me. Palace will look after you. Long as Boss isn't kept up after midnight.

This time the journey seemed shorter than the first one made by McBrien and myself. Soon, all were whispering at whatever palace gate it happened to be, and the Overguard men slipped my blindfold off while we were still in progress within the walls. I was surprised to see, well dug in, amongst the splendid gardens, a battery of antiaircraft rockets. Who were these rockets intended for? The Americans? Or the internal dissenters, some of them in the army and air force? The colonnade at the end of the driveway was a different one from that of the palace in which I'd first met Great Uncle. I presumed that this was Highgate Palace, the one nearest Martyrs Avenue.

They opened the door of the car and helped me out, and I went up the stairs in my bloodied shirt and pants with Chaddock. A palace Overguard officer, member of the Praesidia and a far more scholarly-looking man than Chaddock, met us inside the door and saluted to Chaddock as he handed me over. But the procedure as I progressed along the corridors was similar now. I surrendered my clothing.

Do I get my passport back now? I asked.

In a while, said the officer. Not tonight.

No distaste showed on the faces of the men who handled my clothes soaked with poor Louise James's blood. But I felt that the astonishment and horror I had brought with me would swamp my coming conversation with Great Uncle, and I confess I was pleased to see them clear out with the mess. I showered, gave a urine sample, had an anal examination, and dressed in the same sort of sterile costume I had been put in last time, and dipped my hands in permanganate. This time, however, there was no stop in any anteroom. Stumbling, accompanied by two Praesidian guards, I was taken at a good clip along corridors, and unlike last time there was now no dim office or bureaucratic corridor, but a hallway which seemed to be all gold cloth, and in its midst double doors, molded with tigers and dauntless fifteenth-century hunters. If Great Uncle had greeted me like a soldier in a bunker last time, this time—so the molded and sculpted doors indicated—he would greet me as a prince.

The two guards either side of the door advanced to meet in the center and pushed both leaves open. One of my own escorts gave me the slightest nudge before peeling away. The room I now entered was prodigious in size, one entire wall taken up by a mosaic of gold, green, scarlet, and blue in which stylized old emperors triumphed above the smiling waters of the rivers. The wall to my left told with echoing richness a tale of forgotten classic gardens and orchards. To my front—it seemed the distance of a football field away—there was a far-off dais, and beyond it an enormous window down which water ran in a copious fall, a triumph of architecture by which light would enter, cooled and refracted, though one could see neither out nor in. On the low dais beneath this marvel sat Great Uncle in a sober, bankerlike blue suit, and the immediately recognizable Sonny in some fantastically lapeled and bell-bottomed costume almost certainly of his own design. I had a sense that I had entered upon a family scene, a dialogue well in progress and not yet done.

From this distance I could barely hear anything, what with the thunder and whispers of the water window. I saw Great Uncle wave to me. I came forward down a carpet like a river, with gold and bejeweled fish swimming towards their master in a stream of vivid blue—just as I now swam to him. I found on that short journey, and to my astonishment, that indeed I was not keen on perishing, even if Sonny told me it was about to happen, giving me moments of preparation. My hands were sweating, my feet prickled as I stumbled along like a giant baby in my immune toddler suit.

Both men stood up as I approached. How extraordinary, I thought. I noticed that Sonny's M16 was propped against the back of his chair. Did it serve tonight as an accessory, or a genuine weapon? I remembered what an NCO had said on Summer Island one night: No one can imagine being dead, but thousands of kids with no talent for it have managed it without any trouble at all. The dead could thus easily imagine themselves dead, but I worried about it in my own case on my way down the carpet.

As I got within shouting range, Great Uncle cried, Alan! Alan! and demanded greater speed of me.

I could not avoid being in some primal way flattered and willing. There is a reason why Great Uncle's portrait is everywhere, the religion of state, on walls throughout the city, in one mural an ancient emperor in a chariot, in another a young radical atop a tank, yelling for true independence. And here he was, standing again, the god in the suit, to welcome me, as it remarkably seemed. At last I reached the foot of the dais. Without inviting me to join Sonny and himself at their symbolic level, Great Uncle reached down to me and embraced me in his arms. It was a huge embrace, typical of northern tribesmen, a sort of wedding embrace, I thought, an embrace of clans united by mutual favors and profoundest blood. I half expected Sonny to get his M16 and let off celebratory rounds into the ceiling. He was said to do that where he lived, on his own island in the river. But it was too early in the night for him. His parties were midnight affairs, his excesses were the excesses of four A.M.

I could smell Great Uncle's cologne, Tommy Hilfiger, the same I had smelled on Captain Chaddock.

He released me in a way that sent me staggering back a little. This is a splendid book, Alan, he said. Pearson Dysart are over the moon!

He pointed as if the astral body were above us in the huge chamber. It's a wonderful tale. The Clancys are a classical family. I know such people.

He laughed and pointed to Sonny.

My son hasn't read it, of course. But he rejoices too, in his way. You have done a wonderful thing for the state and the people. Come up. Sit down.

When I had risen a step or two, he pointed to a footstool, on which I tried to sit with some dignity. It was a strange thing. A book stolen from Sarah, yet gaining praise from the tyrant. And that was good enough for the moment. For an instant I felt like a king, though I knew that had I looked I would have seen Sarah's haglike, valid disappointment in the falling water behind Great Uncle.

It was the best I had to give, Mr. President, I told Great Uncle, for that was true. Yet I involuntarily made a cleansing gesture at my chest, remembering tortured Louise James, shuddering to death on the pavement for Private Carter.

Forgive me. I'm a little confused and overwhelmed, Mr. President.

He laughed.

I said, A friend of mine was attacked this evening by the mother of an old comrade. It was Louise James. You remember her father, Mr. President?

I've heard something of that attack. I'd rather talk about Clancy, said Great Uncle, waving the name of James away to the extent that I knew it to be accursed to him. I've heard a rumor, in fact, Alan, that you might have let Mrs. Carter loose. Yet that has its good side. James will not go back and broadcast her possibly malicious views.

I absorbed this.

Whereas, he continued, Clancy is a great hero of the people.

A revelation in the presence of a tyrant is a terrible thing. I thought of how Captain Chaddock was to protect me from all hostile influences, including those within myself. And yet he had let Mrs. Carter, a creature I had in my way created, hang round my apartment door for weeks on end.

Great Uncle, I said, you are not implying that Mrs. Carter was . . .

I am implying nothing. I'm saying that Louise James will not report her minority view.

I must have wavered on the footstool.

Are you all right? Sonny asked me, as if he might have a pill which would rouse me.

Thank you, sir. Yes.

Sonny patted the arm of his chair in a hyperactive way. Tell him about the Yankee writer, Pop!

Oh yes, said Great Uncle, back in spacious form. Pearson Dysart has paid a leading U.S. novelist to read it and he declares it a classic and comments how real it is . . . in the troubles faced by the characters . . . compared to most American writing, which is all about disenchantment and the frustrations of love. Above all, he said it will change attitudes towards the sanctions.

Great Uncle's profound dark eyes glittered like those of . . . well, of a proud great-uncle. I consider you have performed your duty fully, he said.

Sonny tapped the arm of his chair again. Good job, he said.

And to show my appreciation, Great Uncle continued, I have ordered that preparations be made for you to live from now on in a special and splendid villa at one of the palaces. You'll be given the location soon. An announcement will be made that you have been created bard of my tribe, and of the people.

Was he making a joke, prior to expressing a total rejection of my work and asking Sonny to shoot me? Elaborate spoof as it might be, I felt a peculiar onrush of panic. And in the face of both possibilities—that he was and was not joking—the blood seemed actually to want to escape my veins.

So what do you say to that, eh? asked Sonny.

Yes, I answered stupidly, trying to frame the word "Thanks," and producing just the one bleated syllable.

I . . .

Great Uncle raised his hand. No, he said, you have done your service and this is a reward. You will be Shostakovich to my Stalin, Molière to my Sun King. You will be able to write and publish under your own name. You will be my storyteller laureate.

Sonny beamed in a distracted way at my good fortune, and stole a look at the huge watch at his wrist. Perhaps he wanted a fix, perhaps it was drawing close to time for his night's saturnalia. I became aware that after Great Uncle died this edgy Sonny would be my master, at least until the army rose and killed him, and me in my villa too, if the villa itself were not also a joke.

I am overcome, sir, I told Great Uncle nonetheless. Naturally I shall have to make preliminary arrangements.

Take your time. The workers are still at the villa for another week to ten days.

I nodded, hoping he did not see how happy that made me.

In the meantime of course, beamed Great Uncle, you have been assigned an automobile and driver to look after all your needs and be at your call.

I expressed even more thanks as best I could.

Tell me, he then further asked. Did Captain Chaddock treat you well?

I wondered whether the question was somehow the springing of the trap. But despite the unanswered matter of any culpability of Chaddock's in the slaughter of Louise James, I said, The soul of discretion, Mr. President.

I even think he'll miss you, chuckled Great Uncle, as if he had recently had quite a talk to Chaddock.

Oh, the President continued, clicking thumb and forefinger together in self-chastisement. I didn't tell you that Mr. McBrien's been appointed cultural attaché in Paris. The French have always had a soft spot for us. After World War I they hoped we'd be their puppet state. But the English got here first.

Great Uncle smiled within his godhood, far above the curious passions of the English and the French.

I am delighted at McBrien's good fortune, I told him. I believe he sometimes found it challenging to deal with me.

Ah, said Great Uncle, looking at Sonny. The artistic temperament. I know all about it. If it were not for the demands of the state, my son would have been an artist.

Sonny grinned crazily at me in echo of his father's grin.

Well, they'll take you home now, Alan. And thank you.

I rose as the President did, but again, an apparently forgotten item came to his mind.

One thing! he said.

He looked to Sonny, who half yawned and reached down into his boot to extract a *chardri*, the national dagger.

Oh, yes, I said, full of fear and crazy boldness, exposing my wrist to let erratic Sonny induct me with the three promised cuts. At each lusty incision, I thought of Louise James, so recently dead and worthy of memory, but swept from my mind by these potent, sharp-edged entities with whom I shared a crown room.

I was to be made the emperor's caged canary.

The Overguard dressed the notches in my wrist and gave me a suit of nondescript army fatigues to wear home—they would deliver my clothes to me, dry-cleaned, later, they promised, as if it meant a great deal to me. Chaddock met me at the palace door and led me down the steps.

Going home with the blindfold on, I asked, Captain?

Present! he told me.

Was it you brought Mrs. Carter along to kill Louise James?

What?

I think you heard me the first time.

There was a long pause. The engine hummed. I imagined the Overguard exchanging glances.

How could anyone organize a thing like that?

While I was upstairs with her, I explained, you or someone go to the old woman. You say, Look, he's enjoying a woman. Your son will never enjoy a woman! That knife, too. It didn't look a Mrs. Carter sort of knife . . .

Stop, said Chaddock softly to the driver. When obeyed he left the front seat and opened the back door for me and ripped my blindfold off. Get out, Mr. Sheriff!

I obeyed him, too benumbed to feel fear or abandonment, being reduced, it seemed, to the mere span of my three small sores of gouged flesh, the only three small voices of pain which proved I had emerged from the confrontation with Great Uncle. I got out of the car under my own power though, without any involvement one way or another by my backseat escorts.

He took me to a high wall which rose above us to the crumbling villas of an old suburb named Saltash.

Don't know what you're saying, sir, he said softly. Really don't.

It was a great temptation to believe him.

Wouldn't be so snaky, he assured me.

I couldn't honestly say he would be.

Say it was a set scene. Then someone else arranged it. Someone higher. And more secret. See? Okay. Don't talk in front of my men like that. Might get back.

Illogically I held up my bandaged wrist. I've got the marks, I told him. I'm in the clan now.

Back in the car, he said.

I accepted his logic for the moment, and rejoined the limo. As we arrived outside my block of flats, I saw the corner of the fatality had already been hosed clean of Louise's passionate and decent blood.

I took note of that, and then entered the building trembling. There was the old sofa only she had used. In my living room would be minor untidiness, the mark of our failed adventure of the flesh.

Behind me, Chaddock called, All right, Mr. Sheriff?

Yes, I said, dismissively.

I rose up the stairs alone as he watched, entered my apartment, and sat most of the night regarding a rumple our hunger for each other had made in a red and blue mat by my desk. I could not absorb any more phenomena than that; I could not bring my mind to more comprehensive exercises. And my heart creaked now for the inconsolable spirit of Louise James.

Even that next sleep-deprived day, I began to consider my options. I rang McBrien to begin with. He had heard about the James tragedy and hoped I had recovered. He had intended to call in and see me about it and other things, but he'd been all day at the ministry being briefed by experts from other government departments, and had been packing all night. He and Sonia were off in four days. Their child would be born in a top-class Parisian hospital.

And thank you, thank you, Alan.

What's your flight number?

He gave it to me.

I'll try to see you off, you miserable bastard, I told him, just to make sure you are at last off my back. You are absolved of my care now?

You're your own man, yes. But don't do anything that will reflect badly.

What if I do?

He thought about it. Please, just relax. Enjoy the rewards. I intend to.

Louise's body was still at the morgue, and Andrew, who had undertaken a campaign to have it sent back to relatives in Houston, with whom he had already spoken by phone and who were more than willing to pay that expense, asked me to come around to discuss it, perhaps to employ me as a witness to the crime to write to the authorities and plead that the body be released.

On the way to Andrew's, I told my driver, I'll be going to the airport tomorrow. To see a friend off.

Oh, he said. I'm sorry, Mr. Sheriff. The airport's a place I'm not permitted to take you.

The airport? How many other places?

None, he told me cheerily. Just the airport for now.

That's good, I said, because later in the day I wanted to go and see a friend who helped me out with a book. He's a barge captain down in Ibis Bay.

Certainly, Mr. Sheriff.

Since the airport's out of the question, we might as well go in the morning now.

For I trusted McBrien's Air France flight to be off in time.

Do you know a fellow named Captain Chaddock? I then asked him. A captain in the Overguard?

My driver said, I haven't had that pleasure, sir.

Well, I said, you're bossier than he is.

The driver chose to laugh and drove me to Andrew's place. Grace answered the door. What's wrong with your wrist? she asked me.

A graze, I told her.

The three of us, Andrew, Grace, and I, sat together in the pleasant afternoon uttering the necessary clichés with which the death of the young and the handsome needed to be honored.

What I'm expecting next, murmured Andrew, is that they'll come and ask for her program tapes. But I've already had them remastered, so that we can post them out to PBS. I mean, there's already a lot of speculation in the American papers about this death.

Admirable Andrew. I accepted from him the name and address of the appropriate official in the Ministry of Justice to whom I should write about Louise. I thought I had one literary service left in me. This one.

I wrote my plea that night, and slept lightly but at length. In the morning I checked with the Air France office to see that McBrien's plane had left. It had. So I went down to my car and driver.

We drove up over dusty Beaumont, by the hopeful markets, past the women gathering their tainted water, Mrs. Clancy-like, as children worth a dollar yelled after us. Men in ragged clothes were busy on pittance-paying tasks of an ill-defined nature. The broken promises of the world and of regimes were seamed into their faces like grit and legible in their bent backs.

We parked at last by the teahouse and the fuel-sodden soccer ground. You're free, I told my driver. Take some time off. Come back in two hours.

In fact I doubted he would go, and was delighted to see him edge away past the oil-sodden soccer field and into a side street. I feared he might not go as far as I hoped.

I set off across the pier and went looking for McCauley's barge. It was as I remembered when I'd done it with McBrien, a slog over many decks. Some backtracking and sidetracking, until the barge, *Joanna*, presented itself.

McCauley's deckhand, Bernie, was all I found aboard. Pity you came all the way out here, he told me. McCauley was back on land, in the teahouse. So I hiked and vaulted hoses and barrels and gunwales back ashore and approached the oily awning of the teahouse, hoping to look as if I merely sought refreshment.

McCauley, himself grimy and seamed, but appearing wise to the earth, was drinking Turkish coffee inside the place with a man who had the air of being the proprietor. Seeing me approach, he muttered something, and the proprietor rose and went back to his zinc counter.

I smiled broadly at McCauley. Do you remember me?

Yeah. You were going to make a film about us.

Some problems arose with that. But you're still in the business.

Why not? Sit down if you like.

As soon as I took a seat, I leaned across to him. I told him, You have to get me out.

He immediately rose. Don't you damn well dare say that to me here or anywhere.

They've taken my passport.

Why should I care? What's wrong with your wrist?

A graze, I told him.

For God's dear sake, don't even say these things here. Come out the back.

He rose and led me through a bead curtain to a yard where there were a number of rooms for rent by truck drivers and bargees, and a pungent toilet and washhouse. From the door of the washhouse, the bitterness of human ammonia emerged boldly to take on the general air of oil.

We entered deep into the room, a shower in one corner, grimy underwear hung diagonally, the undercleaned toilet in the other rear corner. I followed, standing amidst lank, damp laundry.

Who was that fellow who brought you? I saw you start out looking for me.

A driver, I said. I don't know him. Why didn't you come out and tell me not to waste my time deck jumping?

Hell. I knew you'd get me into trouble. And you're still trying to.

The driver hasn't even seen you. He's off somewhere.

Oh yes?

Yes. I want you to put me in one of your barrels and ship me out.

Prime crude, he laughed. Don't be an idiot. You'd smother.

Punch a hole in the top for air, I urged him.

What makes you think I do this sort of thing? I don't do this sort of thing. And never have. So what gives you the damned right to say otherwise?

Nothing, I hurried to say. I'm pleading with you to consider the idea, that's all. If you can transport oil in a can, it struck me you could ship someone human. Me. I'm not saying you do these things. I'm saying you could! That's all! I spread my hands, pleading.

Can't be done, McCauley calmly declared. Sorry. It's not my business.

I'm pleading, I told him. I'll pay whatever's in my means.

McCauley promised, halfway like a confession, If you're a grass or a troublemaker, I'll finish you myself. He certainly had the meaty, hairy hands for it.

We know all the Overalls, he further told me. We've got them right here, in our pockets. They'll believe me, not you.

That's not the question. I'm asking you to do this one thing, once.

What's your name again?

I told him. He wrote it down.

Stay here in the teahouse. Don't make a single call, or the owner will spot it and you'll be gone. I'll be back in an hour. Read a book or something. Write one for all I damn well care.

He went to leave, but stepped back again into the pungency from the doorway of the washhouse. He was full of a wild irritation. Look, if I normally did this stuff, ask yourself whether I'd still be skippering a barge. No! I'd be driving round like some fucking prince.

He shook his head and withdrew again, and gestured from the door. Go on, go back and drink tea. I hope your damn bladder bursts.

I sat in the shop, dejectedly drinking tea and reading a newspaper. The hour, even though it proved in the end to be only forty-five minutes, was interminable, of course, but I was full of a kind of patience, since that was one of the few virtues left to me to practice. I kept looking out at the pier to see if my driver had returned.

At last, McCauley came down the stairwell behind the zinc counter and, glancing all around, crossed the room to sit with me.

So, he told me, my Overall friends say your girlfriend was stabbed.

She wasn't my girlfriend. And they have the killer.

But you're scared they might let the killer go and turn to you, aren't you, old mate?

His eyes glittered and I could tell he was relieved that I had a normal, predictable criminal motive, not a volatile, political one. He even put a fraternal hand on my shoulder. Look, he said, I had a lot of trouble—this twenty-two-year-old . . . He exhaled, a near whistle, to show how close-run a thing that had been for all participants.

Did you kill her? he asked.

No, I was walking with her.

But did you pay the person who did do her?

No. I swear.

But then it struck me he would respect me more if there were a lingering doubt about that.

They're all mad, you know, he told me. Women. They're all mad.

I shrugged. It would not hurt me to convey the idea that I was an ordinary fellow beset by woman troubles.

I just about came to the conclusion, he told me. Live with one woman and live in one lunatic asylum. Mess around with three and live in three asylums.

I understand, I assured him, trampling on Sarah's sage residual presence.

Suddenly he was right up to my face, and full of spit. If you're playing a game with us, he told me, you'll be laughing where your throat is, my son.

I nodded.

All right. It'll cost you five thousand U.S.

Where in the hell do I get that?

You've got a U.S. dollar account, don't you? I thought you were a swank.

Yes, but the authorities would be notified if I took out that amount.

Say you went to a certain branch. What if you had the name of a sensible fellow at that branch?

It might be a help. I don't want to get arrested at a bank.

I'm not involved, declared McCauley. I'll be protected by the local Overalls, so you needn't even expect to be believed if you say my name.

I understand.

He began writing out the details in block letters on a card, and passed it to me.

Say you want the money for a car. So the rest of today and most of tomorrow, you'd better go looking at cars for sale. You'll all but close a deal, too. The next morning, day after tomorrow, go to the

Bay View Café at Beaumont, near the Eastside markets. Do you know those markets?

Very well, I assured him.

Be using the toilet at nine-thirty. This won't be easy for you, you know? Not that I know anything anyhow.

That's okay. I can get to that bank branch, no problem.

Holy God, I mean *after* that! That's when it won't be easy. You'd better be able to handle claustrophobia.

Okay. I'd rather not suffocate, though.

No guarantees. But someone will do his best to prevent that.

Drop me to any ship, and as soon as I'm out of that barrel, I'll claim asylum.

Yeah, yeah. What would I know? Why do you think you'll be on my barge?

Please, make it yours.

For familiarity would be a comfort and a kind of guarantee.

We'll see, said McCauley. By the way, nothing to do with me. But if you want to take out more than five thousand, you can. But put the excess in your sock, so they don't take that too.

They?

The people you'll be dealing with. Nothing to do with me.

All this was, of course, very much in the tradition of some of the films I would have liked one day to have the chance to subtitle. But the glamour only attends a film. There's no glamour in anticipatory fear and plans in which any minute shift is lethal and in which the escapee doubts the capacity of his own mind not to go crazy during the process. The most piteous creature on earth is the one contemplating unlikely flight, and without documents.

I went out again and found my driver had returned to the pier but seemed to be asleep in his car. Thus began a day and a half of tedious and earnest car hunting. I took my driver's sagacious advice and went and saw a friend of his who owned a large yard of vehicles behind a two-storey house in Beaumont. He was selling cars somewhat cheaply, particularly the older models. In some cases inflation had reduced their value to a couple of hundred U.S. dollars. I particularly liked a white Toyota, like Captain Chaddock's. One could make a journey up north in such a sturdy vehicle, I told my driver and his friend. I saw the anticipation of kickback in my driver's eyes.

And no shortage of petrol, said my driver's friend.

But I made the driver take me to other dealers too. I ran hot and cold over this model and that, still conveying to him that the white Toyota probably had my vote.

On the morning itself, I invited my driver upstairs for coffee, on the supposition that yesterday's car hunting had made us compadres. He seemed so flattered by the gesture that I indulged the hope someone more senior than he would be blamed if I vanished.

As we sipped away, I was aware of carrying ten thousand dollars on my person, divided into wads of five thousand each, one in my breast pocket for handing over, the other, according to the absurdity of this drama, in my right sock. The only thing I carried which resembled a document was a folded-up dust jacket from the American edition of my book.

There's a great place I used to go when I was younger, I told the driver. The Bay View. By the Eastside markets. Do you know that place?

My driver said he did.

And so he took me, and so it befell me.

At nine-thirty, breakfasted lightly and having drunk as much fluid as I could, I went to the men's toilet. As I urinated and waited very calmly for any changes to be rung, a young man stood at a urinal near me. When I had finished, he zipped his own fly and turned to me.

Finished? he asked.

Yes, I said.

Do you have the money?

Are you the man?

Of course. Hurry!

I pulled out the five thousand and he leafed through it.

Very well, he said. The lid's on fairly tight, but when it's time to get out, our man will release you. Okay? You run up onto the deck of the tanker yelling, I seek asylum, I seek asylum! The captains are bound by international law to take notice.

I understand, I said.

As I was still nodding, he punched me vigorously on the side of the jaw. What a big wrist you have, I thought for a second. But this was no bar-brawl punch, which merely confused the sight with sudden lights. I had no time for further thought. I must have simply dropped where I stood.

Unconscious of its beginning, I made the journey in a barrel. In that I woke in fear and pain and confusion, jammed upright in an agonizing position, light entering through five minuscule holes in the lid. We were static. I could feel no rocking of water so I must have stood on the dockside. Though there was some form of padding in the barrel, it gave little comfort. Immediately ill, I found by chance with my hand a liter bottle of water which had been mercifully included.

Since they had left me my watch, I knew it to be eleven o'clock, and clearly daytime, but staring at it, I felt my head expand and shrink with pain. I had been uncomfortably located, my knees and back holding me upright, but however I moved, I could not get a painless position nor achieve a full kneeling one. McCauley had promised it would not be easy.

Heat grew within the barrel. Little by little, I was able to shed my jacket and had an urge to douse myself with the remaining water, but did not know whether I would be suspended in pain and thirst like this for another day. I went into a stupor and woke to the outer world as my barrel was toppled sideways. I could feel but not see the abrasions this movement brought. I was rolled and rolled over planks, keeping my elbows in, crazed with giddiness, sometimes my conveyance falling from one surface an inch or two, or in the worst case, five or six inches, to another. When it stopped, I was sick again and became insufferable to myself. And then, upright, I heard McCauley's voice but could detect mere threads of light. I had found my bark of exile, humble though it might be. I could feel the tug and the suck of the river on which *Joanna*, or whatever barge it was, rode. But another barrel was placed atop mine, and I felt a panic of claustrophobia. The people involved had my money, it occurred to me. There was no reason they would regret it if I perished on a tanker's deck or in a hold, buried amongst the piled-up barrels of crude.

I suffered unutterably and banged the sides of the barrel, but I knew justice had been done—I was buried with my few possessions. I slept miserably, and I woke to darkness, and the fluorescent dots on my watch said nine o'clock. I rationed the water, and lost all sense of my own putridness. I propped myself to my knees again and urinated in the bottom of the barrel. I banged its sides, but the padding numbed the sound. I beat against the lid, and it resonated dully, as if it lay in the bottom row of a pyramid of barrels.

Thus hours of panic passed. I could have brought a pocketknife, a plain utensil to end all the fear and wasting ahead of me, but I hadn't thought I would need it. I began to rave, and the dots on my watch meant nothing more than the random cells of some insect. My barrel swayed and I began to hear the gluey crude moving all round me, and I began to sing a song about it, some oceanic plaint that made sense to me at the time. I finished the water, tried to piss in the bottle, and waited for my air to run out. *Why the oil?* as the medic had asked in "The Women of Summer Island." What was the oil doing, this Satanic honey, out at sea and separating me from the sweet air of earth?

At some stage beyond all time there was new movement and

jolting all around me, and sharp noises around the lid of my barrel. In glittering early air, McCauley looked down at me, Bernie peering over his shoulder, curious to see what had befallen me.

God, you stink, said McCauley.

Oh yes, I admitted.

The two of them dragged me out. I wavered on the deck, and sat as Bernie hosed me totally with seawater.

Barrels rose on pallets from the deck of *Joanna* up the side of a red and white tanker. McCauley pointed to the stairs which led up the side of the ship.

There it is. Look lively.

I caressed him as if he were my lost father.

Get away, you mad bastard, he said. Go on! Up the steps, yelling *asylum* all the way.

I swayed up the tanker's ladder, howling the word. They called the captain, who accepted me with a shrug. I spent three months in a psychiatric ward in Greece. Everyone shook their head at me, even the nurses, and said, Without documents, and stateless.

after-tale

And you see, said Alan Sheriff, isn't that the saddest and silliest story you ever heard?

He was finishing the tale for which he had made such claims under eucalypts in the detention center. It had occupied us some weeks, but Alan Sheriff had been determined to tell it.

How did you get to this country? I asked. Without documents?

I bought fake ones in Greece.

And the book?

It was published under Great Uncle's name and did medium well, but no one believed he'd written it. So I read in *Time* magazine. The thing is, your friend—Alice. She thinks I can be innocently attracted by her breasts? I have two ghosts to stay my hand. Does she think that if I get a temporary protection visa, I'll ask her for a date?

We're naïve, I said.

I looked at the other folk in the yard—matriarchs in the encompassing Middle Eastern or Afghan robes in which they had made their long escapes; a few solemn Sudanese gentlemen, philosophy aching in their eyes; young Palestinians in jeans who could have passed for Italian waiters except for a darkness in their faces.

I wonder, I said, shaking my head as if to rid it of the extraordinary impact of Alan's story. I wonder if all these people have saddest and silliest stories to rival yours?

Oh no, he said. He grinned at me. Some of them have been involved in genuine tragedy.

acknowledgments

The concept of this novel arose as a result of reading "Tales of the Tyrant" by Mark Bowden (*Atlantic Monthly*, May 2002).

a note about the author

THOMAS KENEALLY is the acclaimed author of more than two dozen books, including *Schindler's List*, which won the Booker Prize and inspired the film; *The Great Shame: The Triumph of the Irish in the English-Speaking World*; *American Scoundrel*, a biography of Civil War general Dan Sickles; and most recently, *Office of Innocence*, a compassionate novel about a young priest during World War II. He lives in Sydney, Australia.

a note on the type

This book was set in a digital version of Monotype Walbaum. The original typeface was created by Justus Erich
Walbaum (1768–1839) in 1810. Before becoming a
punch cutter with his own type foundries in Goslar and
Weimar, he was apprenticed to a confectioner, where he is
said to have taught himself engraving, making his own
cookie molds using tools made from sword blades. The
letterforms were modeled on the "modern" cuts being
made at the time by Giambattista Bodoni and the Didot
family.